Beneath the

Gnarled Oak

T. L. Howard

Copyright © 2017 T. L. Howard

All rights reserved.

ISBN-10: 1629860182

ISBN-13: 978-1629860182 (Publishing Inspiration)

T L H o w a r d

DEDICATION

*Dedicated to my father who inspired me with
the desire to write, and by his own example,
proved it was possible.*

*Also dedicated to my younger brother,
Gavin, who originally inspired the idea
behind this story.*

ACKNOWLEDGMENTS

Special thanks to my editors :
Joan Templin Haeberle
Jenna Howard Weiler
Heather Rubert
Stephanie Bowman

And to my family who have supported me and
encouraged me to write, thank you!

Chapter 1

AS WELCOME AS THE RELEASE OF DEATH upon a withered brow breathed nightfall across the dusk-lit town of Pravda. The streets lay in a perfect grid of cobblestone and timber frame homes, nestled among wide rolling hills and a vast forest to the northwest.

The weary eyes of a small ragged figure beckoned the darkness to settle swiftly. He watched the fading daylight stain drifting wisps of cloud with vibrant hues of pink and gold against the deep purple and blue backdrop of the night sky. He leaned against the rough, rippling bark of a wind-beaten oak tree which stood not far from the edge of the town. The breeze that penetrated his filthy jacket carried the crisp chill of early autumn with pervasive scents of ripened fruit and fall squash from the surrounding lush gardens. Amber-tipped leaves rustled above, caressed by the last rays of the sun as it dipped below the horizon.

The hills, with their tall grasses and sparse groves of trees, appeared menacing in the shadowy blue-gray glow of dusk. Thick grain fields lay in an intricate patchwork across the cultivated valley. Only a single lane cut through, carving its way from the larger towns to the east, the dirt path shifting to paving stones at the brink of the town.

For the lone boy beneath the gnarled oak tree, it was the moment of perfect sanity, the unrest settling as stars danced delicately in the darkness above.

The sweeping of the sidewalks had been completed scarcely an hour earlier, the daily routine relentlessly unbroken. Trimmed hedges lined the hand-laid walkways which led to delicate wrought iron gates, barricading the path to painted porches and carefully carved wooden doors from which, here and there, a mother stood calling out for her children to come inside. Bright yellow light spilled through the open doorways as rosy-cheeked children slipped off their shoes and made their way into the glowing warmth.

Doors were closed, bolts slid into place, and curtains were drawn, setting the world within each dwelling far apart from the one without. Pravda and its people had their invariable routines, the steady rhythm in which life progressed.

Leaving behind the weathered oak, Will made his way past the hushed dwellings along Merril Lane toward Main. He again walked the familiar path he and his father had tread those few years ago when they first entered the town. The memories of that day were far more bitter than sweet as Will's mind returned to that hot summer afternoon.

Will had been just a small boy in oversized trousers and a shirt that bulged where it was tucked in at the waist. Frayed sleeves had been rolled several times to expose his little hands. Against his chest he had carried a meager bundle with his few boyish treasures. In his father's left hand was clasped an empty water pouch and a simple leather-bound book.

Day after day, they had walked the dusty roads, drifting over the land—as buffeted and battered as a broken mast carried over the churning sea, helpless to the torrents of nature—in their case, human nature. No place to rest—lost and of no proper use.

The sun burned down with the searing heat of midsummer that day—late noon, early August. Will's hair lay matted and soaked beneath his gray woolen cap. Sweat dripped from his disheveled hair and rolled down the side of his face, trailing through the dust that covered every inch of his exposed skin.

As they approached the town, little Will pulled the cap down over his eyes and watched only the flapping of his lace-less boots knocking against his ankles with every step. There was little to see as his eyes trailed along the tidy cobbled streets.

They had passed through many towns. Will needn't lift his eyes to know of the disapproving stares of the ladies with their crisp-pinned hair and ribboned Alsatian bonnets, or the deep creases appearing beside the noses of the men in their silk top hats as they looked heavenward, praying the two strangers had no desire to stay. The children, he knew, were peeking out from behind their mother's long, tidy skirts, snickering at the ruddy appearance of the two lost souls before them. The pattern was familiar to the weary father and son, and their presence was undoubtedly unwelcome.

Will's father cleared his throat hesitantly as two polished shoes drew near.

"Might I ask, sir, a moment of your time?" His father's voice was rough from the dry heat and too little water, yet it carried hardly a hint of the weary anxiety that lay heavy behind it. Will watched the shadow that spilled from his father's form onto the uneven stones before him. Removing his hat, the shadow gave a small, defeated bow.

"Forgive my intrusion, sir. I do not come looking for charity. I am of a mind to work. Is there any employment to which I might find hire?" he inquired.

A low, gruff voice grunted, "No, certainly not. I'm afraid there is nothing we can offer you." The polished shoes turned quickly and retreated another way, the rhythmic tapping of the hard soles fading down the street.

Will felt his father's hand on his shoulder quivering slightly. His father was silent a moment before he let out a deep breath.

"No need to worry, Will," he said wearily. "We'll try at the mercantile store. Perhaps they will have heard of something there."

Yet the chance never came to ask. They had hardly begun ascending the painted wooden steps of the mercantile store when the door swung open. A man stepped out onto the porch and planted himself firmly on the top step.

"Sir, I am afraid I must ask you to leave."

The voice was snide and unwavering. Not daring to look up into the man's face, Will felt a bitter, swelling hatred clenched in a thick knot deep inside him for the polished, high-laced oxfords that stood where his hat brim could hardly block them from view.

"Please, forgive me, I just came to inquire..." Will's father began, his voice strained.

"There is nothing for you here." The man turned abruptly and the thin screen door slammed behind him.

Will could not bear to see his father's face. Discouragement and anger burned in his throat as salty tears stung the corners of his eyes. They stood for a moment, defeated and despairing. Will's ears caught the hum of talk in the streets around them, of strangers passing ignorant judgment. Silently, the father and son turned and left.

Will's father attempted once or twice more to solicit hire as other men hurried by. Yet, as the sun began to dip low toward the horizon, they found themselves sitting beneath a gnarled oak tree on a grassy hill between the town and a farmer's field.

Not a word was spoken between father and son as the brisk night air settled over the rolling hills. When darkness fell, Will left his father's side and stole his way back through the narrow streets. He returned an hour later with some scraps that had been set out for a family pet. A small, crackling fire lit his father's tired face, his eyes red as they were each night when Will returned. The food was bitter with a stringy grit that was hard to force down, but at least they had a few bites each to ease the tormenting hunger. The day had not been entirely wasted.

Will curled up in the roots of the old oak. His father removed the filthy coat that he had worn through the heat of the day and tucked it tightly around Will's small frame.

"Maybe tomorrow our luck will change," he said softly, brushing the hair away from Will's dirt-stained face.

"Yes, Father. Perhaps it will." He tried to make his tired eyes smile as his stomach gnawed painfully and his legs and feet ached. "Maybe tomorrow." Will let his eyes drift closed with only the faintest hope for what the new day might bring.

* * *

Had it only been two years or three, perhaps, since that night? Will wondered as he continued through Pravda. His small legs carried him silently through the dark town. He made his way down Crestwood Street, through the park, and over the mayor's hedge to the thick tree line where the tangled woods began. It was a dark evening and difficult to see with no moon in the sky, but he well knew the way. Will traveled deep into the forest as the night air grew chill, traveling far into the overgrowth until he came to a large thicket. Children often played in the woods, and hunters took advantage of rabbits and wild game, but it was rare that anyone ventured to this particular section of the woods and none attempted to pass through the rise of uncontrolled thorny bushes which grew nearly as tall as the smaller trees and many meters thick. For Will, it was his haven, his stone wall.

Behind a wispy pine near the thicket lay a mess of strewn pine boughs. Will pushed them aside, exposing a small opening in the ground. He slid inside, crawling into a crudely dug tunnel that passed only a few feet below the thorny rise of bushes. He emerged on the other side where a cultivated bit of land lay hidden within.

As a small child, this had been his fortress; now, though he was not yet twelve years of age, it was his home. Here, through the summer months, he worked steadily for long hours—building, plowing and planting.

Now, as fall set in, it was time for the harvest.

Chapter 2

THAT FIRST NIGHT IN PRAVDA three years earlier had been especially restful for the small boy after the long day on the road. Little Will awoke stiff and cold, still cuddled in the roots of the old oak tree with his father's worn coat tucked around him and his stomach grumbling its complaints after the pitiful dinner of gritty meat the night before. In the hazy light, he could see his father's thin figure a few feet away near the smoking remains of their fire.

Will's body ached from lying on the cold, hard ground. He sat up and rubbed his hands together to regain some circulation.

"Father?" he whispered. Will was hesitant to wake him if he was still asleep. Will had watched his father growing far more pale over the last several weeks with a weariness that deepened the lines in his face and the circles under his tired eyes. A few days ago, a slight trembling had begun to shake his father's frame with each step he took.

Will pushed away the coat that had been tucked around him and laid it over his father's resting form. Shivering in the frosty morning air, he ran through the dew-soaked grass into the silent streets of the town in which they had arrived the evening before. He soon returned clutching several rotting apples that he had found in the refuse pile behind the mercantile store.

"Father, look!" he called out when he had nearly reached their camp. "They aren't so very bad. We can easily cut out the good parts to eat!"

Any fruit was a treat, and apples in particular were a favorite. Will almost skipped the rest of the way to the tree, excited to present his father with even this small reason to smile. His heart warmed in hopeful anticipation. Perhaps today would be a day of wonderful luck after all! Perhaps the apples were a sign that things were about to change at last.

"Father, look!" he called out again.

Bending down, Will put a small hand against his father's shoulder to shake him awake. His father lay quiet and still on his side, an arm resting across his face.

"Father, it's morning, and today truly will be a better day. Look and see!"

His father continued to rest peacefully. Will shook him harder. "Father, you must come and see what I have! We'll have a feast!" Will reached up and pulled his father's arm away from his face.

Will screamed. The apples tumbled to the ground.

Chapter 3

THE LAST RAYS OF SUNLIGHT cast strange shadows over the misty hills before sinking below the tree-lined horizon that evening. Little Will walked slowly into the town. He did not make his way toward the rubbish pile behind the mercantile store, nor did he check the dish set out for the dog. He had seen what he needed. Near the stable of an old plow horse, his little hands grasped the splintering handle of a battered shovel.

It was to be a long night after an even longer day. He had eaten nothing. Little Will had lain curled up next to his father's lifeless form as the sun drifted across the sky. The small child spoke for hours under the shifting shadows, reminding his father of the many dreams they had built up with every step of their long journey as they tried to begin a new life. Will told his father of the memories that were so precious to him, memories of a time when life had been so different—of last Christmas as they sat beneath their large pine tree, decorated with many beautiful lights. He told of the peace he had felt each night as Father tucked him into his small four-poster bed while Mother sang him to sleep with an Irish lullaby.

Will told his father how he had loved walking to the town hall in Bradbury where his father had once worked; how he had loved sitting in the great chair behind his father's desk while his father took the small, hardwood bench; how they had spent hours in that office together sharing peanuts and discussing matters which Will enjoyed pretending to understand.

Will spoke of all the wonderful things they had ever done together—the many evening walks and the fishing on the river, his father pointing out the geese flying south for the winter or north at the start of each new spring.

"Winter will come each year, my little Will," his father would tell him as the geese honked their salutations overhead. "It may be harsh, cold, and so very dark at times. It may even seem as though there will never be an end to it, but spring will always follow, and summer will come again."

All through the day, Will spoke, not daring to stop even as his voice grew hoarse and raw. Dusk fell and darkness enclosed the young child and his father. Will nestled closer against his father's stiff body.

"Father, you promised me." His voice trembled. At last, tears filled his eyes and tumbled into the dry earth as he buried his face into his father's cold neck. "You promised me that though things had become so very bad, we would get through it as long as we had each other. You promised me that you would always be here for me. You promised that someday things be even better than before." Will gasped. "Oh, Father!" he turned and wept against his father's stiff shoulder. "Oh, Father, please come back. Please come back!"

Yet, at even just eight years of age, the young boy knew some things could never be undone.

The next morning, gossip circulated the town. The filthy boy who had been seen with that hopeless, ragged man now knelt alone beneath the old gnarled tree, hardly moving. He must have been neglected, left to starve and die, or perhaps abandoned in hopes of the town's generosity—left to become a burden to them, they surmised.

In their quick judgment, they failed to see the blistered, bleeding fingers and palms of the boy's tiny hands, nor did any draw near enough to see the trickling tears that fell into the freshly turned earth.

Chapter 4

HOW THE YOUNG BOY SURVIVED that first winter was anyone's guess, but only he could have told you about the small knot in the wood by the window of the one-room schoolhouse through which a thin branch could be slid to unhook the window latch. He also would be the only one to tell you that the old plow horse in the stable near the edge of town made for great company on the long, cold winter nights. In these two places, Will passed most of his time as the snow gathered into high drifts.

Earlier in late summer and into the fall, he had pleaded with the butcher. "I can work hard. I don't need much, and I'll do whatever you ask. Please, sir!" But the butcher, the shopkeeper, several farmers, and even the street sweeper only waved him away irritably, insisting that he leave them in peace. They were busy, or they had little enough as it was, they told him curtly. Even the sight of him seemed to upset the town folk. Will soon began to avoid the guilty glares and pitiless scowls.

"Someone else will take care of the child," he heard whispered as he was turned away.

Will realized early on that this "someone else" did not exist. Still, he was determined to find reason to believe that things weren't entirely dismal. Saturdays and evenings were by far his favorite. During those hours, he would often sneak his way into the schoolhouse—the fraying bindings of the books beckoned to him irresistibly. He was careful to return each one before school began the next morning, afraid the book's absence might be noticed.

Will never had to ask to know that he was not welcome at the school, but having already been taught to read as a student in Bradbury, he now discovered that he had the freedom to continue learning on his own in the best way he knew how. The stories lining the schoolhouse bookshelves pulled him away into other worlds far from the lonely one in which his shivering, hungry body remained.

If the moon was full, he often read well into the night. On darker nights, he settled himself behind the hedges of one of the large stone homes in a patch of bright yellow light spilling through a gap in the curtains. Will could lose himself for hours in the strange assortment of literature that he found on those dusty shelves. He counted it a blessing that the town was too small to build separate buildings for a library, a church, and a schoolhouse. They had all been combined into one accessible room for a boy with a small stick who knew of a knot in the wood near the window.

There is much to be thankful for, Will reminded himself each evening as he settled in with a book. Even food wasn't so difficult to come by if he was up earlier than everyone else. Fallen fruit waited to be gathered and vegetables lay hidden in the damp earth, although he was careful not to take more than he felt he must. Will knew it was wrong to take without asking, but he had no idea what else he could do.

Each day throughout autumn, Will returned to the stable at the edge of Pravda and divided the produce he had gathered, hiding some away for the winter and keeping just enough for his scant meals that day. During the night, he visited the refuse pile of the mercantile store and rubbish bins behind several of the larger homes, where occasionally there was something to be gleaned. He then hid himself in the barn behind one of the large haystacks where he waited for Farmer Merril to feed and water the old plow horse and clean the stall. When the farmer was gone, Will crept from his hiding place and sat himself in the freshly tossed pile of straw.

"Hi Jimmy!" he greeted the old horse each morning with a small gift, perhaps an apple core or a bit of carrot. Jimmy nuzzled him a warm hello while he munched the offering.

Jimmy often lay down to rest when Will crawled into the stall. As winter settled in, they shared what little warmth there was to be had in the rough-hewn barn. Jimmy could only lie down for a few hours at most. The rest of the day, the old horse stood as if on watch over the sleeping boy who lay wrapped in a large, filthy gray coat, nestled deep in the straw.

Toward late afternoon each day, Will would wake. With no one else to talk to, he confided his secrets in the weary four-legged creature. These one-sided conversations varied. He described his mother in her long silk skirts and his adventures with his father. As he wound the stories into the frosty air, they carried away a little of the emotional weight that seemed to constantly crush his small frame. But the dark hours grew long and the stories became few. The void of having little to discuss was filled with the wild imaginings of a new sort of life, the kind which could only be thought up by the loneliest of children.

One moonlit night while out on his usual trek through Pravda, Will found a tattered arithmetic book in the schoolhouse fire bin. It was soaked with mud and many of the pages were torn or missing altogether as though it had happened to have found itself in the center of a school-ground fight, likely leading to the quarrelers receiving a severe lashing before the book had been tossed into the bin. Will proudly showed it to Jimmy the next morning.

"I once learned some of this, you know," he told the old horse. Will flipped through the book then laid it open on the floor, attempting to brush away some of the filth before peering intently at the figures written on the first page.

"Look here. I'll show you," he said confidently.

Will spent several weeks working through the tattered schoolbook. He drew out the equations in the dust on the barn floor and explained to Jimmy how each problem was to be solved.

"It's like a riddle or a mystery," he said pointing. "You just have to know what clues you are looking for."

The long, cold hours passed far more quickly as Will worked through the equations, at times pausing and pacing before returning to his calculations, only to scratch his head a while and begin pacing once more. His first time through the book, he wasn't sure he had solved all the problems correctly, so he went back through twice more until he was confident that he understood.

Will then added the tattered book to a small collection of strange and varied items that he kept hidden in the empty stall behind an old plow and other rusty equipment. He stored his treasures in two broken crates which he had salvaged from the burn pile behind the mercantile store.

A store of food, some of which had begun to rot before the cold weather set in, spilled out of the larger crate, consisting of an assortment of fruits, vegetables, tubers, and stale bread. He lined the second crate with clean straw, upon which he laid the bundle he had carried with him on the long journey to Pravda. Beside it lay his father's knife and a few things he had scavenged from rubbish piles around the town. His father's book lay neatly wrapped in yellowed second-hand paper and tied with a bit of twine. The book was given a special place on the top of the pile.

Will little understood the dire predicament that had redirected his life. The bitter struggle of each day was a constant reminder, yet he longed to believe against his own knowledge. He imagined his father was somehow still alive and out searching for work in the nearby towns, searching for a comfortable place for them to live, a place to build the plans they had dreamed up for months as they walked the miles of dusty road together. His mind knew what his heart could not accept. He had scavenged the bit of paper to wrap his father's book, setting it aside until the day his father would return, its secrets still hidden within—the written words of his father still alive and waiting to be discovered. Will's powerful, young imagination alone kept him rising from his straw bed each evening to search for food.

Each morning before Will slept, he filled his father's water pouch with snow and placed it beneath the manure pile to thaw. He then stored the food he had gathered that night in the larger crate. He began to worry as the food to be scavenged grew scarce while the snow banks gathered higher around the town. Shivering in the cold air, Will returned to the stall each morning with only a few new scraps. He then wrapped himself tightly his father's coat, hiding in the empty stall and waiting until the farmer's footsteps faded away.

Even with the shelter of the stable and Jimmy's warmth, the winter grew bitterly cold. With almost no food left to be gathered, Will carefully rationed what he had stored away, eating as little as possible. His stomach gnawed painfully the first week or so, but with time, he grew accustomed to the aching hunger, allowing his imagination to fill the void as best he could.

A few weeks after the first snowfall, the temperature dropped sharply. Will continued to return to the barn after scavenging each night but found he was unable to fall asleep for hours as he rubbed his frozen, wet feet. He soon learned to build a nest of straw under Jimmy's belly. Though he still never felt quite warm, he awoke less often.

Through the darkest, coldest part of winter, Will hardly left the barn. There were no scraps of food left to be gathered. He still had enough of a supply in the crate to last him a few weeks if rationed carefully, but he longed for the books that had given him some company in the long, lonely hours of the fall and early winter. The silence that engulfed the barn under its blanket of snow seemed unbearable. Unable to stand the stillness beyond the second day, Will worked up his own stories late into the night, telling Jimmy of treasure-filled caverns, great battles, heroes, and villains—always concluding with a great victory before the tale came to an end.

Each dark, cold day dragged by. The snow piled high with an occasional warm spell melting a little of the ice before another northern storm passed through. Will felt lost in time in a frozen, bitter wasteland. In the fall and early winter he had paid close attention to the days of the week as they passed, which had been vital for knowing when the schoolhouse would be vacant. Now, with the drifts piling up the sides of the barn and the days growing ever shorter, he lost track entirely. It wasn't until evergreen trees began to appear, twinkling with lights inside nearby homes, that he realized it must nearly be Christmas again.

The memories of the previous Christmas were strong and wonderful—the last of the good times before life suddenly changed. The memories ached inside of him. It seemed strange to him how fast his old life had crumbled. Now, here he slept, alone in a barn with an old plow horse who was his only friend and only a bit of rotten fruit to keep him alive. Will could hardly help but peek through the barn door each evening as darkness fell. He loved to see the small lights twinkling inside the houses near the far edge of Pravda.

The loveliest sight was the red brick home near the town square. The curtains remained wide open to display an elegant blue spruce lit with dozens of gleaming lights and decorated with several glittering ornaments. Will could not see it from the doorway of the barn, but he always made sure to pass by it multiple times whenever he went out. Yet the temperature continued to drop severely and the snow lay in high mounds. Leaving the shelter of the barn now required a great deal of warming up when he returned—an especially difficult task when the barn had little heat to offer.

The temperature continued a steady descent over the next few days until Will hardly dared to open the barn door enough to peek out. Will shivered day and night, piling fresh manure around him to keep warm until he barely noticed the rancid smell.

On a bright, clear night with a slant of moonlight peeking through a gap in the door, the temperature plummeted deep into the negatives. Will's mind was foggy and blurred, drifting in and out of consciousness as something bumped heavily against his small body. His skin burned and his lungs ached. Jimmy's large nose continued to prod against his side.

For several minutes, Will ignored the persistent nudging. His head pounded fiercely and the blood throbbed painfully in his temples. The sharp piercing cold that burned against his skin and lungs was too much to endure. His body was weak from shivering for weeks on end and every muscle ached.

Jimmy pressed his head against Will's shoulder. Will groaned but did not open his eyes. Jimmy pushed hard against Will, knocking his thick skull against Will's tiny head until at last the small boy stirred. Great white puffs of air rose from Jimmy's large nose which nuzzled insistently against Will's stinging face.

"Jimmy, what is it?" Will asked weakly. His voice sounded hoarse and strange. He tried to pat a thick patch of straw beside him, but his body wasn't working quite right. Jimmy understood and folded his legs, laying himself close to the boy. Will slid as much of his body under Jimmy's belly as he could and cuddled his face into Jimmy's warmth.

His hand hardly responded as he struggled to pull his father's large gray coat over his stiff body. Having exhausted his strength, he sank into darkness. His mind was too clouded to even wonder if he would make it through the night.

———————————

Jimmy lay warm and still with Will tucked beneath him. It seemed to Will as though he had been asleep only a short time when excruciating pain raged through his body. Waking in agony, he buried his small face into Jimmy's long hair and sobbed. The pain intensified with each moment and his cries turned into an anguished scream. His frozen body was waking up.

Chapter 5

SPRING CAME EARLY TO PRAVDA that year after a hard winter, dark and bitter cold as it had been, but for no one was it quite so harsh as it had been for the little boy who had taken up residence in the stall of an old workhorse.

Will welcomed the sun with open-armed relief. He was giddy with delight as the days lengthened and the snow melted away. He had grown quite weary of being shut up inside the barn for days on end with nothing but his constant shivering and hunger to occupy his mind. Though he still visited Jimmy each night, he was most content out of doors where he could run as far as his small legs would carry him. His muscles were stiff and weak for a time, and his lungs burned as he ran, but he soon gained strength. Will felt as though the doors of a dark prison had been thrown open at last. He ran across the empty fields, over streams, and through the forest, exploring farther with each day that passed. He climbed trees, swam in the streams, followed animal trails, and spent many afternoons lying out in the warmth of the sun. He slept under the stars most nights, if the weather was fair. When it rained, he slept beneath the old gnarled oak.

Will grew more accustomed to sleeping at night, although he still woke long before sunrise to scavenge for food. His old habits of sneaking into the schoolhouse to borrow books continued as ever before, but he had recently discovered the book roster. Every few days, Will signed out a book or two under the name of Charles Willet whose name appeared more than any other on the list. Will hoped the discrepancy would go unnoticed as long as the books were returned within a day or two.

If the weather was warm, the schoolhouse window was often left open to let in a fresh breeze. Will gathered a large, flat stone, a few bits of chalk, and a broken glass bottle in which he kept the chalk. He hid them beneath a flat gray stone beside the rock foundation of the single-room schoolhouse. There he sat, concealed behind a thick bush growing directly beneath the window, listening intently.

Miss Faux was a tall, straight-laced woman, her hair streaked with gray. Will often saw her walking between the schoolhouse and her simple timber frame home near the center of town. Her hair was pulled back in a tight bun and her plain skirts were immaculately pressed above her polished high-heeled boots. She might have seemed an imposing creature to her students, but to Will, she was merely a voice that drifted through the open window.

Though her voice was slightly nasal and rough, she had a lovely way of accentuating consonants and deepening long vowels. As often as Will discovered the window to have been opened, he perched himself between the foundation of the school and the large trimmed bush to listen in on her lectures. His vivid imagination placed him inside the room at a desk surrounded by the other students as he took part in each day's lessons.

Will tipped the broken glass bottle toward his hand. The bits of chalk fell through the opening. He liked arithmetic quite well. He marked the equations on the stone and found that he could often solve the problems before any of the other students were called on to give an answer. If anyone had been passing near the bushes during that portion of the lesson—and had been paying close attention—they would have heard soft whispers of, "I knew it!" and "Yes, got it!" and an occasional "Aw, shucks . . ."

Will often found himself getting frustrated at his exclusion. Unable to see the blackboard, he couldn't be sure what Miss Faux had written unless she repeated it out loud. Still, he found he was able to keep up quite well, although he did feel somewhat lost in certain subjects, especially when it came to learning the correct uses of pronouns and adverbs.

Ultimately, his favorite part of the school day was history. He loved the stories Miss Faux told the class. Laying back in the dirt behind the bush, he watched the clouds drift across the sky as he listened intently. When a question was asked, Will whispered eagerly,

"1812!...King George the Third! John Smith!..."

Meanwhile, a dull voice from inside the classroom answered, "I don't remember, ma'am."

Though Will longed to be inside the small room, he felt pleasantly relieved that he never had to worry about demerits or receiving a lashing for the mistakes he made. Miss Faux wasn't nearly as hard-handed as Mr. Grantie, the headmaster in Bradbury.

At first, Will wished there was someone who cared at all whether or not he was measuring up. Still, with time, he found that he was quite content to work outside behind the bush in the warmth of the sun and the fresh spring air. It was much easier to concentrate when there was no punishment for falling short of the teacher's expectations.

On rainy days, the window remained tightly closed. It was

such a disappointment when Will woke to a dark, overcast sky. He had always loved the rain, but now it meant that he would be entirely excluded from that day's lessons. On those days, he visited Jimmy and read as the hours passed by. If it was a light rain, Will spent the entire day exploring deep into the forest, returning wet but refreshed.

Windy days also proved to be means for his exclusion since the window to the school house would again remain shut. Will didn't mind the wind otherwise. He could usually be found on those blustery spring days down by the edge of the woods on the west side of Pravda, sitting rather well-concealed in the high branches of a maple tree with a book in hand and a supple willow branch to chew on.

A small milking barn was in the process of being built on the dairy a little to the south of the town. From his vantage point, Will could see the work of the men just below the hill. Thick logs were brought in from the forest on long wooden wagons. He often looked up from his book to watch the hard labor the men put in to prepping the timber, removing the bark, and cutting the deep grooves by which the logs were layered to form the walls. The sides of the barn rose slowly as the weeks passed. A substantial layer of mud was applied in all the gaps between the logs and a roof was added. It wasn't nearly as fancy as the brightly painted timber frame barns around Bradbury, but it did seem rather fulfilling to the little boy in the maple tree to watch a solid structure rise from the empty plot of ground near the feeding stalls.

The last Saturday in May began warm with bright blue skies and a light mist hanging near the river. There was no school on the weekends, so Will climbed into his favorite spot, concealed in the leaves of the maple tree. He had with him a thick volume that he had checked out from the school house under Charles Willet's name, but his eyes kept darting up to see the final touches being made to the exterior of the new building.

Only a light breeze from the west swayed against the highest branches of the maple tree, rustling the growing leaves, but as the sun reached the highest point in the sky, a terrible wind rushed over the hills and tore through the fields. Behind it came a severe lightning storm which ushered in thick, dark clouds.

Will slid down from the branches of the maple and skirted the town just inside the tree line of the forest and across the edge of the fields to the barn. He hid out of sight behind an old shed as the wind whipped his face. Farmer Merril hurriedly unharnessed the sweating old plow horse and led him back into the waiting stall before retreating into the farmhouse as sheets of rain erupted from the dark sky. Will was soaked before he closed the barn door on the darkening world outside.

Rain poured down all through the evening and into the night. Will woke with a start. The drumming of the rain had grown into a harsh thundering that beat against the roof and sides of the aged barn. Will hurried toward the door and peeked out. The torrential rain had developed into thick chunks of hail which banged loudly against every exposed surface. The wind howled and shrieked as the pounding hail pelted down.

Will reached out through the door and picked up one of the hard stones of ice. He retreated to the safety of the stall and showed it to Jimmy, who seemed agitated and wary of the cacophony clamoring around them. The thundering hail eventually died down and the rain returned. Will sat in the corner of Jimmy's stall reading aloud. The beating of the rain occasionally grew so loud that it drowned out his voice while great claps of thunder rumbled in the sky above them.

The rain continued throughout the following day, pouring

in torrents. Restless, Will opened the barn door a few inches and sat against the wall. He watched the streaming droplets pour from the sky.

Great claps of thunder echoed through the town. Will climbed into Jimmy's stall. Jimmy lay upon the straw, his ears twitching. Will cuddled up against his warm belly, listening to the downpour clattering against the roof and the sides of the barn. The rhythm of the rain and the gentle movement of Jimmy's sides heaving with every breath lulled Will back to sleep.

The next sound, aside from the rain, was the barn door creaking open on its rusty hinges.

Will woke to a soft, flickering glow filling the barn. He jumped up and slipped through a loose board between the stalls. He settled the board back into place as Farmer Merril unlatched the door to Jimmy's stall. Will sat against the rough wood and listened to the routine sounds of the farmer cleaning out the stall and replacing the old straw and hay.

Will nearly jumped at the sound of Farmer Merril's soft voice. In all his time hidden in the second stall, Will had never heard the middle-aged man say a word. The farmer let out a long sigh. "Well, old boy. The field is a mess, to be sure. I suppose we'll just be glad we hadn't finished the planting, but we'll be set behind a good three weeks by the time we're able to plant more seed, and then we'll be left to the mercy of a late fall." Farmer Merril sighed again and settled the pitchfork back into the large pile of straw near the second stall. The flickering light faded as the barn door clicked shut and Farmer Merril returned to the house.

Will crawled back through the loose board and sighed. "Jimmy, I just don't think I can stand this rain much longer." Standing up, he patted Jimmy's neck in the darkness. "I suppose it's not so bad, but we're both stuck in the dark. I don't know how

I would dry out once I got wet if the sun doesn't come back out soon." Jimmy pushed his large nose through the fresh pile of hay. His ears twitched as Will spoke.

Dropping down onto the clean straw, Will sighed. "I suppose the rain has to come, and it's not bad to have some rain, really." He looked up into the darkness where the rain pounded mercilessly on the roof overhead. Jimmy munched his meal contentedly. Will climbed from the stall and opened the door a few inches. He sat near it peering out into the downpour.

"It's a lot like life, Jimmy," he whispered. "It may be dark, cold and wet now, but we know the sun will come again." Will sighed bitterly and leaned his head back against the rough wood behind him. "It just seems," he said, looking up at the dark sky, "that sometimes the rain never wants to stop."

Day and night had nearly run together under the thick, black clouds. There was only a dim glow that came and went as time passed. Will sat by the door, squinting at the words on the pages of the book he had borrowed before the storm had blown in. Will's legs ached from sitting on the hard ground near the barn door. He realized that it must nearly be nightfall. He couldn't read any longer no matter how much he strained his eyes, and still the rain poured down.

A strange sound from the stall made him look up. He heard it again and jumped to his feet. Standing on tiptoe, he peered into the stall, "Jimmy? What's wrong?" he asked as his eyes settled upon the immense figure of the distressed horse.

Jimmy lay on his side, his head thrashing. Will threw open the stall door and dropped to his knees at Jimmy's side. He pressed his hands against Jimmy's neck, trying to calm him. The white of Jimmy's eyes caught the dim glow of light from the door. They looked wild and strained.

"Jimmy, Jimmy! What's wrong? Oh, Jimmy!" But Jimmy only whinnied and grunted in pain, still thrashing his head.

Jumping to his feet, Will ran to the barn door and threw it open. He dove into the pouring rain and dashed for the farmer's house. He pounded on the door.

The door opened moments later. Farmer Merril stood surprised, staring at Will.

"Sir, please, something's wrong with Jimmy . . ."

The farmer furrowed his brow and stared hard at him. "Boy, I don't know what you're talking about. I've got enough trouble of my own to worry about just now."

The farmer spotted the barn door, which stood open with rain pouring through it. "Boy! What were you doing in my barn?"

Shoving Will aside, he ran to the open door. Will tumbled into the mud. Jumping to his feet, he hurried after the farmer.

Farmer Merril stood staring into stall. The old plow horse writhed in pain. The man fell to his knees.

"Please, sir, you have to help him!" Will cried.

The farmer leaped at him. "Boy!" he roared, "Tell me what you've done to my horse!" He raised a large, weathered hand and slapped the back of it hard against Will's face.

Will tumbled to the ground, sobbing. "Please, sir, I didn't. . ."

"Get out of my barn!" The farmer's face was deep red even in the faint light. "Don't ever let me see you around my horse again!" The farmer raised his hand again and left a harsh mark on the other side of Will's face. "Get out!" he shouted. Grabbing Will by the threadbare collar of his shirt, he threw him into the rain that poured through the open door. "Get out!"

Will stumbled to his feet, his vision swimming from the

pain that burned from the bruises swelling on his face. He ran as fast as his small legs would carry him, skirting around the town. He paused a moment just before he reached the tree line of the forest. He turned and looked back. Will could see nothing but thick sheets of rain. He raised his face toward the sky, the rain mixing with his tears and dripping to the ground. "Please, oh, please! Let Jimmy be alright!" he pleaded. Will then turned and disappeared into the woods.

It wasn't until morning came that Farmer Merril discovered a steady drip of rain trickling from the roof and falling onto the large pile of hay—turning it black with mold.

Chapter 6

A DIRE SITUATION could hardly have been avoided. After two more days of continual rainfall, the small, thin boy lay feverish beneath a large maple tree deep in the woods. The sky began to clear, but a steady dripping continued all around as water slid from the leaves to the muddy earth below.

Though his body was soaked, Will's throat was dry and his skin burned. He screamed as nightmares turned into illusions. Delirium crept over him. He curled into a tight ball, weeping as massive red giants with large, weathered hands struck his face, shouting, "Get out, boy!"

The voices screamed in his mind. He felt the searing pain across his face. "Please!" he cried. "I didn't do it! I didn't do it!" He tried to raise his arms against the attacks, but his body would not respond. "Please, I'll go, I'll go!" he wept. His small body writhed in pain. "Jimmy! Jimmy!" he cried out, wondering why his only friend had abandoned him to the giants.

By the time he awoke, his body was weak, but the fever was gone. Will found that he could hardly move. He pushed himself backwards along the wet grass and slowly propped himself up against the rough bark of the maple tree, gasping for air. His stomach turned. He retched the bit of water that had trickled into his mouth, a thin stream burning against his throat and lips as it dripped to the ground. The earth twisted in front of him and he fell hard onto the damp earth.

Steadying himself, Will waited for his vision clear. With great effort, he peeled his wet shirt from his damp skin and pulled it over his head then laid it on the thick grass beside him, panting and shaking. He leaned his head back against the tree and rested a moment before working to remove his trousers.

Will found it a small bit of relief that he had run so far into the woods. He crawled into the sun, nearly naked except for his threadbare underclothes. He barely made it beyond the shade of the tree when his arms collapsed beneath him. Burying his face under his arm, he drifted off to sleep.

The sun beat down on his weary body and he awoke with agonizing burns across his back and shoulders. His stomach twisted with severe hunger. He realized it must have been nearly three days since he had last eaten and his mouth and lips were parched, having only drunk the dripping rainwater since he had first collapsed beneath the maple tree.

Hearing a stream somewhere nearby, Will's head cleared a little, but every bit of his body ached. He reached for a nearby branch and pushed himself to his feet. He swayed a little as he gripped the rough wood in his hand. The bright sunlight made his head pound and the warmth burned ever hotter upon his red back. Closing his eyes, Will made his way toward the stream, one slow step at a time.

The sound of the rushing water led Will to a thicket of wild thorny bushes that grew high and dense. Moving along the edge of the brush, he came to a place where the stream poured out of the prickly mesh and continued on its way. He lay down for a few moments on the mossy bank, longing to rest his eyes and sleep a while longer, but he knew he had to eat and the water called to him to quench the burning in his throat.

Pulling himself to the edge of the river, Will cupped a handful of water to his lips. The ice cold water ached against his teeth. He drank slowly. It burned as it touched his throat. He let it drip down his cracked lips and over his chin and back into the stream. It took several minutes to get much into his belly, but eventually the water began to revive him.

A glittering flash in the water caught his eye as he lay on his side, resting on the bank. It flickered then disappeared. He saw another. Will raised his head a little and watched. Several silver-scaled fish, some large and others quite small, swam through the clear water. Will had no hook nor any bait. He reached his hand into the water and tried to wrap his fingers around one of the smooth bellies, but it was fast and slipped through his grasp. He tried again and again and again. Exhausted, his head drooped back to the ground and his hand rested in the cool water against a rough jutting stone. As his hand drifted lazily in the water, he felt something smooth resting beneath the stone. It didn't move as he carefully his fingers along the slippery belly. Will clasped his fingers tightly inside the gills and flung his arm out of the water. The fish twisted through the air and lay flopping on the ground.

"I'm so sorry," Will told the fish, "but I am grateful to have you all the same."

The small fish made a messy but delightful meal.

Will's strength began to return. He camped the next few days near the stream. Twice a day, he slid his hand beneath the rocks until he felt the smooth belly of a fish. If he moved too fast, the fish swam away. Will practiced for several hours until he could easily slip his fingers into the gills and toss the fish from the water. He kept only a few for eating and returned the rest to the stream as soon as they had been caught.

Will found great satisfaction in being able to provide his own food. He didn't feel nearly so guilty robbing streams as he did robbing home-grown gardens and fruit trees.

He hadn't been anxious to return to Pravda since the incident at the barn, but he knew he would have to return soon—before Farmer Merril discovered the broken crates in the second stall. Still, as frightened as he was of being seen by Farmer Merril, he wasn't the reason Will most feared to return. Will wasn't sure he could bare what he might find when he opened the stall door where his only friend had lain sick the night he left.

Nearly two full weeks had passed since Will had run from the barn when a harsh realization came to him. He had been lucky enough to survive that first winter with a barn for protection from the weather and a horse to keep him warm. With no shelter, time was growing short. Will estimated that little more than four months remained until the snows came. Without some sort of refuge, he would never survive. He would have to build a shelter.

The idea of having a stream near the shelter appealed to Will. He followed the flowing water a good distance in both directions in search of a secluded place. Having traipsed along the bank of the river, he could find no spot where the trees grew thick enough to be well-concealed ,aside from the thicket which seemed impenetrable. He was already far from town, but he had seen the hunters venture even farther into the woods at different times of the year. Will returned to his campsite by the vast thicket. He threw another fish from the water for his dinner then settled down for the night as the sun set below the tops of the trees.

Waking suddenly out of a deep sleep that night, Will felt disoriented in the darkness. Only a sliver of the moon hung in the sky above him. A loud grunting near him chilled his blood. Will slowly turned his head to see an unexpected visitor at his camp-site. Not far from where he lay, a large body thick with fur pawed through the scales and guts that had been left from the fish.

Heat racing, Will stared at the bear. For all the time he had spent in the woods, the fiercest creature he had seen was a large black moose that had eyed him warily before moving on, but a bear was different. Will knew nothing about the massive creatures and the last thing he wanted to do was to learn in the middle of the night.

The boy rolled to his stomach and slowly crawled toward the stream, keeping an eye on the creature. Distracted with the fish, the bear didn't look up. Will reached the bank and slid his body into the bone-chilling water. He had planned to cross to the other side and get far enough beyond it that he could run, but as he slipped into the water, he saw an opening in the thicket where the stream deepened beneath the brambles. The top of the stream bubbled through the thorns, but there was an opening in the branches below the surface of the water.

Will drew in a deep breath and pushed his head below the surface. He tried to swim, but he was heading up-stream and only managed to slip backwards in the attempt, finding himself even closer to the bear. Will grabbed desperately at the rocks beneath him and pulled his way against the current. It was slow progress —far too slow. His lungs screamed for air and his head began to pound. Will pressed his face up into the thorns. The sharp barbs tore at his skin, but his mouth broke through the surface of the water. Will gasped in a few breaths then dove under the water once more.

The next time Will raised his head, no thorns dug into his skin. Dragging himself from the stream, he listened for any sound of danger but heard nothing aside from the churning of the water.

He felt disoriented. Will had been certain that the thicket continued much farther than he had come, but he could see nothing beyond a few shadowy shapes of large trees.

Stripping off his wet shirt and trousers, Will lay down beneath the nearest tree. He tried to rest, but hours passed before he had shivered away the water and his eyes finally closed.

Will awoke confused and half naked beneath a large maple. His underclothes were still damp and his shirt and trousers lay in the mud near the water. It took him a moment to remember his late night excursion up the stream. He stood quickly and looked around.

Startled and amazed, Will discovered that he had not passed beyond the thicket, but directly into it. He found himself within a large clearing between two small streams. The two streams started as one at the head of the clearing then divided and curved away from each other with an overgrowth of bushes and trees on the far side of each of the streams. Between the two streams was a wide, open space with tall grasses that looked as though it flooded several times a year. A few trees grew in places where the ground rose a little higher. Birds sang from the upper branches of the trees, but there were no other animals—and there were no other people.

Will estimated the space within the clearing to be nearly three times the size of Pravda's town square and was completely surrounded by a thicket that rose close to ten feet high with trees, brambles and wild brush. Will circled the clearing several times, hardly daring to believe his luck. Flooding would be a problem, he knew, and he would have to find a way in and out, but he couldn't have asked for a place better suited to his needs.

Will excitedly spent the day mapping out his plans for the meadow, using the mud of the riverbank as his drawing board.

His excitement grew until he was nearly giddy with delight as new ideas flooded his mind. He could not have felt more joy had he been given a kingdom. By nature and a little luck, Will had been given a large, safe parcel of land, all his own.

The next morning, Will awoke at the break of dawn. In the cool, crisp air of a bright June morning, the work began.

Chapter 7

THE FIRST WEEK IN THE CLEARING passed quickly. Fresh dew glittered in the early hours within the walled-off enclosure as Will worked his way from one side to the other, preparing and clearing his hidden bit of land. Swimming in from upstream and leaving downstream made accessing the clearing fairly easy, though Will found it necessary to cut away some of the brambles and clear away several large rocks. The only difficulty remaining was the unavoidable damp clothing that clung tight against his skin as he traipsed through the forest looking for fallen logs to use to build his shelter.

Will walked far into the thick brush looking for usable wood. With patience and a great deal of exploring, he came across a variety of fallen trees, each of which he dragged back to the stream. Will broke away the large branches from each log and rolled them into the water before returning to his search for more wood. When he arrived back in the clearing each evening, a mess of washed-up logs lay along the banks.

Will shivered and stamped his cold feet to regain circulation as the chilly breezes of the early mornings made the wet clothing much less tolerable. It took until late morning before the river water dried from his clothes each day, and it was late into the evening after returning that he managed to dry out once more.

After the first cold, wet week of searching the forest, Will decided it might be wise to spend a day or two creating an alternate entrance into the meadow. With his plans solidified and lacking only the tools necessary to complete the project, he decided that it was finally time to make a trip back to Pravda.

The first day after discovering the clearing, Will spent most of the morning and afternoon hunting for logs and sending them downstream into the meadow, but as the sun dipped nearer the horizon, he turned toward the town. By nightfall, he sat just inside the tree line, waiting until the last light was extinguished. He stood in the quiet darkness and shook bits of leaves and dirt from his clothing.

Once night had fully fallen, Will cautiously made his way toward the old barn. He paused a moment at the door and said a short, desperate prayer. Taking a deep breath, he pulled open the barn door. Something shifted in the stall. Will hurried over and unhooked the latch.

"Jimmy!" he gasped. He slipped inside and wrapped his arms tightly around Jimmy's neck. Jimmy snorted happily.

Will buried his face into Jimmy's mane for several minutes, breathing in the familiar smell of his dearest friend. "I can't stay, you know," Will told the old horse, releasing him. "But I'm glad you are alright!"

Jimmy nuzzled him. Will embraced his friend once more and stroked his large nose. Jimmy lay down expectantly. Will smiled and settled himself against the large, weary creature. The small boy sighed contentedly.

"Oh, Jimmy. How I've missed having someone to talk to! I suppose you know what it is like to feel such loneliness, here in this dark, drafty barn all alone. There are times when I think it is more than I can bear! And yet, somehow, I find that I make it from that day to the next, and to the one after, but how I wish that things were so different!"

Will paused, looking up at a small new patch in the roof above them. He sighed, "But what good does it do to think in such a way? It does no good, Jimmy. I come here, find you alive, and have many wonderful things to tell you about a secret place—all my own, and the first thing I tell you is how lonely I have felt. That won't do. Things—well, at least many things—are so good. I can even catch fish with my bare hands—you should see it! I still am uncertain how it is even possible, but it truly is so."

The heaving of Jimmy's side against Will's back brought to the small boy such an enveloping sense of comfort—the gentle contact and movement from another living creature there beside him. Closing his eyes, Will was surprised at the peace and safety that filled him for those few moments.

Will allowed his body to rest for a time in the warmth and security that surrounded him in that simple stall. It seemed hardly a minute or two later that Jimmy shifted and began to stand. Will stood and hugged the old horse tightly around the neck. He felt a deep ache and a burning in his eyes and throat as he held his old friend close.

"I didn't have much, Jimmy, but I at least had you. It is nice to have a place all to myself, but I would give it up if only I could stay in this stall with you through the coming winter."

Will reached out his small hand and stroked it along Jimmy's neck. "Thank you for everything, Jimmy. You were that someone who watched over me when no one else would." Will patted him gently then turned away.

Will lifted the loose board between the two stalls then climbed into the space in the second stall. With relief, he discovered that the two crates were still intact. The little bit of food he had left behind had rotted in the summer heat, but everything else was in about the same condition as when he had left it, only now hidden beneath a thin layer of dust and straw. Will even found the book he had thrown as he ran to get the farmer that terrible night. It had landed beside the old plow and was filthy, but not ruined.

Will took the crate with the rotten food and emptied it behind the barn. He stacked the two crates together with his precious belongings tucked inside. He carried them along the outskirts of Pravda and hid them in the shadow of a thick pine near the edge of the woods. He picked up the book from off the top of the pile and stole his way silently toward the schoolhouse. Will easily unhooked the latch of the window and pushed his way inside, leaving the book in its place on the shelf and marking it off on the roster.

Will knew the thicket was a good distance from Pravda, but that night as he carried the heavy wooden crates, it seemed much farther. When at last he arrived, he hid the crates beneath a bush then swam back into the clearing and fell fast asleep.

The next night, Will traveled back to the town. This time, he borrowed the same shovel he had used nearly a year earlier to dig a hole beneath the gnarled oak tree. Now, he set out to dig a passage beneath the thicket. He chose the spot well. An ugly, twisted pine stood among several other trees on the east side of the thicket. Just behind this particular pine, Will began to dig.

Though he got tangled several times in the thorns and bushes as he climbed in an out, Will dug with the enthusiasm of a nine-year-old, but his strength began to wane long before the hole was complete and the long handle of the shovel became a hindering nuisance in the cramped space. He kept finding it necessary to dig deeper as thick roots blocked his path. He was just deciding he would soon have to quit for the night when the hole began to fill with water.

Will hurried out of the hole, damp and filthy, but still quite pleased. He ran back to Pravda under a full moon with the shovel slung across his shoulders. He replaced the shovel and savored the long walk back. He slipped into the river from upstream then stripped off his outer clothing. While shivering away the chilly water, he caught and ate a large fish. Will then curled up in the shadow of the largest oak in the clearing and fell fast asleep.

He borrowed the shovel again the next night and worked to reroute a section of the stream, allowing him to finish the tunnel. Most of the night was spent diverting the water. He had just replaced the shovel back in the shed and returned to the woods when a glow appeared on the eastern horizon.

The sun was high in the sky and burning down when he awoke. Will went back to work, building a wall of boulders and twigs where the stream had been diverted.

It took several days for the tunnel to dry out. Will waited only until the water was gone before he finished the passageway in a muddy mess. He emerged inside the clearing, filthy and triumphant. Although the roots had been troublesome to work through, they created a fibrous network that held the soil in place around the tunnel.

The tunnel was little more than the smallest of the preparations that would be necessary before winter arrived, but an easier entrance made the rest of his workload much easier.

A large pile of long, thin logs lay gathered and stacked near the center of the meadow. Will cleared a square of grass on what he deemed to be the highest level of ground. He knew it would not be enough to keep the stream from flooding into it, but for now, it would do.

Will set about stripping all the remaining branches from the driest logs. It took a great deal of time. Many were far too stubborn to relent to his persistent efforts. His hands grew blistered and bloodied from the harsh work, but it was invigorating to see the success of each day's labor.

After removing the branches, Will began a futile attempt at using his father's knife to debark the trees. The knife soon grew dull and the tip broke against a thick knot in one of the logs. Will stowed the knife back inside the smaller crate then set about striking a large black obsidian rock until it boasted a sharp, jagged edge. Even with the obsidian, it took many hours to strip each log, working from the longest to the shortest and laying them out in order.

Will had never built anything very sturdy, and certainly no sort of shelter. He had watched men building the new milking barn, but he couldn't have lifted the heavy timber they had used. Still, he decided to try layering the modest-sized logs he had brought into the clearing. As hard as it had been to strip the bark with the obsidian, Will found it nearly impossible to cut the grooves needed to do the layering. He finally gave up on using the stone and sneaked back into town late in the evening.

Finding the shovel had been easy enough, but finding a saw took him nearly three nights of searching. Will finally came across an old jagged blade that lay covered in rust inside a rickety shed. He hoped that its absence might go unnoticed for perhaps a few weeks until his project was complete.

Will returned to the clearing with the rusty saw and began again with fresh determination. Progress was slow, but aside from building his shelter, the only thing he had to worry about was eating occasionally and sleeping. The small boy worked mostly at night when it was less likely that anyone would be in the woods and the sound of the saw would not be heard. In the muddy clearing, the walls of a small cabin began to rise.

For weeks, Will continued to gather, scrape, carve, and build. With each passing day, the progress of his hard labor began to show and his excitement grew. He worked feverishly as June turned to July and July grew late. There was still far too much to be done. He had not yet even begun to store food for the winter.

August came and the night air grew cool. The walls were mostly up, yet there was neither a door nor a roof. A cold snap blew in with heavy rains. He realized that it would soon be too late to gather a decent supply of food.

Will cleared away the grass from a large patch of ground in a high spot in the clearing. He packed mud over the area and gave it a few days to dry. Each morning he caught as many fish as he could find hiding in the two streams. Using his father's knife, he cut the pink flesh from the bones and laid it out to dry on the hardened mud. In the evenings, he continued to search for branches and logs to cut down and break into firewood. For just one night each week, Will scavenged in the village for food and other supplies.

One clear, moonlit night, he found two small metal buckets in the rubbish pile behind the new milking barn. Will could hardly contain his excitement. One of the rusty buckets had a large hole near the top and was missing the bottom entirely. The other had a large crack down the side. Will took them back with him to the clearing. He took the worst of the two buckets and beat it into the rough shape of a shovel blade. He then pushed a thick stick through two holes he had made in a line down the middle and beat the metal around the stick until it held secure. It was neither sharp nor very strong, but it was far better than nothing. The other bucket was set aside until he could decide how to best put it to use.

In one corner of the cabin, Will carefully shoveled out a deep hole, in which he began to store the fruits and vegetables he gathered. He created a large shelf that extended from one wall at the back of his shelter to the other for storing the dried fish.

At last, it was time to start building the roof. One log after another, Will layered the saplings toward the center of the room. The roof took on a unique, square-shaped form as he crossed the logs one way then the other, with each layer using slightly shorter timber and rising upwards until only a small opening in the center remained. It was less than sturdy initially as he propped several logs beneath the opening to hold it up, but he would soon build a fireplace with a chimney to support the misshapen roof.

The cabin was far from perfect with its odd shape and disproportionate walls, but to young Will, it was beautiful. It was his own. He alone had built it. Still, he worried, studying the odd little structure, wondering if it might not withstand the winter winds and heavy snows. He hoped that perhaps the large oak that stood just beside the small shelter might be helpful in protecting it from the worst of the weather.

The roof had been a difficult and challenging endeavor, yet the door proved to be the trickiest part of the project.

Will stripped the nails from the two broken crates. He straightened each nail as best he could, though it proved nearly impossible to do much to improve them. He cut and built a frame then sawed some logs to fit. He laid the thin logs together and realized with sinking disappointment that he would still be several nails short. Will nailed as many to the frame as he could, growing frustrated as he fought the bent nails. When at last the final nail was in place, he looked uncertainly at the large gap that still remained.

On his next trip to town, Will searched for any sort of used nail that wouldn't be missed, but he could find nothing but a single rusty spike that had been snapped in half and would do little good.

Twice a week now he continued to search for anything he might be able to use, but the weather was growing colder with each passing day as October came with its seasonal rains. He was running out of time. He spent each day mudding the walls and roof of the small cabin, both inside and out, adding dry grasses to help it hold.

He was exhausted by evening as he searched for firewood. Will had returned the saw a few weeks before and was only able to gather wood that was already small enough to be used without having to be cut up.

The first snowfall came early that year, but it melted by mid-afternoon that same day. It was now late October. The walls had been mudded and the roof thatched, but a small hole still remained at the top of the ceiling in the cabin. The door, with its wide gap, still had not been fixed in place. Hinges, Will knew, would be even less likely to be found than a handful of nails.

He was now spending three nights a week gathering food and scavenging around the town.

On one especially dark night after a terrible windstorm, Will came across a shamble of wood near the center of town. He recognized its crushed form as being the old privy that had recently stood behind the town hall. A large branch lay splintered on top of the mess with several of the boards broken and smashed beneath it. The small, mutilated building had been set near a wood pile, left to be rebuilt at some future time, but seemed to have been left neglected as the second snow storm set in, falling heavily.

Will's fingers were bright red from the cold as he left behind a shapeless pile of weathered planks. In his arms, he cradled a wrapped bundle of nails and two precious hinges. He disappeared into the forest, the snow covering his footprints.

Chapter 8

WILL DUG A SMALL FIRE PIT in the center of the cabin and surrounded it with river rock. Through the first part of the winter, he did not yet dare light a fire since there had been no time yet to build a chimney. The air had grown intensely cold by now. His hands grew painfully stiff and bright red as he plunged his fists into the icy stream to gather the needed stones for this final project. The mud dried slowly and it took over three weeks before the rounded fireplace and chimney had been completed.

The weather grew icy with fierce, penetrating winds. A thick storm settled around Pravda and tormented the weary town and surrounding fields and woods. A great and welcome relief filled the little cabin hidden within a rise of brambles when at last a fire blossomed within the oddly-shaped hearth, crackling merrily, its dancing light brightening the otherwise dark room.

Will stepped out into the snow and watched a while as the smoke rose from the chimney. A thin, soft wisp drifted into the ash-gray sky—not enough to draw attention, he hoped, although perhaps he would let the fire burn only at night and use the coals to keep warm through the daylight hours. He went back inside, relieved at the glow of warmth that greeted him.

The winter snow fell heavy in the forest and fields. At first,

Will felt a great deal of freedom having his own place to enjoy as he pleased without having to always worry about being seen, but it wasn't long before he began longing for his old surroundings—particularly for his old friend Jimmy. Will hadn't spoken to a single human being since his terrible, brief conversation with the farmer. He hadn't had time to worry about being lonely through the busy summer months as he struggled to create a means for survival, but now, winter had come and the silence grew as thick as the drifting snow.

Will found much to keep him occupied. Each morning, if there was no blizzard, he went hunting. He had little success for the first several weeks. His father had shown him a few techniques during the long months of their journey together, but even his father had little skill and Will found that trying it on his own was far more complicated than their weak attempts had been during their travels. Will experimented with ideas for snares, setting them in several parts of the forest. It took a good deal of practice and a lot of error, but at long last, on a bright, crisp morning, he checked his makeshift traps and discovered a small rabbit caught in a line he had rigged. Will had no idea how to skin a rabbit and it proved to be a rough sort of job, but it was a nice change from his supply of fish, fruits and vegetables. He roasted the misshapen bits of meat over the fire and chewed the meat contentedly throughout the day.

The fur pelt cleaned up well in the icy water of the stream, but he knew nothing of preparing the hide. Will snuck into Pravda that night and worked a stick through the knot in the wood near the window of the schoolhouse, unhooking the latch. He had seen a book on basic hunting and hide tanning beside a large volume on architecture that had also fascinated him. Will borrowed both books and carried them back with him. He made a mess of the first rabbit's hide—scraping holes clear through—but a second hide from a rabbit caught later that week gave him the chance to improve his technique, and the soft pelt, though a little shredded, became a comfortable resting place for his head each night.

A large pile of grass picked near the end of autumn made up his bed in the corner and his father's worn coat provided some warmth on the long nights, but the grass had grown dry and brittle and rather uncomfortable. As the days passed and his traps became more successful, Will lined his bed with fur pelts of various sizes and colors and piled them over himself each evening for added warmth on the wintry nights.

The cabin was cozy and much more comfortable than the stable, but the long, dark hours settled painfully over the small boy, lonely and far too quiet. He felt as though his identity as a human being would soon slip away and only the instinct to survive would remain. The thought frightened and troubled him. He longed for someone to talk to, anyone who might save him from the empty void that expanded the distance between him and all other existence of life.

Occasionally, a warm wind blew in from the south. On these days, Will wrapped himself tightly in his father's old coat and walked to the village. He often climbed the giant spruce on the northern end of town and sat quietly hidden among the thick pine boughs. He nestled deep into the branches and watched the people bustling around below. Children played and called out to one another, lost in the merriment of the fresh snow and their exuberant freedom between school and work. He soon learned their names and a great deal about each one of them.

Gavin was a smaller boy with sandy blonde hair and a bright smile. His best friends were Billy, a rounded sort of boy with short legs and plump, dimpled cheeks, and Noah, who was pale with curly red hair and freckles. They teased the girls, but not unkindly—especially pretty Leanna with her dark brown bobbing ringlets and her bright ruffled dresses. The rowdy boys of the town, Mark and Joshua, were not much larger, but they seemed always agitated and ready to push and torment whoever was nearest them. They were constantly reprimanded for fighting and causing mischief, though they rarely seemed to take much notice as they coaxed each other into even more devious deeds. They hardly seemed intelligent enough to cause any real trouble, Will observed, but they were an obvious nuisance.

Sitting huddled high in the branches of that great blue spruce was something akin to a social feast for Will, observing all that played out before him. Having spent so much time alone throughout the previous year, he felt quite content as he watched the mayor walk the half-block to the town hall, his large belly making him waddle slightly with each heavy step. Will also contemplated the odd sight of Deputy Cornelius strutting through the streets with a well-polished badge glinting from his crisp, clean coat, while his head swiveled ceaselessly like a dizzying dance atop his scrawny shoulders.

Will especially loved watching the ladies when they came out in their brightly adorned dresses and long, black fitted coats. Their elegant posture and soft manner awed him and he felt absorbed watching as their skirts gently flowed behind them.

Miss Eleanora was the loveliest of all of the women in the town below him, and it was evident that Mr. Murdoch, the postman, had noticed. Mr. Murdoch seemed interested in nearly any young, available female, but Miss Eleanora was his obvious favorite. It also seemed clear that Mr. Murdoch knew only too well that she went to the mercantile store on her lunch break each day as his route took him in a strange pattern that landed him crossing her path no fewer than four times each way.

Unfortunately for Mr. Murdoch, Miss Eleanora seemed far more attentive toward the absent-minded Mr. Carter, the town clerk. Mr. Carter didn't seem to notice much at all as he rushed from the town hall, nearly bumping into Miss Eleanora each time due to his fogged-up glasses and her rather impeccable timing.

Frail Miss Margery was the oldest person in Pravda. Her white, wrinkled hand shook as it gripped the arched cane that she used to get to the store once each week. She stayed at the store much longer than seemed particularly necessary to pick out her regular small supply of groceries. She then returned to her house with slow, careful steps while Charles Willet followed dutifully behind carrying the recently purchased items, listening as the the elderly woman described in quite matter-of-fact tones her opinions regarding the state of the town—whether to her approval or otherwise, depending on her demeanor for that particular day. Charles Willet walked along saying nothing.

Charles Willet was the son of Mr. Willet, who owned the mercantile store. Charles was a quiet boy with a shy smile. He often passed between the schoolhouse and the store carrying twice as many books as anyone his age.

Will discovered with surprise the steady appearances of unsightly bruises rising on Charles' thin, unclad arms and occasionally on his sallow face. Will had seen Mr. Willet enough to have reason to believe him to be a hard-handed man, yet it was difficult for Will to imagine that a boy so soft-spoken as Charles could ever behave poorly enough to deserve the colored marks that adorned him.

Will wondered at it. How much he would have given to have anyone that might have cared for him, but Charles walked slower and slower the closer he came to the mercantile store until he reached the doorstep, dropped his head, and made his way inside. Perhaps, Will thought, if being alone was the alternative to Charles' obvious fear of his father, then it wasn't nearly so bad.

And then, there was young Bonnie. Will had first noticed her on the third warm winter day as he hid in his usual place high in the large spruce. A southern wind had blown in that morning and some of the heavy snow began to melt.

A small, poorly dressed boy named Jason appeared at the door of the farmhouse that Will knew only too well. Jason picked his way down the muddy lane and stopped at a gate not far from the farmhouse, where he waited each day for Jonathan, the carpenter's son. Jonathan soon appeared and together the boys dodged puddles as they made their way up the avenue. They had nearly reached the main street when Jason gave an excited whoop. He reached down and scooped up a bright, polished nickel that had been left exposed by the melting snow. Jason showed it to Jonathan then grasped it happily against his chest, but his expression quickly changed to one of horror. Mark and Joshua approached and stood in front of them glowering.

"*Thank* you for finding my nickel." Mark said. He narrowed his eyes threateningly. "I'll take it now." He held out his hand and stepped forward.

"No. It's not yours. I found it." Jason backed away, his small face scrunched with a surprising mixture of fear and determination.

"You found it where I dropped it, now give it to me, or I will be happy to help you." Both he and Joshua took another step forward, cornering the boys against a slushy bank of snow.

A small figure with long, dark knotted hair and wearing a faded dress suddenly appeared. Her arms held a thin shawl wrapped tightly around her bony shoulders. Her tired brown eyes took in the sight of the four boys. She took three calm steps forward until she was nose to nose with Mark, a frightening glint in her eye. She never spoke a single word. She just waited silently, staring into Mark's twisting face. Mark's fury radiated and the veins in his neck and forehead bulged, but the young girl maintained her composure—unmoving and silent.

After a moment, Mark spat at her then laughed scornfully. "You stupid goat-face. Why don't you try talking for once! Prove you've got a brain somewhere in that ugly head." He walked away snickering with Joshua.

Bonnie watched the two bullies leave before she turned and walked away, never taking a second look at little Jason, who still clutched the prized nickel against his chest, and Jonathan, who plopped with relief into the mushy bank behind them.

Will was stunned at the brief encounter. He pondered on it for the many hours that followed until darkness settled over Pravda that night. He had seen many unusual things in his few years, but nothing that captivated him in quite the same way. He supposed Bonnie was nothing as pretty as Leanna, but he somehow felt drawn to her. He began to watch for her, noticing as she walked the streets silently, hardly ever looking anyone in the eye and never speaking. Bonnie was silent—"mute or dumb" the other children called her, but Will wondered at how little else they all seemed to notice in young Bonny.

Adults brushed past her in the streets, hardly seeing the poorly clad girl, yet Bonnie seemed to notice everything. Unwittingly, and surprising to even himself, she began to teach Will to see as well.

Will had come even earlier the next morning, climbing to his place in the tree and settling among the branches. He shivered in the damp, chilly air. Only a slight glow lit the eastern horizon when a slim, solitary figure headed toward Pravda, coming up the footpath on the far side of town.

The path she traveled broke through the tree line to the west, where a part of the woods skirted the edge of the town. Bonnie's father, Will supposed, must be Mr. Wilson, one of the lumberjacks whom he had seen working on the new milking barn earlier in the year. Mr. Wilson had a run-down cabin not far inside the forest. He also knew that Clyde Wilson was reputably the town drunk.

Bonnie traipsed through the snow, barely visible in the pale light. She was the first of the children to set out to school and the last to arrive. Her path was hardly direct.

Her first stop that morning was at old Miss Margery's home. No lights were on inside the dwelling. Bonnie made her way up the walk to the front porch. She wrapped a cold, red hand around the crooked straw broom that rested near the front door. Within moments, the light snow that had fallen during the night was cleared from the walkway and the broom once again rested in its place beside the door.

Bonnie was turning to leave but paused and looked up at the roof above the porch, where a stream of water dripped steadily down onto the walkway below. She climbed onto the porch railing, slipping a little in her worn boots. She wrapped one arm tightly around a post and balanced on tiptoe as she reached up to the rain gutter. She pushed her frozen fingers against the thin metal until the gap slowly closed and the dripping subsided. She then slid carefully back to the ground. Picking up her books and the small bundle of sticks she had carried with her, she headed on her way.

Bonnie stopped next at a small, well-kept cottage a few doors down from Miss Margery's place. She knelt in the snow and began rolling two thick snowballs. She placed the largest in front of a thin window on the east side of the small green cottage and set the second snowball on top. She plucked a stick from the bundle she had brought with her and used one of the sharp ends to carve grooves into the smaller of the two snowballs. She added lumps of snow here and there and shaped the form tenderly with the tips of her frozen red fingers. When she turned to leave, a beautiful, pure white snow-bunny sat several yards away from the side of the house, directly in front of the window.

Bonnie picked up her bundles and set off once again. The thick bundle of sticks that she carried made Will especially curious, but he hadn't long to wait. Bonnie knelt in front of another house and untied the strap of cloth binding the twigs and branches together. She then tossed the bits of wood around the snowy ground beneath a large maple tree. The tree was tall and full of thick branches. It added an elegant look to the yard in which it stood beside a beautiful brick home, but the strewn branches that she tossed made little sense to Will, scattered haphazardly across the snow.

Bonnie made a few more stops and arrived at the school just before the bell finished tolling in its spire.

Will watched the town curiously, keeping a close eye on the homes that had been given special attention by their silent visitor that morning.

The sun had barely risen when the door of the small green cottage was flung open. A tiny girl with crutches emerged from the house, followed closely by a woman with thick braids neatly pinned to her head. The little girl had been bundled in a thick coat, hat, and mittens. She struggled through the snow with her crutches, hurrying as quickly as her little arms could move. Her skin was unusually pale and her thin legs jutted out at odd angles beneath her.

She called excitedly to her mother, beckoning her to follow. They came around the corner of the cottage and the girl pointed to the bunny, smiling.

"He was there when I woke up, Mother. Isn't he wonderful?" she asked.

Her mother pulled the girl into her arms, a tender smile on her lips. "Yes, Annie. He is lovely."

She kissed the pale forehead of her small child. They sat in the warm sun for several minutes, watching the smiling face of the beautiful white bunny before the mother lifted tiny Annie into her arms and carried the small girl back inside.

At another dwelling nearby, a thin old man appeared late that morning, stepping out onto the doorstep of the handsome brick home. It was the home of Mr. Gordon, the most ornery old man Will had ever seen. Will often observed Mr. Gordon shuffling around Pravda. The elderly man walked slow and proud with an obvious limp, but he used no cane.

Mr. Gordon hobbled down his front steps around high noon with a large basket in his arms. He made his way to the tree in his yard and began collecting the sticks that lay strewn beneath.

Mr. Murdoch, the postman, leaned casually against the white picket fence as he greeted the old man. "Mr. Gordon, it is delightful to see you."

"Well, it is no great pleasure to see you," Mr. Gordon stated simply, still picking up sticks.

Mr. Murdoch's head jerked slightly, glancing over his shoulder. Will followed his gaze and saw Miss Eleanora coming up the street.

Mr. Murdoch raised his voice a little and said loudly, "Why Mr. Gordon, wouldn't you like some help picking up those twigs?" His head jerked again, obviously trying to sneak a glance to see if the lovely Eleanora had looked their way. She hadn't.

"I don't need help from you or from anybody else. I never have and certainly *never* will. I can take care of myself just fine, now get away from my fence and be off with you." Mr. Gordon glared at the mailman and snorted. He went back to collecting the sticks, grumbling, "Man can't even gather timber in peace..."

Mr. Murdoch seemed flustered and turned rather pink in the face. Miss Eleanora had nearly reached them. He took a deep breath and gave it one last try.

"Are you sure you have enough wood there?" He nodded cordially to the bundle Mr. Gordon placed in his basket. "I would be happy to..."

The old man straightened suddenly and faced the mailman squarely. "I said be *off* with you! I don't need any more wood and I certainly don't need your high-and-mighty assistance. Good day!" Mr. Gordon said firmly. The old man turned abruptly. Grabbing the handle of the basket, he hobbled back inside his home, slamming the door behind him.

Mr. Murdoch blushed scarlet as Miss Eleanora passed by, but Miss Eleanora had not seemed at all aware of the embarrassing encounter. Her eyes were drawn down the street to where Mr. Carter had just emerged, slipping awkwardly down the steps of the courthouse. The poor fellow landed ungracefully on the sidewalk with his thick-glassed spectacles askew.

Will smiled as he watched the scene below him. Everyone had their routine in Pravda. Change was rare. The town seemed to flow to its own steady, unalterable rhythm. The passing of life would hardly have been noticed in the simple consistency of each week. Every citizen played their same role day after day as Will observed from above, yet none of the proud folks who passed below him seemed half so remarkable as the young girl who walked the streets of Pravda each morning before the glow of dawn.

Though her route varied a little each day, the intent of it was always the same. She walked the silent path of the angels, creating small miracles which often escaped notice—or would have, had there not been a young boy curled up in the boughs of a large blue spruce on the north end of town.

Chapter 9

A WALK AT DAWN and a walk at dusk occupied much of Bonnie's life. Will watched with curious wonder and uncertainty at the strange pattern in which the ragged girl passed her days. Even more surprising, he discovered that she did not seem to limit herself only to those who were weak, or to those who seemed kind and perhaps more deserving of good will.

A pure and unexpected moment of confusion which later led to a much greater understanding struck Will one snowy morning as he sat nestled high, not in his usual blue spruce, but in a tall pine further to the west. The wind was unusually calm and great flakes of snow tumbled from a blanket of clouds above, whispering softly as they dropped to the earth. The town lay peacefully asleep in the predawn hours of the winter morning.

Bonnie arrived even earlier than usual. Dawn was still nearly an hour away.

Will had seen her disappear behind the mercantile store in the darkness a few times before, always on mornings when heavy snow was falling. Each time, she carried a small bundle in her arms and arrived even earlier than her usual routine. On this snowy morning, he had chosen a towering pine to the northwest. He held fast to the trunk of the tree with cold, red hands. The branches weren't quite sturdy enough to support his full weight, but the height and location of the tree afforded him an excellent view.

Bonnie arrived at the edge of Pravda with her ragged shawl tied around her shoulders and the usual small bundle held tightly between her thin arms and her chest. She trod lightly over a narrow snowy path that led out to a small yard behind the mercantile store. She paused at the broken fence and glanced cautiously around before continuing her journey. She soon reached the base of a sturdy maple tree that stood skeletal and majestic in the glittering snow.

Bonnie slipped the bundle into her skirt pocket and reached for a low branch. Her bright red fingers wrapped tightly around its slick surface. She climbed the tree with surprising ease in her long skirts and worn shoes before sliding herself onto a branch halfway up the tree. She balanced herself with one cold red hand. With the other, she eased the bundle from her pocket. Setting it on the branch in front of her, she carefully unfastened the cloth that bound it. Delicately, she lifted three long strands of tinkling glass, each tied with a length of string.

In the dim light from a distant lamppost, Will could see her slender form shivering beneath the tattered shawl. He watched with fascination as she tied the three strands onto a branch above her head. She knotted them close together and gave a quick tug to each one to ensure that the strands were secure. A gentle breeze drifted around them and the glass tinkled merrily, the lengths of glass bumping against each other, sparkling faintly in the dim light.

Bonnie cautiously slid back along the branch and made her way down the trunk of the tree. Without a look back, she continued on her way, her footsteps soon hidden beneath the falling snow.

Will watched her retreating figure until she turned a corner at the far end of the block and disappeared from sight. Still curious, he chose to remain hidden within the pine. He watched anxiously for any movement from the rear of the mercantile store below, but all was quiet, and dawn was still a good half hour away.

When at last the sun rose and the clouds began to thin, Will peered through the pine boughs and looked again toward the maple tree. The sight was extraordinary. Will drew in a sharp breath and sighed in wonder. There, spinning in the breeze, were hundreds of strands of glass tied to the branches, twinkling and glittering in the morning light.

Will remained hidden among the branches of the pine as the sun began its ascent higher into the sky, a soft glow behind the clouds above. His arms ached and he shivered violently as wet snow slid from the higher branches onto his exposed skin, yet he could never have imagined the scene that soon unfolded before him.

The door at the back of the mercantile store opened with a slight creak of wood on metal. A figure stood beneath the porch roof a moment, nearly hidden in the shadow it provided. Will pressed himself nearer the trunk of the pine, hoping the branches were thick enough to conceal him from view.

In the shadow of the porch, he recognized the tall, thick figure that stood motionless. It was Mr. Willet—the angry, hard-handed man who had turned away Will's father on the steps of the mercantile store when they had first arrived in Pravda—the same man who left dark, colored bruises on the pale flesh of his soft-spoken son.

Mr. Willet remained stoic for several moments, standing in the cold, damp snow on the porch, staring out toward the large, skeletal tree. After a time, he timidly stepped from the rickety wooden stoop and made his way toward the great maple with slow, heavy footsteps. He glanced back a time or two to be certain he was entirely alone. When the burly man reached the base of the tree, he placed his hand against the rough bark of the trunk and raised his head, peering up at the high branches. His eyes swept over each snowy limb, searching for several minutes. At last, Mr. Willet's eyes fixed on the three new strands of glass tied to a narrow branch several feet above his head. He took a great, shuddering breath and fell to his knees in the snow.

Mr. Willet buried his head in his hands and wept.

Chapter 10

A HARSH WIND blew in a fierce blizzard across the rolling hills of Pravda and through the trees of the forest nearby. Will found himself stuck inside his small cabin for nearly a week with little to entertain himself aside from the imaginations that grew stale with time and the constant, listless loneliness.

He stared dully through a crack in the door at the cascading snow while the fire crackled behind him. The cabin held strong in the rushing gale, blocked from the worst of the weather by the nearby trees, for which he was grateful, but the constant howling of the wind and the overwhelming absence of all human interaction began to overpower him.

Will searched the room for something with which he could busy himself. His eyes lit on the growing pile of fur pelts in the corner near his bed. He stared dully at them through bleary, tired eyes, the crackling fire making him sleepy as he leaned against the cool logs behind him.

An idea slowly took form in his mind. He sat up, a dull yet growing excitement stirring within him. He pulled the makeshift shovel into the shifting light cast by the fire and stripped away a tiny piece of metal. He clasped the scrap tightly between his fingers and laid it against one of the flat stones of the hearth. Will dug his palm around another smooth stone until it came free. Careful to avoid contact with his fingers, he beat the bit of metal until it was nearly perfectly flat with a narrow point at one end. He studied his handiwork for a moment then slipped one end into the white coals beneath the fire. He waited impatiently until it was soft from the heat. Will pierced a hole through the white-hot end and left it to cool near the snowy gap in the door.

The cracked metal pail lay at an angle on its side, holding water for Will to use as he pleased. Will stripped off his shirt and placed it in the water to soak. He slid the pail onto the stone hearth near the fire. The water took several minutes to grow warm. When at last it was suitable, Will knelt by the pail and scrubbed at the filthy, frayed cloth until much of the dirt slipped away. He regretted having no soap as the cloth was still far from clean, but it showed a remarkable improvement by the time he finished. He wrung the water out onto the dirt-packed floor and hung the shirt over the side of his bed to dry.

Will sat at the head of his bed and carefully sorted through his sizable collection of furs. He selected several of the softest and most beautiful among them. He set them aside and piled the rest back together in a heap out of the way. He then cleared a space in the middle of the floor and began to sketch out his ideas in the dirt. It took him several hours of drawing and wiping away each imperfect attempt before he developed a design that satisfied him.

Will laid the furs carefully over the drawing and began to cut each one to fit.

Night fell too quickly. Will's eyes grew heavy amid his excitement. With begrudging acceptance, he ate a bit of dried fish and a carrot from his reserve then tucked himself into bed for the night.

The small boy slept soundly until the fire died down and

the air in the cabin grew piercingly cold. Will slipped from his bed and shivered violently as he stoked the fire. Already awake and mostly rested, he went back to work in the flickering light.

By mid-day, he had finished cutting the furs. Will pulled his damp, over-sized shirt toward him and extracted several long strands of thread from the bottom. A few of the strands broke, but others slipped out easily and proved to be quite strong. Will threaded his makeshift needle and eagerly began to sew.

The delicate work with the thick furs was far from simple, especially as the imperfect needle proved to be far more cumbersome than he had anticipated. Will found himself stopping several times during the first couple of hours to reshape the fine point and to beat down the flattened tin of the thin shaft even more. He also found himself undoing a stitch more often than he left it in.

At long last, he had nearly finished the project when he decided the stitches still weren't quite small enough. Will ripped out each stitch and trimmed the edges then started over. Several days passed filled with moments of intense frustration interwoven with pride at his growing success before the project was finally complete.

He held it up for inspection and studied his work. It wasn't perfect, but it was good. Will retrieved his father's knife from its place in the crate against the wall. Using the sharpest part of its edge and the broken tip, he carved seven small, round buttons from bits of wood. He pierced two holes through each one using the heated tip of his hand-fashioned needle then added the wooden buttons to the front of the sewn project for the finishing touch.

The storm had cleared for only a few hours as he worked, but it settled in again before nightfall. Now, as morning approached, Will waited impatiently for it to pass once more. When the sky cleared at last, the snow lay piled in huge drifts surrounding the cabin. Will pushed and shoved at the door, but to no avail. He knew it would likely be several days before the snow would melt enough that he could travel.

He sighed and paced his small space irritably for a time. After a few hours, he turned back to his collection of furs. Will selected a few more, smaller this time, and began yet another project. This time, he finished much more quickly, although it required even greater patience to make a warm, soft pair of gloves.

Will had hardly completed his second project before he set about on still another, yet this project was very different in its structure and function. Will began building himself a pair of sturdy snowshoes. He had seen hunters using snowshoes quickly trudging over the snow in the woods while he struggled through the drifts to check his traps.

Lashing the sticks to form the frame proved to be a frustrating process as Will struggled to bind them securely. The thread from his old shirt was far too weak to hold the sticks in place and the wood would snap back, often leaving a painful welt on Will's thin arms.

Will tried for nearly an hour before he finally gave up and thrust the wood into a corner. He dropped onto his bed eating a bit of dried fish and brooding over the failed project.

The fire died down to bright embers that popped and cracked in the hearth. Will watched the waves of heat rising into the chimney. His eyes grew heavy in the peaceful warmth of the fire. Will stood and stretched and began preparing for bed. He organized the piles of fur across the bed to give him added warmth for the chilly night. When he turned back, he noticed the scraps of fur from his earlier project. A simple idea lit in his mind.

Will swallowed the last of the fish and once more pulled out his father's knife. He sat in the middle of the pile of scraps and began cutting until he had several long strips, scraping away the fur the best he could with the worn blade. Will retrieved the branches from the corner and, using the strips, he again set about to lash the wood together. It took a firm hand to band the wood into place, but with a lot of patience and a bit of practice, the knots he tied eventually held secure.

It took him nearly a full three days to finish the first snowshoe and less than two to make the second, having now gained a better understanding of the process.

The high drifts began to melt as he worked through the long, cold winter hours. With welcome relief, Will finished the snowshoes and made his way back into the outer world, feeling refreshed and revived in the cool, clear air. He spent much of the next day shoveling snow from the tunnel. Then, after nearly two weeks of confinement, he set out toward Pravda several hours before dawn.

The crisp, early morning was bitter cold with a cloudless, starry sky sweeping through the darkness above him. The snowshoes made traveling much easier and offered a welcome relief to the constant trudging through the drifts that had before greatly slowed his pace.

Will felt an immense merriment growing within him as he continued on his way, carrying the two bundles in his arms. He walked steadily though clumsily, not yet having grown accustomed to the new snowshoes, while already deciding on new improvements that he would add to them upon his return to the cabin.

Will wore his father's old coat, which was still far too large for his small frame. It trailed over the back of his snowshoes and swept along behind him as he walked.

Little Will arrived at a run-down cabin on the west end of

town about two hours before sunrise. The cabin was dark and still. He trudged to the rickety porch and carefully set the bundles to the side of the door. He stood a moment, staring at the ramshackle dwelling before quickly turning to leave. He had barely made it through the front gate when he paused. In all the days that he had observed Bonnie from high in the blue spruce, she had never stayed to watch the effect that she had made on those around her, but Will couldn't help himself. He looked around him and selected a tree a short distance from the cabin. The trailing coat wiped away the shallow prints of the snowshoes behind him.

Will slipped off the snowshoes and climbed to a high, sturdy branch. He shivered with nervous anticipation. His bursting excitement kept the blood pumping warm through his veins in the chill morning air. At last a light flickered inside the cabin. A short time later, the sound of a bolt sliding over metal carried to his ears. Will held his breath as Bonnie's slim figure emerged, wrapped in her usual thin shawl.

Bonnie closed the door behind her. As she turned to leave, the two wrapped bundles caught her eye. She hesitated, glancing around the silent woods that surrounded the cabin. She then knelt in the fine layer of snow beside the misshapen packages. Will looked down from above, biting his lip as he watched.

Bonnie slowly reached out a thin hand and delicately pulled away the faded paper from the larger package. She stared, her eyes wide with wonder. Her hand stroked the soft, white pelt. Slowly, she lifted the beautiful fur coat with both hands. Her breath came out in a soft gasp. She stared at it for several minutes. Hesitantly, she slipped the shawl away from her shivering frame and dropped it to the snowy ground. She then pulled the new coat around her petite shoulders and slid her arms inside, fastening the soft fur coat with the hand-carved wooden buttons at the front.

Nearly a perfect fit.

Bonnie's smile was bright with excitement as she picked up the second, bundle. She pulled away the thin paper revealing two beautiful, soft gray mittens. She held them against her face, feeling the fur against her cheek. Bonnie stood, wearing the coat and holding the mittens in her hands. She looked around, peering into the trees beyond the fenced yard, but seemed to see nothing in the dark wooded space. Gently, she slipped her hands into the gloves. A tinkling burst of laughter escaped her lips and filled the silent night air. She clapped her mittened hands together and twirled beneath the starry sky, lifting her hands above her head as she turned.

Bonnie sighed happily as she came to rest against the railing of the steps. She covered her face for a moment with the soft warmth of her mittened hands. She breathed in slowly then smiled as she looked up at the starry sky.

"Thank you," she whispered into the darkness above her.

Will almost gasped in surprise. He stared down from his hiding place high above her. He was almost certain he must have imagined it, the first words he had ever heard her speak. Then her voice rang out once more, bright and sweet as she sighed happily, still staring up into the starry night.

"Thank you."

Chapter 11

WILL WAITED until he was certain Bonnie was gone before hurrying down from the tree and making his way back to his little cabin, unable to stop from grinning in delight.

He checked his traps on his journey back and discovered several rabbits and a beautiful ring-tailed raccoon. He spent the rest of the day skinning the animals and prepping the flesh. Will now had far more meat than he would need for the winter and felt rather content each time he glanced at his substantial store of provisions.

Will packed some of the meat from his earlier trappings that had already dried and wrapped it in paper. He woke early and set off on his trek over the snow, but this time, he headed east toward the opposite end of town—to the old farmhouse.

Will stood in the darkness, staring at the slightly crooked front door. It seemed another lifetime ago that he had run from Jimmy's stall to alert Farmer Merril of the horse's ailment the night his only friend had become ill. Will shook his head and turned toward the barn and made his way inside.

"Hi Jimmy!" he said as he climbed into the stall. Jimmy greeted him happily and nuzzled his soft nose against Will's shoulder. Will held out an apple that had only partially rotted.

Jimmy ate it contentedly.

"I can't stay long, Jimmy," Will told him, "but, how wonderful it is to see you! And can you believe it? I now have my own cabin with a fireplace and a bed—and even more food than I can eat! See here? I brought some dried meat for Farmer Merril."

He held out the wrapped packages then set them aside as he sat near his old friend.

"I've done a lot of thinking, Jimmy. I suppose I should have tried to understand why he was so upset the night you got sick. He must have been angry only because losing you—his only horse—would have meant that he would have no way to take care of his family—no way to plow and harvest the fields, and food can be pretty hard to come by if you don't have money enough for it, except I'm learning how now. I'm not sure Farmer Merril would know what to do. It would be so hard, I think, to have to worry so very much. Don't you think so, Jimmy?"

Jimmy nuzzled him. Will pulled out another apple and gave his the old horse a long hug.

Will left the stall and secured the barn door behind him. He then made his way across the snow-covered yard to the small farmhouse. He slipped the package of meat onto the porch. This time, he did not stay to watch.

Chapter 12

BONNIE CONTINUED HER USUAL ROUTINE, walking the town twice each day. Will began a similar tradition of his own, but he made the journey through Pravda only once, waiting until darkness had fallen each evening. The more he observed, the more he began to see that it was far too great a job for Bonnie to do alone. He walked the empty streets while it was still dark then climbed the spruce before Bonnie arrived. He stayed to observe for a while before slipping back down to the ground and returning to the woods to check his traps.

Will felt such a change taking place within himself, something surprising yet not at all unwelcome. The more he watched, the more he saw—and the more he saw, the more he understood and grew to care.

Later, on the same morning that he had left the dried meat on Farmer Merrill's doorstep, he noticed old Miss Margery standing on her porch looking entirely forlorn and miserable. She held a white shaking hand around the banister of her steps, but she never made her way down to the mercantile as was her weekly routine, being Wednesday and fine weather. Instead, she slowly sat down on the steps and cradled her head wretchedly in her hands. Many of the town folk passed by, but no one seemed to give the slightest indication that they had noticed the poor woman.

Will watched, puzzled, until he noticed the broken shaft of wood laying in two pieces behind her. He also noticed an extra limp as she stood and turned wearily to make her way back inside. He realized she must have fallen and broken the cane, but she seemed all right otherwise.

Will climbed down from the tree and hurried back into the woods. He took his time returning to the cabin, checking his traps and searching the ground as he went. He walked an extra mile or so past the tunnel, circling around until he came across a couple of thick, hardy branches that looked sturdy enough for the job.

He returned to the cabin and set to work using the sharp obsidian to strip and shape the wood. The maple seemed rather well-suited to the need it was destined to fulfill, being lightweight yet strong. Will worked late into the night by the dim glow of the crackling fire. He finished at long last, his knuckles raw from the work. He sat back with a satisfied nod of approval then used one of the newly carved staffs to push himself to his feet. He tested each one. Both easily held his weight.

Fighting exhaustion, Will strapped his snowshoes to his feet and set off into the night, hurrying to reach Pravda before sunrise.

When the sun rose later that same morning, a lonely widow opened the door to a welcome sight. The two simple carved branches were to her much more than mere shafts of wood. She had been given back her independence and mobility. Miss Margery smiled as her white, wrinkled hand gripped the newly fashioned cane nearest to her. A spark of delight lit her eyes. She looked around her, but seemed unable to make out a reason for the strange occurrence.

Will suddenly realized that, though the gift he had left behind would be of great use to Old Miss Margery, there seemed still to be an unexplainable tenderness in her expression. Perhaps, he realized, in her difficulty, nothing meant more to her than knowing that someone had noticed her troubling need and had cared enough to reach out to her, a lonely old widow.

Miss Margery's weekly trip to the mercantile was a day late, but her routine remained otherwise unbroken.

Chapter 13

WARM SUNLIGHT began to melt the mounds of snow across the forest floor as spring drew near. Will followed the example of several of the women he had observed and created for himself a tap for the sugar maple trees and gathered the sweet syrup into his cracked pail. Throughout the previous year, he had collected a few discarded broken jars and bottles, creating a store of them, which now came in quite useful. Some of the bottles had cracks near the bottom and were only useful for storing dried goods, but nearly half a dozen of them had cracks a little higher up which allowed Will to store a little of the sweet syrup in each one. Four of the bottles were only jagged at the top, with fragments missing through the neck, but otherwise they were sturdy and functional.

Snow dripped sulkily from the branches and swelled the streams. Much of the ground within the bramble enclosure had grown marshy and well-saturated. Will spent much of his day digging and gardening, starting with the areas on the highest ground where the earth was not entirely sodden.

He brought out his store of seeds, which he had gathered from his garden-plundering the year before. He now had a variety of fruit and vegetable seeds, though many had been unavoidably mixed together and took him a great deal of time to sort out before planting. Carefully observing from the branches of the spruce above Pravda to see when different items were planted, Will imitated the local gardeners accordingly.

He took great pride hilling up rows and diverting the water for easy irrigation. The spring runoff soaked large areas around the streams as well as the lower part of the cabin. Will spent nearly two weeks building diversions and walls to protect the area from constant flooding. He used a mixture of old straw, clay from the riverbank, and loose gravel to secure the stones.

It was a long and exhausting project, requiring many large stones. With steady determination and a great deal of hard labor, the clearing eventually had a complete wall circling within the borders of the streams. He left one spot open on each side where a round boulder remained easily moveable for irrigating the garden, allowing him to open or block the waterways as needed.

The days continued to lengthen and the spring breezes grew quite warm with the summer solstice drawing near.

Will usually spent the dark hours before sunrise walking the town, followed by his usual hour or two observing from above. On his way back each day, he checked his traps before he went hunting. He carried a simple bow which he had fashioned during the long winter months, using rawhide from a deer he had found dead in the snow months earlier.

He was far from good as a hunter and found it necessary to be constantly making adjustments to the bow. Still, he was improving and the bow responded better with time. Will searched for bits of obsidian during his treks through the woods to use as arrow tips. Each discovery of a fragment of the black stone was a rare find, but occasionally luck was on his side. He shaped the stones then added each one to a thin, sturdy shaft of wood, which he then place in his simple handmade quiver.

The garden blossomed through the summer and produced delicious fruits and vegetables that offered a welcome change to an otherwise unbalanced diet.

Will struggled to keep the weeds down in his large garden plot. The grasses native to the clearing made constant attempts to return where he had only days earlier rooted them out. He dedicated a couple of hours each day to taming the rows, burning the pile of pulled-up grass and weeds each night.

While still observing from the large spruce in Pravda, Will soon discovered that stubborn old Mr. Gordon also struggled to keep his garden free of the pesky weeds. The old man was bent over painfully for hours, struggling to stand afterwards though very little progress had actually been made. The weeds were overrunning the man's little plot of land, yet he was far too proud to ask for help.

Once a week, under the cover of darkness, the young boy spent an hour or two before dawn in Mr. Gordon's backyard doing what the old man could not—pulling weeds, cutting the grass, and occasionally trimming the hedges.

It was a glorious summer for a ten-year-old boy. Due to both necessity and opportunity, Will spent a great deal of time working, yet he also allowed himself an occasional break for swimming, reading, and exploring. On particularly lonely days, Will returned to the village around dusk—often sitting beneath the gnarled oak tree near the open fields until the last glow faded from the horizon before returning to the clearing.

Summer passed and fall settled itself solemnly over the rolling hills. Will collected the produce from his garden and placed a stack of logs around his new fruit trees to protect them from the winter storms. The winter snows began to blow across Pravda as the wind tore away the last few leaves that struggled to remain aloft in the trees. Will once again settled in for another long winter.

It was a mild winter, much to Will's relief. He visited the town nearly every morning, leaving packages of dry meat from his growing supply on doorsteps around the town. He had become quite adept at setting traps and moderately skilled with a bow. In late November, he managed to bring snare a young elk. The meat supplied him well and provided plenty to share with several families in Pravda—including Bonnie and her father.

Will selected several large strips of venison, a bit of rabbit, and a few of his best fillets from the trout, all of which he wrapped neatly in salvaged sheets of paper that had been discarded from the schoolhouse. He dropped off the packaged meat while making a visit to Pravda. Nearly every week now, Will acquired enough meat to provide him with enough to share, and the cabin on the west end of town, as well as several others, were routine stops before the sun rose each Friday morning.

Will's daily walk through the village energized him. It gave him purpose and a sort of social interaction.

On the occasional day that Will couldn't make it into Pravda due to inclement weather, he spent several hours working with the excess furs, cutting and sewing them into soft, warm winter attire. He had taken so much thread from the hem of his shirt that it was nearly the right length for him now, and would soon be even too short.

He also now found it necessary to stoop a little when entering the low door of the cabin, and crawling through the tunnel became far more cumbersome as his limbs put on a little length and his shoulders grew ever so slightly. Still, even had he not been growing and using the shirt for thread, it had become so threadbare that it was hardly worth wearing anyway.

Will devised a new sort of plan to which he dedicated the majority of his efforts whenever he was neither in the village nor sleeping. By early December, he had amassed six beautiful fur coats of various sizes and several delicately sewn pairs of gloves.

Will left one of the coats, made of soft gray rabbit fur, on the doorstep of Farmer Merril's home, cut to fit the slender woman that gave every bit of warm clothing she had to her young son, Jason, and to her hard-working husband. She was not well dressed and was often looked down upon by the wealthier women of the town, but Mrs. Merril took no notice. She worked hard in the fields beside her husband and helped with the harvest in the fall. She was rarely seen in the winter due to her lack of warm clothing. Young Jason never looked particularly well-dressed in what she was able to give him, but he was warm.

Along with the coat, Will left a hand-stitched pair of mittens. He hoped with all his heart that the gifts might fit her well. He had done his best to guess her size, but it was very difficult to know.

Later that morning, he watched the town from his usual position in the large spruce. To his wonderful delight he saw the thin but lovely woman—smiling as he had often seen her in the warmer months—now holding her son's hand and taking a blissful walk in the beautiful fur coat. She was no longer trapped inside by the bitter cold of winter and the crisp air brightened her eyes.

Her son wore the mittens, but the coat looked lovely on her thin frame. Will grinned with the elation of a successful triumph. She walked the streets cheerfully with Jason smiling beside her, enjoying his mother's felicity. The other women stared. Their jealousy was obvious to everyone but the lovely woman who saw only the perfect winter morning and a new sensation of freedom.

Will had also brought with him two more coats—one sized for a very small, young person. It was made of soft, white fur and adorned with carved wooden buttons. The other matched but for its larger size. He left both at the well-kept little green cottage.

The family didn't seem particularly poor, but little Annie had been looking far paler with each month that passed. She could no longer walk on her own and had to be carried everywhere she went. The child and her devoted mother took a walk each afternoon whenever the weather warmed enough to melt the ice. Annie seemed desperate to take in as much of life as she could. Time for her was not a gift Will could give, but he longed to do something that might give her a bit of joy in the short time that remained as his heart ached, watching her fight a battle she would never win.

The blue spruce was near enough to the cottage for him to hear a slight gasp when the door opened. A woman's voice called within, "Annie, a gift has been left for you!" The young mother reached down and tenderly lifted the package into her arms before disappearing inside.

The gentle mother and delicate daughter soon appeared in their lovely matching attire, carving only one set of footprints up the short path to the gate.

"Oh, mother. There are angels, aren't there?" Annie said, reaching up and stroking her mother's face with the soft fur of her new mittens.

"Yes, Annie." The mother pulled the little girl close to her breast. "I truly believe there are."

Chapter 14

THREE COATS STILL REMAINED back at the cabin. Will packaged these into a large rawhide bag made from the small elk. He also packed a large supply of meat and a bit of fruit for the long journey, then, tying the bag around his shoulders and strapping the snowshoes to his feet, he slung his bow across his back and prepared for the long journey ahead.

For the first time that winter, he put out the fire—and for the first time since entering Pravda, Will set off toward a new destination, far beyond the town he had grown to know so well.

He reflected on the strange passage of time as he tread several miles through that cold winter day. Nearly three and a half years had slipped by since he and his father had first arrived in Pravda. Will could hardly remember many of the cities they had come through, but he knew that they had walked a great distance from the previous town before arriving at Pravda. Will wasn't sure how far he would have to go, and with the snowy winter season, he made extra preparations for the journey.

Will trudged through the wooded areas until he came out into the rolling hills where he took up the path carved by sleighs used by the mail carrier and delivery drivers. It crossed through the cultivated farm land, large fields now hidden by the deep snow, and over several bridges. By nightfall, he could see the lights of a large town, perhaps even a city, in the distance. He stopped to rest and slept, taking shelter at the base of a tall pine. It took a long while for Will to get comfortable enough, sitting on the cold ice, before he was able to drop off to sleep for a short time.

Will hadn't slept but a few hours when he woke in the middle of the night, soaked from the snow beneath him and shivering with cold. He groaned softly as he stretched his frozen, aching legs and rubbed his hands together to regain some warmth and circulation. He was just leaning back against the rough bark of the tree when he heard an eery sound that prickled the hair on the back of his neck. He judged it to be several hundred meters away, but Will's heart pounded furiously. He pulled the bow over his shoulder and slid the strap of his bag over his head, securing it around his neck and left arm. The sniffing was coming nearer and Will detected a low growl.

Will silently reached for the lowest branch just above his head. His frozen hands struggled to grasp the thick bough. Each finger ached from the cold as he pulled himself upward. He had just reached the second branch when a piercing howl split the silent night air. Will forced himself up faster, fear and exertion pumping warm blood into his limbs. He dug his feet into the wet bark of the tree and strained his muscles. His arms burned and a cold sweat broke across his forehead.

Several snarling wolves ran into the clearing as Will hoisted himself onto a large branch partway up the trunk. He watched fearfully as the pack circled the base of the tree below.

A large gray wolf with grisly fur jumped and snapped at his dangling legs, but Will was out of reach.

Will gasped for breath, more from fear than from exertion

as he watched the wolves below. The cold air froze his wet clothing against his skin. The night sky shifted slowly overhead.

Will struggled to remain alert. His body ached from the cold and from his uncomfortable position on the branch. After several hours, most of the wolves had lost interest and wandered away in search of easier prey, but the two largest wolves still remained.

Will steadied himself against the trunk of the tree with his left hand and pulled the bow from around his shoulder with his right. He had never liked wolves with their ferocity and their roaming packs. He strung the first arrow. The wolves looked up and growled. Will let the arrow fly.

The arrow hit just behind the left ear of the largest wolf. It fell to the ground without a sound. The second wolf whimpered and nosed its companion then howled and turned its back on Will and disappeared into the woods.

Will waited another hour until he was sure the entire pack was long gone before he climbed down from the tree. He kept an arrow strung in the bow and carried it ready in case of another encounter.

Several hours later, Will reached the city that he had seen from a distance. A wooden sign, embellished with carvings and a clean coat of paint, hung at the edge of the precinct with the words "Welcome to Bloomfield" inscribed artistically in the center. He replaced the arrow in his quiver and slung the bow over his shoulder.

Will soon realized that he was the focus of several strange looks as he hesitantly made his way into the city. He was certain that he was not at all a pleasant sight—particularly since he had not had a good bath since winter had set in, although on occasion, he had heated a bit of water in his cracked pail and scrubbed a little of the grime away. Still, he was given a wide berth as he made his way up the main street of Bloomfield.

How long had it been since he had spoken to anyone? Will wondered. The thought of it made him very nervous, but he was determined. He approached a burley man who had paused in his task of unloading a pile of wood from a small wagon, but when Will asked directions to the nearest store, the words came out barely coherent. The man looked puzzled and wiped a bit of sweat from his brow as he stared at the young boy. Will just shrugged and decided he would try to find the building on his own.

As it turned out, there were several shops and stores of various kinds. Bloomfield was a beautiful city several times larger than the small town of Pravda. It took Will most of an hour, but at last he found a large general store which had been built next to the post office only a few blocks from the town hall. Will took a deep breath and squared his shoulders. He walked determinedly up the front steps and into the store.

Two well-dressed men stood arguing near the counter. They stopped abruptly the moment Will stepped inside.

"Just what do you think you are doing in here?" asked one of the men, presumably the shopkeeper.

"Excuse me, sir, but I have something you may wish to buy." Will tried to sound confident. Before the man could think of a response, Will slipped the bag from his shoulders and pulled one of the fur coats from inside. He held the coat out for inspection.

Both men stared in astonishment. They each fingered the fur and inspected the small stitches that held it together. Finally, the other man spoke. "You're only a child. Wherever did you get such a beautiful coat?" he asked.

"I made them, sir."

"Them?" the shopkeeper asked. He looked up, surprised and curious.

Will nodded and pulled the other two coats and several pairs of gloves from the bag. He laid them on the counter for the men to see.

"You made all of these? Surely not by yourself. You didn't steal them, I hope?" The men took a good look at the boy, the rawhide bag and bow slung across his back. They shook their heads in apparent acceptance of his claim.

"How much would you take for them?" the shopkeeper asked.

"I…" Will paused. "I don't know, sir. Perhaps you could tell me what they are worth."

The man went to the till and pulled out several coins. "There, I think that should do."

"*Herbert!*" the other man chortled. "I'm surprised at you."

The shopkeeper blushed crimson and doubled the amount.

"Tsk, tsk," the other man said, "that still isn't even a quarter of what these lovely items are worth."

The shopkeeper turned purple and veins bulged at the side of his head. He growled and dug a fist into the drawer. He counted out two more handfuls of coins and pushed the large pile toward Will.

"Will that do?" snarled the shopkeeper, more at his friend than at Will.

The other man laughed, "I should say that is a little more like it, though I still believe you could do better."

Will stared at the pile of money in front of him. He nodded fervently. "Yes, sir, and thank you!" He scooped the money into his bag then hung it again over his shoulders.

He turned for the door, then paused and hesitated before turning back. "If it's alright, sir, might I get some thread?"

"I would certainly think you can afford it now!" the shop-keeper glared at his friend.

"I also would like to purchase some new clothing, if you might have some in about the right size."

The shopkeeper's face was still a little red, but his tone softened. "Well, I would certainly agree that you need it. Let's see what we can find."

By the time Will left, he carried with him two sets of under-clothing, a pair of trousers, two shirts, three pairs of warm socks, a sturdy pair of shoes with a little room to grow, two bars of soap, three sewing needles, seven spools of sturdy yarn, a notebook filled with clean paper, two pencils, a new sharp knife, and a flaw-less tin pail. His bag bulged and he looked especially odd, but Will could hardly have been happier as he left Bloomfield licking a sweet stick of lemon candy the shop owner had given him.

Chapter 15

WILL MADE TWO MORE TRIPS to Mr. Herbert's store in Bloomfield before the end of winter. Each time, he filled his rawhide sack with fur coats, hats, and gloves and returned with a few tools and several other necessities.

Spring softened the frozen ground and turned the area around the stone wall into a marsh while the rest of the clearing stayed mostly dry. Will extended the garden plot and planted several seeds for fruit trees around the perimeter near the wall. A few of the trees from the previous year had survived the winter, yet it would likely be another year or two before any fruit could be harvested.

Will tapped the maple trees for syrup and boiled it down, preserving it in bottles he had brought back on his third trip from Bloomfield. He continued to improve his little clearing—creating a wonderful oasis that he could call home. A momentous hunting trip in early summer proved especially rewarding, although perhaps in a rather unusual way.

Will set off along one of his most common paths—through the thick foliage to the east and over the river by means of a crumbling fallen log. He had barely gotten beyond the churning sound of the water when he became aware of a faint humming not far off. It took him some time to locate the source, the soft roar of the river behind him making the task more difficult. He finally discovered an old maple where the sound grew loud enough to cause him to pause and search its boughs. There, on a thick branch several feet up, hung a swarming beehive buzzing with life. Will had seen the man-made hives on the south end of Pravda. He knew little, but he hoped it would be enough.

Carefully, so as not to upset the swarms, Will cleared a space beneath the tree from all needles and leaves. He searched about until he had piled together small bundles of sticks and a large branch which he piled together. The bees seemed to be growing nervous with a boy moving about below them. Will found himself running to the river several times to apply mud to a new welt on his exposed skin. Even with these uncomfortable interruptions, he soon had a small fire crackling at the base of the tree. As the flames grew, he added wet needles and damp leaves to the center. The fire smoked terribly, drifting up around the hive. The buzzing slowed and finally became weak and faint.

The process was delicate and rather tedious, but with the careful patience of a boy who could only imagine the sweet addition which the bees could offer his little hideaway, Will managed to successfully relocate the hive into one of the larger trees in the clearing.

The furrowed garden bloomed thick and full in the heat of summer. Squash, vegetables, tubers and berries added a cheerful burst of color to the small clearing. The many fruit trees near the stone wall continued to grow straight and full, anchored against the wooden stakes Will had pounded into the ground.

Will found a peaceful, solitary contentment each evening as he sat amid the tall grasses by the door to his small cabin, watching the glow fade in the sky above him. Crickets and bullfrogs hid in the foliage around the stream, calling out into the deepening night. The air cooled beneath the starlit sky while soft breezes rustled the leaves in the trees and vines around the clearing.

Once the garden had been planted and the land cultivated, with a brand new axe in hand, Will decided it was time to build himself a real cabin—larger and far more sturdy.

In a single day, Will found that he could chop and strip three logs on top of his regular routine of visiting the village and working his own bit of land. Still, even with the new axe, it took him until mid-summer before he managed to gather enough logs to begin to build.

Though still small, Will's arms had strengthened a great deal in the past two years, yet he struggled to lift the logs on his own. As the walls rose higher, he found it necessary to work one end of a log into place and brace it with ropes while he lifted the other end into its groove. It was exhausting work and left him weary within a short time, but it became a little easier day by day as his strength continued to grow.

Proper tools made the job a great deal easier than his first attempt to build a cabin. Will dug a large pit inside his old dwelling and added several shelves along the walls. He reapplied mud to the walls and braced the already weakening structure, turning it into a food cellar. He built the new cabin onto it, the old doorway connecting the two.

Will built the walls of the new cabin shoulder high before taking a needed rest for a couple of days to return to Bloomfield for more supplies. He gathered up the last set of fur coats and gloves left from the winter and took his journey to the east.

Mr. Herbert greeted Will warmly as he now did whenever Will dropped by. He now offered Will far more for the winter furs as the quality of Will's sewing increased. Mr. Herbert even occasionally shared ideas for adding certain buttons or a rounded collar or even a little black trimming along the edges. The coats had sold well, as had the gloves and hats. There was certainly a viable market of which they both made great use.

"You're a little early, coming in during the warmer months," Mr. Herbert said pleasantly as he shook Will's hand.

"Yes, sir. I came for something in particular. I am building a cabin and I would like some framed glass for a window," Will explained.

Mr. Herbert paused, stepping back and staring thoughtfully at the boy. "You are building a cabin, you say?"

Will nodded.

Mr. Herbert furrowed his brow, pondering and saying nothing, then he smiled and shrugged. "Well! Turns out, I don't have any of that here, but I know where you might be able to get a bit of glass. Have you brought more coats, then?" he asked.

Will set the rawhide back on the ground and showed Mr. Herbert the stock of goods he had brought with him. Mr. Herbert happily paid him a large sum.

"Right, then," Mr. Herbert said, grabbing his hat. "Come with me and we'll see about getting you a bit of framed glass."

Mr. Herbert led the way up through Main Street and down a side road that led to the blacksmith's shop. A thunder of loud blows—heavy metal upon metal—sounded from within. He nodded to Will and stepped inside.

"Stanton, do you have a moment?" he shouted over the din of pounding metal.

The noise ceased. A man covered in soot and bulging with thick muscles stepped into view holding a red poker iron and a hammer.

"Why, Jim Herbert. Are you stopping by for a visit in the

middle of the day?" Stanton noticed Will and cocked his head smartly to the side as he studied the strangely-clad boy.

"You see, Stanton," Mr. Herbert motioned to Will, "this boy is looking for some framed glass. You mentioned to me a week or two ago that there had been some ordered in for the courthouse that didn't fit quite right. Was it sent back?"

Stanton shook his head. "No luck sending it back. It must be in storage somewhere. The courier had been none too happy about transporting the glass the first time. He wasn't anxious to take it back without being paid mightily for the service. Mayor Ringwald is hoping we might find a buyer." He nodded to Will. "What size do you need?"

Will held out his hands to about twice his shoulder width. "I suppose about this big—though it can be larger or smaller. I'll just build around it, so long as it's not too big."

Stanton looked at Mr. Herbert questioningly.

"Boy says he's building himself a cabin," Mr. Herbert shrugged.

Stanton nodded. "Wait just a moment then." He disappeared into the back and soon returned, having relieved himself of the tools and apron. He then led the way to the city building and strode inside. The clerk stared through his interior window at the soot-covered blacksmith followed by the shopkeeper and the young boy with a rawhide sack and a bow.

Stanton stopped at a thick, painted door and knocked loudly. There was a shuffle inside the room before the door opened.

A tall, lean man with thinning dark hair and a kind face stood in the doorway. He smiled. "Stanton, Herbert, come in. It is good to see you. There's no trouble, I hope." He glanced curiously at Will.

"No trouble at all, Mayor," Mr. Herbert said. "This young

man's name is Will. He is the lad who has been bringing the fur clothing that has made such a stir in the town."

The man seemed momentarily taken aback. He looked astonished as he looked at Will then back to Mr. Herbert who shrugged. The mayor then nodded.

"I see! Well," he turned to Will, "they have been quite popular around here—and they are lovely. I purchased one for my wife just last Christmas. She has grown quite attached to it." He smiled warmly and shook Will's hand.

"Well, it turns out," Herbert continued. "This boy is looking for some framed glass. Stanton mentioned that there may be some here that, as of yet, has remained unused. Is that still the case?"

Mayor Ringwald raised his eyebrows in surprise. "Why, yes! I had thought we'd have found a use for it by now, but luckily for you, we simply have not managed to repurpose it yet. Come with me. I'll show you what we have, and you can decide if it will do." He led the way out of his office and waved cordially to the clerk who continued to stare at the growing group that again passed by.

Mayor Ringwald led the two men and the young boy outside to a door at the side of the city building and unlocked the bolt that held it in place. A damp, earthy smell greeted them as the door swung open. The Mayor motioned to the others to follow. They stepped down the two shallow steps into a dark basement. Mayor Ringwald pulled a chain, and a single bulb dimly lit the room. He continued toward the back wall. An odd assortment of items lay scattered around the room, some covered with cloth and others stacked in crates. In the farthest corner lay two sheets of framed glass carefully set against the wall.

"What do you think?" Mayor Ringwald stopped and

turned to Will.

The glass was clear and beautiful. The light from the single bulb hanging from the ceiling reflected off the thick, wavy surface, but the two sheets together would be too large for him to be able use both. "They are perfect, but might I only have one? I'm not sure I could use two," he said.

"Well, turns out," Mayor Ringwald said with a smile, "I don't have any other purpose in mind for either of them. I suppose you have the money to purchase it?"

"I think so, but it would depend. How much would the glass be?" Will asked.

Mayor Ringwald pondered a moment then offered a price. Will smiled and nodded in acceptance and counted out the amount.

"Do you live far from here? Did your parents send you to pick it up on your own? How do you intend to get it back?" Mayor Ringwald asked.

"I can move it on my own. I had just intended to carry it," Will told him.

"And how far do you have to go?" Mayor Ringwald studied him.

"About a day-and-a-half's journey on foot," Will said.

"I see." Mayor Ringwald said looking again at the large sheet of glass.

"We could offer you a ride for at least part of the distance," Mr. Herbert said, stroking his chin.

"I don't mind the walk, really," Will told him, though he felt grateful for the offer.

Mayor Ringwald smiled. "Well, then. It sounds like we'd better package it up well so it survives the journey." He searched the damp basement for a case to hold the glass.

Less than an hour later, Will was happily making his way up the street awkwardly carrying a thin wooden box with the thick sheet of glass packaged carefully inside.

"It seems as though you may be needing some curtains to go with that, if that sort of thing appeals to you," Mr. Herbert said.

"Yes, I think that's a fine idea," Will agreed.

They stopped at Mr. Herbert's store after leaving the court-house. Will set the box near the door and began looking through the different fabrics that Mr. Herbert pulled from a back room. There weren't very many options, but Will found he was quite satisfied with a sturdy, light green cloth which seemed perfect for the job. Mr. Herbert complimented his choice and wrapped the fabric in plain brown paper and handed it back.

Will thanked him and tucked the cloth into his sack. He then carefully picked up his package with the framed glass and started off on the long journey home.

It took nearly three full days carrying his inconvenient load before he made it back to the thicket, and then it was an unusually difficult challenge to get the glass through the brambles.

Will chose a discreet spot behind a clump of trees and, using his axe, cut a narrow path into the thicket. It was a great relief to have the glass safely delivered against the side of the half-built cabin. Will worked the brambles back into place so that the path he had carved would soon be overgrown and indiscernible.

Chapter 16

THE PEAK OF SUMMER swept over the rolling hills in a dry blazing heat which soon turned into a more mellow warmth, scented and comfortable as fall again approached. A simple cabin stood sturdy and strong in the center of the clearing. The wavy glass of the window reflected the scene inside the enclosure. Light green curtains hung on each side within the cabin, framing the pleasant view. A warm fire blazed in the hearth against the north wall.

Winter snows followed a pleasing bountiful harvest. With the return of the chill and isolation of winter, Will dedicated much of his times to furnishing the cabin with bits of furniture made from poorly carved logs.

Once satisfied, he then set about developing a better bow and practicing with it for hours on end until the bow snapped and he was forced to make another.

The older part of the cabin—now a storehouse—was filled with an assortment of fruits and vegetables, some dried and some stored in crates stacked deep in the hole dug into the ground and covered with the thin boards that had been used to protect the framed glass on its journey from Bloomfield. There were now jars boasting honey, dried meat, sweet maple syrup, and even some wheat, salt and oil which Will had purchased from Mr. Herbert earlier in the year.

Will felt quite content as he settled for yet another snowy season. He still felt the gnawing pangs of his solitude and the neglect from the outside world, but his greater comforts and his ability to now take better care of himself offered a high level of satisfaction.

Will continued to visit Pravda often, nestling in the branches of the large blue spruce for an hour or two at a time and helping in the night wherever he saw a need.

His stock of fur coats, hats and mittens continued to grow, which offered him a welcome excuse to make the trek over to Bloomfield. He found himself staying a little longer with each visit to enjoy the rare bit of conversation that soothed his loneliness for a time.

Will's collection of coins had grown to a rather substantial amount. He made a rawhide pouch to hold his savings and kept his accumulating wealth on a shelf in the storehouse.

January settled in with the usual dark, bitter cold storms that made Will ache for sunlight and the freedom of the warmth of spring.

Will sewed, designed, built, and filled his time as best he could, but the hours passed slowly. When the sun occasionally peeked through, it offered such welcome relief that Will hardly moved from the pool of light which swept across the dirt floor of his cabin for a few hours before it sunk behind the trees to the west.

Constant work was the best sort of distraction. Will used the periods of stormy weather well and amassed a sizable collection of items to sell. He enjoyed the long walk more than ever after the many hours he had spent in silent solitude. With the passing of a particularly lengthy storm, it had been weeks since he had seen another living creature.

Will stepped into Mr. Herbert's store and found appreciable comfort in the warm greeting he received.

"We wondered when we might be seeing you." Mr. Herbert leaned over the counter to shake Will's hand. "With that last terrible storm that passed through, people have come asking for your coats until we've run clear out."

Will grinned.

Mr. Herbert was excited to see the large stock of coats Will pulled from his sack. He paid Will even more for the merchandise than usual.

"You've added a little extra lining to my pockets, Will. It's time I returned the favor. They've been fetching a mighty high price," Mr. Herbert said. His face suddenly lit up. "Oh, and I have something that I wonder if you just might be interested in taking with you."

Mr. Herbert disappeared into the back room of the store. When he returned, he carried a small crate. There was a soft whimpering sound coming from it.

"I found her by the rubbish pile—abandoned by her mother during the storm, it seems. I'm not sure what kind she is."

Will slowly reached his hands into the crate, hardly able to believe what Mr. Herbert was offering him. Gently, he pulled out a small pup with brown and white coloring and a wrinkled little nose. She whimpered and looked timidly into Will's eyes. Will pulled the dog into his arms, unable to speak.

"She's not trained at all, but she should be just old enough to start eating regular food. She's a bit of a runt, though. What do you think, Will?"

The pup cuddled into a ball and nestled in under Will's

chin. Will laughed and warm tears filled his eyes. He could hardly remember when he had never felt so happy. He stroked the small bundle of fur, hardly able to breath for the joy that was bursting inside of him.

Mr. Herbert watched for a moment. "Well, I think that settles that," he laughed. "What will you name her?"

Will held the small pup tenderly against him and looked down into her tiny face. "Perhaps I will call her Kaeya." Kaeya licked his hand and snuggled into the folds of his coat.

Still holding the little creature, Will searched the store for the items he needed to purchase. Before he left, he wrapped a scrap pelt of fur from his sack around the pup and nestled her into his coat.

The trip home had its challenges. Mr. Herbert had fairly warned him that Kaeya had not been trained. She wet them both a couple of times before Will began to recognize the signs that she was needing to go. She ate well enough, but she had a hard time holding still while Will tried to get some sleep, a particularly challenging task as Will felt it especially necessary to sleep high on a tree branch in case of wolves.

When at last they arrived in the clearing through the tunnel, Will set her down. Kaeya ran over the top of the snow, licking at the flakes that swirled in the breeze.

Will laughed, watching her. How strange and wonderful it was to not be so entirely alone.

Chapter 17

THE WINTER MONTHS PASSED with a far greater measure of enjoyment in the hidden clearing as Kaeya grew. She was playful, yet intelligent. She learned quickly and loved exploring the woods with Will as he went to check the traps. Will kept her on a rawhide leash as they walked and kept his bow strung. He had only ever run into the wolves that solitary occasion near Bloomfield, but he had often seen the mess they made each time they had discovered a rabbit caught in his traps. Luckily, Kaeya didn't seem anxious to wander off on her own.

Will continued to visit Pravda, though now he limited his visits to only a few days a week. Kaeya waited inside the cabin whimpering until he came back and greeted him energetically upon his return.

A new idea for a project had drawn Will's interest during his last visit to Bloomfield as he passed by several of the houses and their little outbuildings. He developed a few plans to suit his own needs and mapped the dimensions in the snow. He then spent the early part of February cutting the wood and building himself a sturdy chicken coop. He also took the needed time to build a slatted crate, to which he added a bit of clean straw and strips of cloth so that he would be able to care for the baby chicks until they were old enough for their new home.

Then, packing several more fur coats to sell, he set off toward Bloomfield to pick up some hatchlings. He didn't dare take Kaeya along until she had grown a little more, fearing she might draw wolves to them. It would be their first time apart for more than a few hours. He knew it would be hard on her when he didn't soon return, but he wasn't sure what else he could do.

Will made a quick trip of getting there, arriving the same day just after night had fallen. He slept in a tree only half a mile from the town and woke in the early morning to the sun rising in the east. Even for a chilly night, it had been a peaceful rest, leaving him feeling ready for a quick trip back, but as Will swung down from the tree, he noticed fresh paw prints in the snow. The wolves had come during the night.

Cautiously, Will pulled out his bow and strung an arrow. He studied the prints and looked through the trees in the direction they took. The wolves' tracks ran parallel to the town. It seemed unusual that the wolves would come so near to Bloomfield, but it had been a harsh winter and even Will had struggled to keep his traps filled.

Squinting hard into the bright morning light glinting off the snow, he watched for any sign of movement, but all was still. He kept his bow at the ready as he set off toward the city. He had barely covered a quarter of a mile when he heard a long, low howl —and a terrified scream.

Will tore the snowshoes from his feet and ran along the tree line where the snow was thin. He heard the vicious sounds of the wolves clashing against the frightened shouts coming from not far ahead.

Bow drawn, Will came in view of a sled filled with wood. A small red-headed boy was perched on top of the stacked wood, shrieking and shaking with fear. A young, nearly identical teenage boy stood on the lip of the sled swinging a thick branch and shouting at the wolves. A large gray wolf dove and caught the older boy by the leg. The boy screamed in agony.

Will ran as close as he dared and raised the bow. Sweat poured down his face. Again the older boy cried out in terror, gripping the sled with all his strength as the wolf started to pulled him into the pack.

Will released the arrow.

The wolf dropped to ground.

Will slung another arrow and shot it straight into the pack. Another wolf howled and fell to the earth, writhing in pain. It whimpered pitifully. Will let another arrow fly. A third wolf fell. The remaining wolves howled and snarled in confusion.

"Leave! Go!" Will screamed at the wolves, running at them with another arrow strung on the bow.

A smaller wolf took a few running steps toward him. Will let the arrow fly. The wolf leapt to the side. The arrow barely skimmed its ear, but the wolf turned and ran. The others followed close behind.

Will ran to the boy, who lay gasping in pain. The smaller boy shook with sobs, watching as Will packed snow around the bloody, torn leg of the older boy.

Will pulled the small boy down from the pile of wood and set him next to his brother at the front of the sled. The little one wrapped his arms around his brother's neck and sobbed.

"It's going to be alright." Will said, but his voice shook even as he spoke the comforting words. He tucked his bag in beside the feet of the two red-headed brothers then shoved the pile of wood off the side of the sled. He kept his bow strung over his shoulder with the last of his arrows in the quiver.

It was a light sled without the load of wood weighing it down. Will slung the rope over himself and pushed through the snow toward Bloomfield. He wished now that he still had his snow shoes. His legs sunk deep with every step and slowed his pace.

As they approached the town, Will shouted for help. The smaller boy joined him, crying out with all his little heart. Several men and one woman came running. Will struggled to catch his breath.

"Wolves!" he gasped. "There were wolves!" he said and pointed at the older boy in the sled.

The men ran to the boy and hoisted him into their arms. The smaller boy ran after them, his flaming red hair soon disappearing from sight. Will collapsed against the sled, panting heavily.

"Are you alright?" Will turned his head. The woman knelt beside him in the snow.

Will nodded. He realized that he, too, was covered in blood —whether from the wolves or from the injured boy, he wasn't sure—likely both.

"Come with me. We'd better get you into something dry. I think a nice cup of tea would do you well," she told him.

Will blushed with surprise at her kind offer. He nodded and pulled his bag from the blood-stained sled. The woman led him up the street past a couple of wood-framed houses to a beautiful white home with a lovely porch and dark green shutters.

"Come on inside. We'll get you cleaned up."

Will suddenly felt very self-conscious. He stopped on the outer step and peered inside the clean entryway. He then looked down at his filthy clothes and soaking boots.

"It's alright," the woman insisted with a smile. "Mud mops

up well enough." She held the door open. Will hesitated before stepping inside.

Will's heart felt as though it had stopped. He stared around him in astonishment. How long had it been since he had found himself inside a real home? he wondered. How many months had passed since the day his life had suddenly changed all those years ago? He shuddered. A flood of memories came sweeping back. He felt nauseated with the overwhelming mix of emotions that filled his body.

The woman opened a shallow closet just off the entryway and handed Will a towel. "Take this and go into that room to the right. Draw yourself a bath. I will look and see if I can find any clothes that we might be able to pin to fit you."

Will stared, surprised and uncertain. The woman only smiled and pointed at a door partway down the hall.

"Go on now," she encouraged him gently. She left Will and headed up the stairs.

Will tiptoed cautiously along the polished wood floor. He tried not to the touch the knob more than he had to, but a thick layer of filth rubbed off onto the varnished metal. He grimaced and sighed then stepped into the white-tiled bathroom. A large mirror hung on the wall above the sink. Will suddenly realized he had not seen his reflection in nearly four years. He almost looked, but he decided to wait to see what he looked like until after he had cleaned up a bit. Will set the towel on the edge of the tub.

For nearly five minutes, Will just stared at the faucet. Timidly, he reached over and turned one of the knobs. Cold water came rushing out. He turned the other and the water grew warmer. He realized that all the water that was going into the tub was draining out through the bottom. He reached down to where a small piece of rubber on a chain was swirling in the rushing water and stuffed the stopper into the hole. The tub began to fill.

Will adjusted the knobs and watched the clean water fill the tub. He peeled the filthy clothes from his body and stared into the steaming tub. When he finally stepped into the bath, he sank in utter relief into the warmth of the water. The heat soothed his muscles and eased the tension in his hands and feet. The crusted dirt that had built up throughout the winter began slipping away from his skin.

A bar of soap lay on the counter near the tub. Will picked it up and rubbed it over his arms. The soap turned filthy and gray. Will kept scrubbing. The tub water grew cool long before he had finished scrubbing the dirt from half his body. He add more hot water to the tub and kept scrubbing.

Once his skin was clean, Will began working at his hair. He scrubbed and rinsed and scrubbed and rinsed. At long last, he stepped from the bath and wrapped himself in the soft, clean towel and pulled the drain from the tub. The water gurgled loudly as it drained away, cloudy with dirt and filth.

There was a knock on the door and the woman's voice called softly to him, "I have some clothes for you. I'll leave them just outside the door."

Will heard her set something down in the hallway then listened as her steps faded away. He slowly opened the door and picked up the bundle she had left for him. The clothes were large, but they had been pinned and rolled up at the sleeves and at the bottom of the trousers.

Once dressed, Will turned around. He raised his eyes at last to look in the mirror.

Although he hadn't been sure quite what to expect, he still was quite surprised. Will stared at his reflection curiously. He supposed he was even kind of handsome for a young boy. He was amazed how much he had grown and how his face had changed. He was beginning to look more like his father.

Will knelt and tried to wipe away the grime he had left on the bathroom floor, using the damp towel. He then folded it and laid it over the edge of the tub.

Will opened the door to the bathroom and looked out. It was very quiet. He felt odd walking alone through a strange house, especially after having not been welcome inside of any home for so long. He made his way back up the hallway until he heard some faint sounds coming from behind a door to the right of the staircase. Will pushed the door open slowly and peered inside.

"Well, look at you! That's a remarkable change, I must say," the woman smiled. "Come on in. I'm making bread. Why don't you give me a hand." She had tied a long apron over the front of her dress. Flour covered her arms up to her elbows. She handed Will a lump of dough while she worked on a larger lump. Together they pounded and kneaded the dough, adding flour as they worked.

"My name is Amelia. What is your name?" she asked.

Will nervously cleared his throat. "My name is Will." he said softly.

"And what brings you here to Bloomfield, Will?" Amelia asked.

"I came to sell the fur coats that I've made and to purchase some baby chicks, if they have any ready to sell."

"Well, then!" Amelia stopped working at her lump of dough and turned to him. "I suppose I do know a little of you." she smiled. "My husband bought me a nice fur coat a year ago last Christmas. It has been so delightfully warm. It's really quite love-ly, so thank you, Will." Amelia gathered the dough into a large bowl and covered it with a towel. She rinsed her hands and motioned for Will to do the same.

"I also heard that you came during the summer to buy some framed glass. Whatever did you need it for?" she asked. She pulled some milk from the fridge and poured two glasses, which she set out with a plate of cookies.

"I was building myself a cabin," Will told her. "It is much nicer to have a cabin with a window than to be stuck in the dark through the winter."

"Well, yes it is." Amelia paused. "But certainly you weren't building the cabin by yourself."

"Yes, ma'am. I built it all by myself," Will said timidly. He felt proud of his accomplishment, and it felt so wonderful to have someone to tell about it.

Amelia sat back, studying Will as she sipped her milk. She pushed the plate of cookies toward him. Will reached out cautiously and took one, watching Amelia's face. She nodded. He stared at the cookie. It smelled delightful and bits of chocolate were visible on its soft brown surface. How long had it been? he wondered. He wanted so much just to hold the moment all to himself. It wasn't the cookie itself, though he was beyond excited to be holding something so wonderful. It was the gift. She had given him something—something she had made—a gift just for him. And there she sat talking to him, noticing him, as though she cared to know more about him.

"Will, don't you have a mother?" Amelia asked.

Will still held the cookie with both hands, staring happily at it, but not eating it. "Yes, ma'am, but she's gone now."

"I see." she said. "But what about your father?"

Will looked up. He realized he had never yet said it. He swallowed hard. "My father..." he began. He sighed. "My father is gone too."

"Gone?" She let out a long breath. Her eyes searched his face. "Will, where has he gone?"

Will looked up. There was something so tender and kind in her expression.

Will looked down at the bit of cream-colored cloth that covered the table. "My Father died. He's buried beneath an old oak tree."

"Oh, my dear Will," Amelia said. "Don't you have anyone to look after you?"

Will shook his head. Then he looked up and smiled. "I'm alright, ma'am. I've got my own place now, and I can hunt." Will held the cookie against his lips and breathed in the delicious smell.

Amelia watched him. She pushed the second glass of milk across the table to him. "How long have you been alone, Will?"

Will paused a moment to think. He still held the cookie tightly in one hand, but he picked up the glass of milk with the other. He studied it for a moment then took a small sip. He let the liquid slosh around inside his mouth. It tasted strange and rich—yet wonderful.

"This August, it will be four years. Father died when I was eight."

Amelia slowly got to her feet and turned away from the table. She stared out through the window above the sink.

Will was intent on enjoying the sweet scent of the cookie, hardly noticing the silence that had fallen.

"Have you been alone all that time?" Amelia asked after a few minutes had passed. Her voice was soft.

"Oh, no, ma'am. There's Jimmy. He's a horse. He kept me

company all through the first winter. And now I have Kaeya. She's just a puppy, so I couldn't bring her along with me."

Amelia sighed and lowered her head. She was still turned away from him, looking out the window.

Will looked up as she turned back to him. She smiled warmly, but a troubled expression still creased her forehead.

"Go ahead and eat up." she told him. "You are welcome to have as many of those cookies as you like. I'm going to put your old clothes in some water to soak."

Will nibbled at the cookie in his hand. It tasted like heaven—like the best sort of memory on the best sort of day.

By the time Amelia returned, he had only nibbled away a small portion of the cookie. She stood in the doorway for a time before speaking.

"Will," she said, "I was wondering if you might come on a walk with me."

Will, still holding his cookie, nodded. Amelia slipped into a beautiful fur coat that Will recognized as one of the first he had made. She held another coat out to him. It was much too large, but she rolled up the sleeves and wrapped it tightly around his small frame. The bottom of the coat hung just a couple inches above the ground.

"There now." she said. "Let's be on our way."

They headed up the street along the rows of thick hedges. Amelia paused as they neared the shop-lined streets.

"We'd better check in on the Bronson brothers—the two boys you helped earlier this morning." She turned down a side street and then another until they were nearly at the edge of town. She strode up to a run-down home and knocked at the door, which soon opened. Many people stood crowded inside.

"I hope it is no bother for us to drop by, but I wanted to ask after the boys," Amelia said to the tired-looking woman who had opened the door.

Will recognized the small, red-headed boy that came running up to them.

"Mother, that's him! He's the boy that shot the wolves. He killed a whole bunch of them! Boy, he looks different all cleaned up though."

Both Amelia and the mother looked at Will in surprise. "You are the boy who saved my sons?" the mother asked. "Oh, child." A sob caught in her throat. She pulled Will into her arms and held him tight. Tears fell from her eyes into his hair. "Bless you, child. These boys is all I've got."

She kissed the top of his head and smiled, holding him tight before releasing him. She wiped her eyes on a damp handkerchief.

"Jacob will be jest fine, as long as we are able to keep out the infection. He had some deep gashes, but the doctor thinks he will heal up with time." She smiled. "And Joseph," she said, picking the smaller boy up in her arms, "has been talking about you and what you did for them. He has hardly paused for breath since they arrived. I hope you will visit again." She placed a hand on his shoulder. "You are always welcome here. What is your name, lad?"

"My name is Will," he told her, a warm flush rushing to his cheeks.

She smiled. "Will—a good name. Thank you, Will. We owe you a great deal."

She looked at Amelia. "Thank you for coming by. I better get back to Jacob now. The doctor is still working to sew up his wounds."

"Of course," Amelia nodded. "Let me know if there is anything I can do."

The streets were quiet except for the soft crunch of snow underfoot from the few that were out and about. For all that had happened in those few hours, it was still early in the day. Amelia led Will back to the center of town and up the steps of the city building. They made their way inside. Again the clerk stared.

Amelia turned to Will and placed her hands on his shoulders. "Will, would it be alright if I asked you to wait here for me for a few minutes?"

Will nodded and found himself a seat on a bench near the door.

Amelia walked to the door of the mayor's office. She tapped lightly on the painted wood then stepped inside.

The clerk watched Will as the boy sat slowly nibbling away at the cookie that he still carried with him.

Amelia was inside Mayor Ringwald's office nearly half an hour before she emerged. She approached Will, who still had not finished his cookie.

"Will, would you mind coming with me for a moment?" she asked.

Will followed her into the mayor's office. Mayor Ringwald smiled and offered him a seat.

Mayor Ringwald sat on the edge of his desk and cleared his throat. "Will, it seems as though you have met my dear wife." Amelia joined her husband who slipped his arm around her.

Will nodded slowly. Surely he had not known they belonged to each other, but it seemed sensible enough to him. They both had a similar demeanor and the same kind ness in their smile.

Mayor Ringwald glanced at Amelia. She nodded and he continued, "Will, it sounds as though you've accomplished some wonderful things. Amelia has told me that you've even built a cabin on your own—with a window and all." He looked rather impressed. His expression then changed and his voice became rather serious.

"Will, we were wondering if there is anything else you might need—that you might wish to have as a part of your life."

Will thought a moment before answering. "I do have plenty to eat, and enough firewood, and a garden," he said, thinking hard. "I came to pick up some baby chicks, though. I think I would like to raise perhaps four or five, but I have enough money to buy them."

Mayor Ringwald and Amelia glanced at each other. "But, Will," Mayor Ringwald continued, "what if you could have more than that. Suppose we could offer you a better place to live."

Will shifted nervously. He had heard about the orphanages. His father had been encouraged to give him up when times got hard. His father had refused.

"He doesn't belong in such a place!" his father had shouted angrily each time the orphanages were mentioned.

Will looked at Mayor Ringwald uncertainly.

Amelia watched his face. She spoke gently, "Mayor Ringwald and I have always wanted to have children of our own. We're not so very old, but it hasn't been something that has happened for us as we had hoped—and even if it did, you would still be welcome to be a part of our family, if it is something you might find agreeable."

They both watched Will intently. Will stared, still holding the little bit of cookie that remained. "You really want *me*?—to *keep* me?" he asked.

"Yes, Will," Amelia said softly, "we really want you."

Mayor Ringwald nodded his agreement.

Will covered his face with his small hands and wept. He turned away and tried to wipe away the tears, feeling a little foolish, but when he looked up, he saw tears in both their eyes as they leaned together, still observing him.

A sudden thought struck Will. His breath caught in his throat. "What about Kaeya?"

Amelia laughed. "We talked about that as well. Kaeya is welcome to come, too. We have a large yard and we can build her a home of her own, if that would be alright with you."

Will couldn't decide whether to laugh or cry so he ended up somewhere in the middle.

That afternoon, when he and Amelia made their way back to the beautiful white house, Will could hardly stop himself from shouting the news to the world. His heart beat fast and free in his chest. He finally had a home—a real home with a mother and a father.

Chapter 18

AMELIA PACKED A DOZEN COOKIES for the trip along with several slices of fresh homemade bread. She asked if she might accompany Will on the journey, but he insisted on making this last trip alone. There was something sacred to him about the clearing surrounded by brambles that hid the small cabin, a garden and a beehive dripping with honey. It had been his place of safety—his refuge—a place only he knew of.

He stopped by the Bronson's home and asked if he might borrow the sled. Mrs. Bronson readily agreed but then hesitated when she heard he was going back through the woods. Still, she would not break her word but allowed him the use of the sled after receiving a promise from Will that he would be careful to avoid any unnecessary danger.

Will managed to find his snowshoes where he had left them, tossed carelessly in the snow a short distance from Bloomfield. He felt his heart race several times, a small sound in the distance making him jump and duck beneath the nearest tree as he strained his ears for any hint of danger. He kept his bow ready, but aside from the fear that plagued him as he trudged through the woods, he had no trouble getting back.

Kaeya ran in circles for nearly an hour after he arrived back at the cabin, yipping joyfully until she was entirely worn out.

"Well, Kaeya, we are going on a trip—and at the end of it, there is a real family for us! We might even have a Christmas tree with beautiful lights—and the lady, she makes cookies with chocolate bits. She even makes bread—real, soft homemade bread. Oh, Kaeya, it is all too wonderful!"

Will packed his ample supply of food and furs onto the sled. He tried to bundle Kaeya, but she refused to hold still long enough, so he attached the leash to her and let her walk along beside him.

Will made his way to a single cabin on the west side of Pravda. It was midday. The children would all be in school. Will walked up the steps of the run-down shack and knocked at the door. There was no answer. Will turned the knob. The door opened.

Will spent several minutes carrying all of the food and furs from the sled into the house. On top of the pile, he left a package of homemade cookies and a pouch with several coins.

Will turned away. He knew it wasn't terribly far between Pravda and Bloomfield, but he felt an ache at saying goodbye to everything he had built. It felt strange to him to realize how much he would even miss all the people he had come to know so well during the past few years, knowing he had never been known by them. Yet, he knew he would miss no one as deeply as he would miss Bonnie, who had taught him to see the world around him in a new and more beautiful way. He supposed it was strange to miss her, knowing they had never even met, but he still felt as though he was leaving a small part of himself behind on the steps of that rickety cabin.

The journey back to Bloomfield was rather peaceful in comparison to his previous trip, though Will continued to jump at every sound. He often imagined that he could hear a low growl or a howling somewhere beyond the next hill. As he settled down to sleep, he discovered that Kaeya didn't quite like the idea of staying in a tree, so it made for a very long, restless night.

Will arrived in Bloomfield relieved and exhausted, but wonderfully happy. For him, it was the beginning of a new life—one in which he would never be quite so alone.

Chapter 19

LIFE BECAME EVEN BETTER than the young boy could have imagined.

Will awoke each morning to the savory scent of fresh pancakes and sausages—unless it was a Saturday. Saturday was muffin day with fresh apple muffins and a sweet molasses topping.

Amelia enrolled Will with the headmaster of the Bloomfield Academy to start lessons at the beginning of the new school year that fall. Will approached his first day back with excited trepidation. He had fallen so far behind. There were great gaps in his education from the years spent in Pravda, but his enthusiasm for learning gave him a significant advantage as he worked through the problems, asked questions, and studied on his own.

Mr. Martin, the headmaster of the Bloomfield Academy, was strict but rather good-natured. He spent the first year creating a unique course of study to bring Will up to the level of the other students. By Will's second year under the man's tutelage, Mr. Martin had pushed Will beyond the standard curriculum. Will's dedication to his studies soon had him surpassing his classmates. He worked hard and studied hard. He felt privileged and excited to be allowed to learn among the other students—able to ask questions and turn in assignments and receive feedback and personalized instruction. He set a new standard, an enthusiastic approach to learning. It was infectious and before long, the other students found the motivation to achieve a similar standard in their own education.

For several months, Will struggled to interact with his classmates. He had rarely had any conversations during the years he had spent on his own, and he felt unbearably awkward. Yet, due to his incredible role in saving the Bronson brothers, he was remarkably popular with his fellow classmates. The story of his bloody arrival in Bloomfield pulling the two boys to safety had spread like wildfire as it had passed through the town, yet the other children seemed more impressed with his skill with a bow than with the heroics of that day, the brothers having spread the story of wolves dropping all around them as Will's arrows flew.

The children were patient whenever Will found it difficult to express himself, and how they loved to hear the stories of his hunting, trapping, and fishing!

Friendships sparked easily. The boys in Bloomfield taught Will to play baseball and worked patiently to teach him the skill of batting and catching. In return, Will showed them the artistry of hunting with a bow. He removed the obsidian arrow tips and attached round gray stones for the boys to use as they practiced.

The seasons passed swiftly through Bloomfield. The children learned and grew as they filled their days with school, sports, swimming, camping trips, and a good deal of hard work.

Will could not have felt more grateful for his new life. He still had many of his old habits. He often retired to the town square in the evenings, sitting on the large wrought iron bench with a friend or two, silently observing those around them and slipping in quietly when help was needed. Amelia, he noticed, was much the same. He supposed it was easy to see why she had been drawn to him—a young boy, so much in need of a family. It wasn't until a few years later that, looking back, he realized how much she had needed him, too.

Chapter 20

MONTHS TURNED INTO YEARS, passing by all too quickly with tinsel-strewn Christmas trees, frosted birthday cakes, hundreds of loaves of freshly-baked bread, summer and fall baseball games, endless piles of books, starlit nights with the bullfrogs croaking, community hayrides, Thanksgiving dinners, main street parades, barn dances, picnics in the town square, and many evenings by a crackling fire with Will's new father and mother, telling stories and solving riddles while Kaeya lay happily at their feet.

Will continued to treasure the memories of his real mother, the aching longing now exchanged for a peaceful recollection. Neither had he forgotten his father, who lay peacefully beneath the gnarled oak on the edge of Pravda. The leather-bound book that had belonged to Will's father lay tucked beneath Will's mattress, still wrapped in the same paper, unopened since that dreadful morning.

Will's eighteenth birthday arrived on a warm spring morning. Jacob Bronson came by for cake and ice cream that evening before the two boys headed off to a barn dance near the center of town.

Jacob still walked with a slight limp, but he was an excellent dancer. Will enjoyed the dances as well, but he wasn't nearly so graceful as Jacob, even with two perfectly functional legs. On their way to the dance, Jacob stopped beneath a lamppost, the light glowing off his dark red hair.

"It arrived just today. I want to show you," he said confidingly. He motioned to a bench along the stone walkway and the two sat down.

Will grinned. "Then tonight is the night! Does Julia know?"

"Not yet." Jacob shifted nervously and ran a hand through his hair. "I have the ring though. I hope she likes it. I want to know what you think. It's nothing fancy, I know."

Will laughed and clapped Jacob on the shoulder. "I don't think she'll care much at all what the ring looks like."

Jacob pulled a thin, gleaming band from the inside pocket of his jacket. He beamed as he held it out. Three small diamonds glittered in the light from the lamppost above them. Jacob and Will had been planning this night since Jacob had turned twenty last fall, but Jacob had struggled to wait until the ring arrived on order from Baltimore.

Julia had been his sweetheart since their third year in school. Lately, Jacob had been spending all of his spare time working to build a small home on a corner of his family's farm. Will and Joseph spent much of their available time aiding him in the project, jesting the anxious groom-to-be. Jacob was good-natured and a hard working man and fiercely loyal. Julia was kind, devoted, and a perfect match.

Jacob tucked the ring carefully back inside his pocket. "What about you, Will? Come the end of term, you will have graduated from the academy. Laura is still vying for your attention as ever she has. I think it's easy to guess she will be at the dance tonight, lovely as a picture."

Will shook his head. "Jacob, Laura is wonderful, but I've never had it in my mind to court her. I just haven't been able to feel that way toward any of the girls I've known here in Bloomfield."

"So, you are still holding out hope for a girl you say has no idea that you even exist." Jacob shook his head, grinning.

"She *doesn't* know I exist. Of that I am quite certain. We have never met—and perhaps when we do, there will be nothing in me that inspires her interest. Yet, I cannot imagine building a life with anyone else—at least until I know that I haven't even the slightest chance of winning her love. One day, if there is that hope left to me, you will meet her. Then you will know why I could never wish for anyone other than her." Will stood and held out his hand. "Come now. An excellent evening awaits you, Jacob Bronson."

The night proved to be wonderful indeed. Joseph Bronson showed up at dusk and gave his older brother a knowing smile. Will danced with several of the local girls from the town, each of them lovely in their bright ruffled dresses.

Just before the final number of the evening, Jacob slipped outside with Julia beside him. Joseph and Will silently hurried ahead of them making sure the bench nearest the river was vacated, on which they left a lovely bundle of wildflowers tied up with a bit of ribbon. The two boys settled behind a tree nearby as Jacob and Julia came up the path. Jacob guided Julia to the bench and slipped the bouquet into her arms. He sat beside her for a short time, talking softly. His hands trembled in the light of the nearest lamppost. His voice shook as he reached into the pocket of his jacket. Jacob slowly knelt down on one knee.

Will had been right. Julia didn't even look at the ring before kneeling down and wrapping her arms around Jacob.

Months later, the young couple was married. Will stood with Joseph at Jacob's side as the bride and groom were pronounced "husband and wife." The celebration lasted well into the evening before the wedding party gathered on the steps of the town hall to wave off the felicitous newlyweds.

Within the week, Will found himself preparing to head off to a new life of his own. Mr. Martin had done a great deal of writing to several of the most prestigious universities with a recommendation for Will to continue his studies under their tutelage. Four had responded with letters of acceptance, two of which included offers for scholarships.

There had been many late nights in the Ringwald household as the small family discussed the different schools and possible careers. Will felt quite content when at last he settled on attending one of the largest of the four universities, pursuing a degree in business and economics.

The late summer evenings grew chill as Will packed two large bags and a box of books with a train ticket set on top. He had only two days left before his departure.

The next morning, Will walked to the post office before the sun had come up and enlisted a ride with the mail carrier on his journey to Pravda. The postman seemed a little surprised when Will asked to be dropped off at the edge of town where the old gnarled oak tree grew, but he obliged the odd request.

"Are you planning to return to Bloomfield by the coach?" the man asked before pulling away.

"Thank you, but no. I think I will enjoy the walk back," Will replied.

The man again gave Will a disconcerted look. He hesitated

a moment then shrugged and clicked his tongue to the horses. The mail wagon quickly covered the last stretch into Pravda to drop off the mail to Mr. Murdoch, who stood outside the post office watching up the street—but not for the mail wagon.

Will smiled. It was still all too familiar to him. At that very moment, a lovely young woman, stepped out of the mercantile store, her eyes drawn toward another part of town, waiting for her desired suitor.

Chapter 21

WILL'S HEART POUNDED and sweat prickled his brow as he attempted to leisurely stroll down the street. For the first time, he wasn't looking at the ground, neither was he hiding behind bushes nor tucked inside the branches of a large spruce. Dressed in a suit and hat, many of the gentlemen gave him a slight bow and a curious look as he passed by. Many of the ladies smiled and curtsied. Not a single face registered recognition of him, but how much he knew about each of them, and what pleasure it brought him to see them all again!

Will walked from one end of Pravda to the other, rehearsing in his mind the words he would say when at last they met. He reached the farthest end of town, and still he had not seen her. Will casually turned back as though this were a planned part of his stroll and made his way slowly back up the street. He had nearly completed his second pass through the town when he saw her at last. She emerged from a small shop dressed in a simple skirt and blouse. It was Bonnie.

She looked as lovely as ever. Will tried to pretend he wasn't staring, but it was so wonderful to see her—and to see her nearly grown into a woman. She was probably seventeen, and perhaps not as strikingly pretty as was Leanna, who had managed to brush by him a handful of times already, smiling brightly up at him each time she went past. Bonnie was so much more. Bonnie was complete. She seemed to define all that was lovely and beautiful about the world in her charming, unassuming presence.

Bonnie had just left Madame Belle Lucille's Dress Shop, where he supposed she must be employed. In her left hand she carried a small sack, which she set just inside the gate of one of the houses on her way to the town square.

Will smiled. In all those years, Bonnie had never changed what he loved about her most.

From a small bag she carried with her, she pulled a book and a sandwich. Bonnie ate slowly while she read, tossing small bits of food to the squirrels that playfully ran around her. Will watched her a moment longer, his heart dancing. He turned suddenly and slipped up the stairs into the mercantile store.

Mr. Willet greeted him pleasantly. "Can I help you find anything in particular, sir?" he asked.

Will tried not to stare as he looked at the tall man behind the counter. Mr. Willet's hair had turned gray and his face was now lined with deep wrinkles, a surprising change in the few years since Will had last seen him.

"I'm looking for something beautiful—something special. I'm looking for a gift."

Mr. Willet guided him to a glass case beneath the front counter. Inside lay an assortment of lovely items—brooches, necklaces, rings, and other delicate and appealing objects.

"May I see that box there?" Will pointed to a small ivory box with delicate carvings etched intricately into its surface.

"Ah, yes. This," Mr. Willet said, opening the glass case and pulling it out, "is a charming little music box." He opened the lid. A tinkling melody played from within.

Will recognized the song. The band in Bloomfield played it every Saturday night at the barn dances as the final slow dance of the evening.

"I believe the song is called "Let Me Call You Sweetheart"—a rather popular tune." Mr. Willet continued.

"Yes, I do think you are right." Will agreed with a smile. "It's perfect. May I purchase it?"

"It will cost a pretty penny," Mr. Willet said, haltingly.

"Well then, how much will it be?" Will asked.

Mr. Willet named the price. Will counted the coins into his hand.

Mr. Willet pulled out a square of brown paper. "I can wrap it for you to keep it safe on your journey."

Will shook his head. "I'll not need it wrapped. Thank you." He picked up the small music box and, giving a slight bow, he departed.

Will reached the park just as Bonnie stood, brushing off her skirt. He practiced his greeting silently as he approached her. Bonnie slipped the book into her bag and turned toward Madame Belle Lucille's Dress Shop. She didn't see Will until he was no more than a few feet away. She looked up at him, surprise evident in the pleasant smile that lit her face.

Will flushed. The words caught in his throat. He stammered, "Miss Bonnie…this…box…I…well, it…" He took a deep breath. "It is a gift… for you, and… I…well…I know you don't… you don't know me and… well, I…I just…that is to say…well, I was hoping…"

Bonnie smiled warmly. "Of course I know you, Will."

Will felt his face freeze. He stood there in silence for several seconds trying to regain his composure. "You…wait, what…you

—you do?"

Bonnie smiled again, the corners of her eyes creased merrily. "Yes I do. You weren't the only one who spent a good deal of time observing the people who walk these streets. There weren't many whom I ever saw climb the large spruce, or live in a stable, or survive on their own as a child in the woods. I was there when you and your father first came to Bloomfield. He called you 'Will' just as you passed by me, but you didn't see me. You had your face turned toward the ground."

Will felt the air rush out of him. The apples he had found, the things he had needed. Perhaps finding them had been wild luck. Perhaps it had been much more than luck. He had never even considered.

Will's heart beat wildly. He slipped the music box into her hands. "Miss Bonnie, I would like a reason to come back to Pravda one day—and if I did, would you ever consider...I mean, we have never talked before now, but just supposing..." Will felt the blood rising to his cheeks. "Well, would you consider it?"

"Of course, Will. I could hope for nothing more."

Will's face flushed again and a bright smile tugged at his lips. He tried desperately to appear calm and collected. "Well, then," he gave her a quick bow, "it may be some time as I am off to the university, but I hope to find that all is well with you when I return."

Again, he bowed. Bonnie smiled and gave him a quick curtsy then hurried on her way to Madame Belle Lucille's Dress Shop.

Will later discovered that he was unable to recall the trip back to Bloomfield, nor could he quite remember the farewell he was given at the train station as he began a new journey of a thousand miles, his mind caught up in blissful turmoil.

Chapter 22

WILL SETTLED INTO THE UPRIGHT SEAT of the steam engine passenger car and watched the scenery pass by. Vibrant fields and forests turned into flat plains as the train followed its long track. The train glided over a high canyon bridge then through a range of high, jagged mountains before dropping down into a blanket of wide rolling hills—even more green and lush than those surrounding Bloomfield and Pravda.

He arrived at the campus late in the evening and found his dormitory just as the lamps began illuminating the streets below.

Will had always seen Bloomfield as a large town, and in many ways it was, but the endless streets and the cacophony of hundreds of automobiles near the university made for a long, sleepless night. Still, Will was excited at the endless prospects that lay before him.

Will developed a rigorous class schedule and maintained a strict focus on his studies. On occasion, he found time for socializing, but most of the cheap entertainment his new friends sought held little appeal to him. He found he much preferred to spend the evening reading in the library or sitting on a park bench observing those who passed by.

The high expectations and requirements associated with his

scholarship challenged Will. Yet, he found that he loved the rigor, and by the end of the first semester, he had achieved perfect marks and had risen to the top of his class.

Even with a strict dedication to his studies, Will could not miss the troubling news that occupied the newsstands and the corridor conversations. The European unrest had developed into a bloody war. Though it hadn't yet reached homeland soil, Europe was plummeting into a dark, vicious battle. Rumors and truth intertwined. Nothing seemed certain but for the fear written into the headlines.

Will increased his class load for the second semester and dedicated even more time to studying, preparing assignments, and completing term papers. With war brewing closer to home each day, he felt a great sense of urgency to secure a degree as soon as possible. Will often heard university students express a vote of confidence in President Wilson for his determination to keep the United States out of the war. Still, Will knew, though many insisted otherwise, America's lack of involvement could not be guaranteed.

Will made a short visit home during the holidays between his first two semesters. He, Mayor Ringwald, and Amelia discussed the concerning state of affairs that swept across Europe, but it was still too early to determine a projected outcome.

The second semester passed as quickly as the first. Will's busy schedule made the time fly by with the intense workload he had taken on, and he soon found himself visiting home for summer break. Amelia greeted him at the train station. Mayor Ringwald had been called out of town for a meeting with the governor but would soon return.

Will took a short trip to the Bronson farm to visit Jacob and Julia—and their new little arrival, Liam—his curly hair as bright red as his father's had been in his youth. Joseph happened to be home for the summer as well, on break from the nearby college. He and Will took a walk through the town, stopping for a bit of ice cream and a long talk.

Will enjoyed the occasional social interactions, but he spent much of his summer break reading newspapers and discussing the situation in Europe with Mayor Ringwald once the mayor had returned from the state capital. The reports that came in were almost more frustrating than they were helpful. Each report often contradicted earlier publications, and all were filled with a false sense of confidence that radiated from the highest governing powers in the nation while yet little evidence substantiated their claims of the assured lack of involvement in the European conflict.

Toward the end of the summer, Will again caught a ride with the mail wagon back to Pravda. He strolled into town greeted by the same polite bows and curtsies with which he had been acknowledged on his visit the previous year. Will waited at the park, standing anxiously beneath a tree until Bonnie came into view.

She noticed him as he approached and smiled. "How are you, Will?" she asked.

Will smiled. Several years of his life had been spent in the same small town as all the people he had just passed on the road. He knew so much about each of them, but not a single resident of Pravda could have called him by name—nor could they have recollected him to be the same man who had entered their town as a small boy in filthy clothes so many years earlier. No one, that is, except Bonnie, who could have told stories of that little boy which would have sounded rather wild but were nonetheless true.

"Hello, Miss Bonnie. I am well—wonderfully well. And how has life treated you?"

They stood a few feet apart near the large blue spruce, a formal air between them.

"Life could hardly be better," Bonnie said warmly. "Are you soon heading back to the university?"

"Yes, I am," Will confirmed. "Would you walk with me?" He offered Bonnie his arm.

Bonnie slid her hand over his elbow. Will's heart leapt. Together they strolled around the town square. It wasn't a long conversation. Bonnie was due soon to return to work, yet it seemed that for that small span of time that all was right in a world which rocked with turmoil.

Will bowed as he said farewell. He placed a folded letter in her hand then left her at the door of Madame Belle Lucille's Dress Shop.

Before passing beyond the gnarled oak tree, Will turned back. He saw Bonnie leaning against the banister outside the shop, reading the letter. She smiled and glanced up, catching his eye. She raised a hand and gave him a wave. Will smiled as he waved back, then he turned to make the long walk home.

Chapter 23

Sweet Bonnie,

I hope it will not come amiss to ask if I might write to you while I am away. There is so much I wish to know about you, and I hope it might please you to come to know me better in the meantime. Amidst the constant clatter of the city, I would be so grateful to hear a little of life, where the days pass on nature's more peaceful clock and where talk of war is not heard so extensively on every corner. I would be most grateful if you could send me a little reminder of the country life as the world seems determined to turn a very different direction. It would give me something to look forward to throughout my university studies and the chaos of our world at war.

There is great beauty, even in the city. Still, it is a far different world from the freshly plowed fields, the wide open spaces, the forest of tall sap-laden trees, and the simple routines of everyday life. The buildings that surround me even now reach more than ten times higher than the town hall and the endless street lamps make it impossible to see the stars. The air smells bitter and people rush about in a constant fury. It seems a strange way of life—one in which I have no desire to remain a permanent part, though I am glad to be here. I have learned a great deal and am amazed at the wealth of information and good entertainment so easily

*accessible. There are several theaters, museums, and concert halls. I
would love someday to show you everything there is to see here. Truly,
the city is worth a visit, but life seems much better lived in the fresh air
of the small country towns.*

*I have enclosed my address, and I hope most earnestly that I might hear
from you.*

Sincerely,

William Linden

Dear Will,

I would very much enjoy a correspondence with you.

*Though I have never been to the city, I am grateful for my life here in
Pravda. There are times, though, when the daily routine seems to have
little purpose—a rather monotonous continuity of custom and circum-
stance. In those moments, I find it necessary to remind myself to have
patience enough to enjoy the simple things. I know I would not want the
life in the city, but it is difficult not to long for an adventure—particularly when the daily tasks develop into a rather wearisome regimen.*

*The night air has grown cool and the harvest has just begun. It is per-
haps a few months away, but there is great anticipation among the children as they await the first snowfall of the year. The change of the seasons is one of the most beautiful things in life. It gives variety to the
months and forces a bit of change into the otherwise constant routine. I
also find it inspiring to look over the golden fields just before the harvest
and imagine them barren and covered in several feet of snow—and then,
throughout the winter, I see the barren fields and imagine them gold with*

wheat come summer. It is incredible to try to imagine the change that occurs each year—a stunning reminder of the beautiful renewal of life.

Some changes are appealing. Other changes leave a gaping hole in the world. It is hard to consider the prospect of war. What is truly accomplished? What is to be gained? Is there not a better means to ensuring there is enough for all? And if we have what we need, why must there be those who determine to look further? Why seek power, great wealth and prominence when it comes at the price of precious life—each of which is of greater value than all else the world could ever offer? There are causes worth fighting for, surely, but are there no other means of accomplishing needed change? What is proven by sheer force and brute strength against another that it should determine who is given what and who is denied that which they seek? Why have war and murder become the means for ending conflict? Such action is no resolution; it only leaves scars that can never be healed.

Even here, there is great talk of the war, though there is considerable hope that we as a nation will remain unscathed in our lack of involvement. So many people are dying, and is there not some lack of truth and due purpose on each side? The very men who might have grown up as childhood friends, neighbors and even brothers fight against each other in the hatred inspired by factious leaders who see their troops merely as units and numbers to be counted for or against the strategy they intend to use in securing for themselves their unjust causes. Suppose we were never to rise beyond the broken battlefields? War is a permanent part of history. Must it be a permanent part of the future as well?

I suppose I must apologize. You've written your desire to hear something more than the conflict that already fills your daily conversations, but I am afraid it is a topic that cannot be avoided if I am to truthfully divulge a few of my daily thoughts. There are moments when it seems as though *all is well. The streets are still swept by dusk, the mail is routinely delivered, and everyone continues about their lives as ever they had. I may at times dislike the predictable events of each day, but there is a greater sanity in its simplicity. Still, I do envy you in your opportunity to attend the university. What is life like in the city? What have you chosen to study?*

I hope this letter finds you well.

Sincerely,

Bonnie Wilson

My Dear Bonnie,

Life here in the city is far different from anything I had yet experienced. As you know, there was little need for an automobile in Pravda, but here, they are everywhere. I love the sight of them, and I enjoy an occasional ride across town as often as the opportunity arises. They never cease to amaze me, and now there is talk of machines that can actually fly—if you can imagine such an idea!

I have chosen to study a degree in economics and business. Once more, I am amazed at society. The means by which it remains afloat seems ingenious, though I have at times wondered at the stability of it all.

The university has a large campus with several buildings—most made of brick and some made of gray stone. The professors are open to questions and, overall, are quite enthusiastic about their subject matter. I have had the opportunity for a great deal of private tutoring, for which I feel most profoundly grateful.

If I could show you only one part of the many beautiful things here in the city, I wish you could see the library. It is several stories high with thousands of books lining the shelves. I have nearly been late to a class a time or two as I find myself lost in yet another novel. One of my favorites is called <u>A Tale of Two Cities</u>. It is a story by Charles Dickens. There is a bookstore two blocks from my dormitory. Perhaps I will see if I can find a copy to send to you.

I could not ask for more than the honest way you have expressed your opinion regarding the situation overseas, and I find that I quite agree. I often wonder how we could have learned so little from the past. Have we not yet reached a level of civilization to instead be intent on seeking the welfare of those around us? Could we not find a better way to understand and resolve differences of opinion before men are sent out as pawns upon the battlefield for such unjustified purposes? Have we no greater sense of humanity than the wolf packs that fight each other in territorial battles, or are we, too, merely animals on the hunt to prove strength and brutality? Perhaps some men are merely wolves, born as animals without such a sense of humanity, for who could otherwise create a need for a deadly conflict? How much greater progress could be made in the world if it simply were not so!

I write this letter from my dormitory room, which looks out over the east side of the campus. From my window, I can see a small park. It lies lit beneath several lamps that line a paved walkway, and at this moment, falling peacefully from the sky are the first flakes of snow ushering in the winter. It is a peaceful change. Even here, it forces people to slow down a little.

Life in the city has its own charm, but I occasionally find myself longing for that more simple existence, sitting high in the branches of a large blue spruce, watching the unfolding of life below.

I have long admired the girl who walked the streets before dawn — the girl who taught me to see mankind in a different way. I could ask for no greater privilege than to hold a small place in your thoughts, as you hold a secure place in mine.

With affection,

William Linden

Dearest Will,

Thank you for the book. I can easily see why you cherish it so deeply. The story is lovely, though I am not yet to the end of it. I think I will likely finish it either this evening or tomorrow, as time permits. I am anxious to find out how all is to be done.

I have long wondered what happened to the young boy who disappeared from Pravda those many years ago. I worried you might have fallen ill. I tried to find you. I spent weeks searching the woods, but I was unable to locate even the smallest sign to indicate where you had been living. I only hoped that the food you had left was a sign that you were well and had only moved on. How wonderful it was that day you arrived again in Pravda — to see you alive and well.

Life in the city sounds captivating, yet I'm sure I would never wish to trade it for life in Pravda. Still, I would enjoy the opportunity to visit someday.

Fondly,

Bonnie Wilson

Dearest Bonnie,

How wonderful it is to think of your concern at the time I left Pravda. I had not thought my absence would be noticed or I would have left some indication of where I had gone. I had been offered a family of my own in Bloomfield. I spent the next six years in the home of Mayor Ringwald and his wife, Amelia. They are as dear to me as my own father and mother had been.

There is something I have wondered all these years. I once watched you climb the large maple behind the mercantile store to hang strings of glass from its branches. I know it somehow meant a great deal to Mr. Willet, but I never understood the reason. May I ask the meaning behind it?

I'm sending along another surprise. This one is titled <u>Les Miserables</u>. It is another of my favorites, but it may take you a great deal longer to complete than <u>A Tale of Two Cities</u>. The characters are developed in such a way that I can see a piece of myself in each one—from the wayward Jean Valjean to the overly zealous Javert and even the wicked Thenardiers, though I do hope I have little enough of them in me. I suppose I shouldn't say much more or I will give away far too much of the story.

Ever yours,

William Linden

My Dear Will,

I am anxious to start reading the new book you have sent. It has been quite a busy day and the hours of daylight have grown short, so I may have to wait until tomorrow to begin reading.

As for Mr. Willet, it's a bit of a long story, but it's one worth knowing, and it comes out of a difficult though cherished part of my past as well.

Mr. Willet's wife, Jeanine, was a rare and wonderful sort of woman. She loved each of the seasons for its unique beauty. She and Mr. Willet would often walk together through the streets of Pravda and deep into the woods. Each time they came across a broken bottle, Jeanine would gather the pieces and string them up in that same tree.

About a year before you arrived in Pravda, my mother passed away. My father turned to strong drink in his sorrow. I was lonely and withdrew from everyone.

Mrs. Willet had seen me passing by the store on my way home from school each day. She must have noticed that I had hardly spoken since my mother's death. One afternoon, Mrs. Willet called to me to come sit with her. She spoke to me, pointing out all of the beautiful things around me.

She continued to invite me to sit with her each day if the weather was warm. She did what she could to fill the emptiness that had been left by my mother's death and my father's absence, to teach me to see the world in a better way. She often talked to me until the sun began to set, her arm around me, holding me tight and warm against her side. One particular day, she pointed up at the tree where hundreds of glittering pieces of glass chimed merrily. "There is great beauty to be found, even in the broken things," she told me, "but you have to wish to see it."

I hadn't known it then, but Mrs. Willet was very ill. She passed away only a few months later.

It was then that Mr. Willet changed. He became angry and fierce, but he was hurting with a pain so deep that it could never be understood by those who have never been forced to travel that road. He had loved her with more love than I had ever before seen. I knew Mrs. Willet would wish him to find joy again in life, and I wanted him to remember to see the beauty—even in the broken things. That's when I first began walking the town at dawn, at least once a week to hang broken glass. The more I walked the streets, the more I began to notice the beauty but also the many needs around me. It has changed so much of who I am, and it was Mrs. Willet who first taught me to see.

If I might ask, there is something I would dearly like to know. Where did you live all those years before you left Pravda? I saw you at times, but I never knew where it was that you went. I often worried for you, yet you looked as though you weren't faring too poorly, even throughout the bitter cold storms of the winter.

With affection,

Bonnie Wilson

Dearest Bonnie,

How remarkable it seems to have known you so long and to now discover that I have known so little. Even in a single story, I find that the depth to which I know you has changed significantly. I wish I might have known Mrs. Willet—and yet, I suppose I do know her, as part of her legacy lives on through you.

We are nearing the Christmas holidays now, and it would mean a great deal to me if I might be allowed to come to see you, perhaps on Christmas

Eve? If I may, would it be possible for me to pick you up at noon for a sleigh ride? I have something I wish to show you.

Fondly,

William Linden

My Dear Will,

Yes. I will look forward to it.

Until then,

Bonnie Wilson

Chapter 24

SUNLIGHT SPARKLED over the icy snow that Christmas Eve. Will borrowed the Ringwald's sleigh pulled by two beautiful black Percheron horses. Bells jingled merrily in the frosty morning. Will could hardly contain his excitement. He slowed the team when he reached Pravda and waved at each person who greeted him as he passed them by. He laughed a little at the curious glances he received. Will reined in the horses near the center of town and tied them to a rail in front of the mercantile store. He purchased a few sweet oranges and a little bough of holly.

"Just passing through, then?" Mr. Willet said as he rang up the total. "It is a rare opportunity to have strangers in town."

Will smiled. "I'm just visiting a dear friend."

Before Mr. Willet could ask any further questions, Will paid the man and left the store.

He placed the holly festively across the front of the sleigh and put the oranges inside the wicker basket set at the back.

Will pulled the sleigh up to the gate of the run-down cabin nestled just inside the woods on the west end of town. His heart raced as he tapped lightly on the door.

He heard footsteps on the floorboards inside. The door opened. There stood Bonnie in a simple but well-kept dress and an overcoat. Her bright smile lit up her eyes.

"Hello, Will," she said. "It is so good to see you."

"Hello, Bonnie." Will smiled. He tenderly offered her his arm. She took it, smiling warmly, and they made their way down the walk to the sleigh. Will pulled out a blanket and wrapped it around her shoulders.

"Are you warm enough?" he asked her, settling a second blanket across her lap.

Bonnie nodded. Will clicked his tongue to the horses and they set off deeper into the woods, traveling slowly to find a suitable trail for the sleigh.

The cool air rushed passed them, chilling Will's exposed face and neck. Bonnie leaned in close to Will and laid her head against his shoulder. Will wrapped his right arm around her and together they watched the scenery glide by.

Eventually, Will slowed the sleigh when the trees grew thick. The sleigh bells jingled as they trotted along at a moderate pace. A wave of memories rushed over Will as the thicket rose into sight.

Will reined in the horses near the tunnel entrance.

"Just a moment," he told Bonnie. Will hopped down from the sleigh and tethered the horses to a low, thick branch. He searched through a box of tools attached to the back of the sleigh until he came up with a small axe. Will found a spot in the thicket, well-concealed by the several pines that grew near and began cutting a path into the clearing. He spent several minutes making certain it was wide enough to pass through. He then replaced the axe and helped Bonnie from the sleigh.

"This is what I wanted to show you," he told her. Will led her to the path he had made passable and helped her through. They reached the clearing and both stood a moment in awe. Will stared at the beautiful haven that had once been his home—seemingly untouched since he had left it so many years ago. The cabin looked quite forlorn, but it still stood strong.

Bonnie gazed in wonder and amazement. She turned to Will. "You built all of this? You were just a child at the time," she said softly.

Will smiled. "Come with me, " he said taking her hand. He led her around the low stone wall. He showed her the trees he had planted, which had grown tall and wild. He showed her the place where the garden lay beneath the snow and pointed to the beehive that looked as though it had been maintained through the years by thousands of bees. Together they walked toward the cabin.

Will pushed open the door. It creaked on its rusty hinges, but moved surprisingly well. Layers of dust coated the walls and floor, but otherwise, it looked very much the same as when he had left it, though chinks in the mud had opened between some of the logs. Yet the framed glass still held together unscathed.

A flood of memories washed over Will as he remembered each lonely winter night and the dozens of fur coats, hats and gloves.

The makeshift shovel lay in the corner, the handle half rotted away. The cracked pail stood on a shelf still holding needles and bits of soiled thread. The fireplace had partially crumbled, but much of it still stood. The bed frame lay splintering and filthy in the corner.

Will circled the cabin and peeked into the smaller room of the storehouse. He felt overwhelmed with the memories of a very different time. When he looked up, there stood Bonnie, her arms wrapped around herself, a tender expression in her eyes. She shook her head.

"I can't imagine the lonely boy who survived out here all on his own."

Will held his hands out to her. Bonnie stepped forward and together they stood, staring out through the window, which was now only framed by tattered remnants of the light green curtains.

"It was a lonely time," Will said, "but there is so much in life that I could never take for granted now that I know what it is like to be without."

Will and Bonnie stepped back outside. They spent a little time building a large snow bunny beside the door to the cabin. As they left, Bonnie slipped her hand into Will's, and together they made their way back to the sleigh.

Chapter 25

THE FOLLOWING SEMESTER passed slowly for Will. He anxiously looked forward to his visit home in the summer.

One rainy spring afternoon, he had just gathered his books and was about to leave a class that had finished for the day when he was approached by Professor Richins, his economics instructor.

Will felt incredulous as Professor Richins outlined an internship opportunity that he believed would benefit Will, sending him to Washington, D.C. during the summer break. Will asked for some time before giving an answer, to which Professor Richins agreed.

Will wrote a lengthy explanation to Bonnie. He received her reply only a short time later.

Dearest Will,

Of course you must go if you have a desire to do so. This is a great opportunity for you. I will still be here when you return.

Yours ever,

Bonnie

Will spent that summer in the capital city working closely with financial analysts, bankers, successful businessmen and investors. His power of keen observation and his dedication to his studies soon won him a place of credit in the eyes of those with whom he worked. He found the collaboration from the various groups intensely valuable to his education and his fresh ideas and opinions gained him popularity with the senators and representatives within the legislature.

As summer drew to a close, Will received many job offers, pending completion of his degree. He expressed his willingness to consider each offer, but everything inside of him felt as though he were being drawn homeward.

The third year was the most difficult for Will as he took on the upper-level courses and a more intense class load than the previous two years, but it set him on track to graduate at the end of the winter term.

Once again, Will was unable to return home when the holiday break finally arrived. He spent the majority of the holidays in the library preparing a lengthy proposal as his final project. Though it would not be due until the end of the following term, he knew that he would have little time to spend working on the paper during the semester due to his increased class load.

On Christmas Eve, a small package arrived wrapped in light-brown paper. A few other packages already lay beneath a waist-high pine that Will had cut down a few miles from town. This particular package never made it under the tree. Will sat on his bed the moment it arrived and pulled away the covering revealing a leather-bound book entitled, *A Christmas Carol* by Charles Dickens.

Will opened the cover and a note fell onto his lap.

Dearest Will,

I hope all is well with you. I found this book in the mercantile store, and I admit I read it before sending it to you. It is enchanting and a new favorite of mine.

My Christmas wish for you is that you may have no regrets in the past, great joy in the present, and a warm home with a brightly-lit Christmas tree each year in the future.

Have a wonderful Christmas.

Bonnie Wilson

Chapter 26

My Dear Bonnie,

We are nearly midway through the semester, and I will soon graduate from the University. I look forward to returning to Bloomfield and making a trip to Pravda the moment I can secure a horse for the ride. It has been so long since we have had the opportunity to spend a moment together, and I hope hereafter to be allowed to court you properly. It would bring me the greatest joy.

I hope you are well.

Most sincerely,

William Linden

Dearest Will,

I wish you the very best in completing your coursework, and may your journey home be swift and safe. I will watch for you each day.

Fondly,

Bonnie Wilson

Yet, as graduation neared, life suddenly changed.

On April 6th, Will celebrated his twenty-first birthday. He took a rare trip into the countryside with several classmates. When they returned, the campus was in an uproar. The United States had joined the war.

Talk in the dormitories continued well into the night. After only a few short hours of sleep, the students returned to their classes much more anxious to hear their professors' sentiments on the war than to continue their studies of business, trade and economics.

Will felt lost in the turmoil. Final exams were still scheduled to take place, and commencement was only weeks away, but he struggled to remain focused. He often found himself drifting even more frequently to the crowded common rooms, where the news blared from radio sets and to the newspaper peddlers selling their troubling headlines down in the streets.

His next letter home carried with it an anguish so deep that it was sent only after a long sleepless night spent walking the banks of the muddy river near the university campus.

My Dearest Bonnie,

I feel as though I have already asked far too much of you, so I will not ask any further. I feel I must join the efforts of our nation to stop this war. An unbearably great number of lives have already been lost in these endeavors, and I believe our cause is just. It must come to an end, but how I wish it might never have been!

Bonnie, I do not know but that I will be called to give my all on the front lines. I cannot ask for you to wait, though I do hope one day I might return.

Know that I love you and that thoughts of you and of the safety of our homeland will be my greatest strength as I stand with the Allies in battle. I wish for you the greatest happiness in life and love, whether at my side, or whether that is never to be.

With all the love of my heart,

William Linden

My Dear Will,

There are times when life asks far more of us than we could ever desire to give. How I wish this conflict had not been born in the world, yet it is here, and we must find a way to vanquish it. I would not hold you from the call. Know that you carry my love with you and that I will pray every morning and night for the success of the Allies and for your safe return.

I will watch for you each day until you return safely home.

All my love,

Bonnie Wilson

Chapter 27

COMMENCEMENT WAS A SOMBER AFFAIR. Many of the graduates had already signed up to join the military, Will among them.

Mayor Ringwald and Amelia traveled to the campus and joined him for the celebration. They then escorted him to the train that would take him away on yet another journey. The next day, Will reported for duty carrying with him only a few clothes, his father's leather-bound book still wrapped in the same paper from many years ago, and a bundle of letters tied with a strip of burlap.

The training began. The strength of the men was tested and their endurance challenged far beyond their accustomed rigor. They were examined in their fortitude and valor. Lack of sleep, the vast change in circumstances, the overwhelming push for quick preparation and the faint understanding of what lay ahead drove the men forward at a maddening pace.

The need was too great and the time too short for a full measure of preparation. Still, it was unlikely that anything could have prepared the men for that initial moment when they arrived in the war-torn areas of France. The shattered countryside left plagues of illness and starvation along with the ravages of fire and trench warfare. The European Allied soldiers were weary and broken from watching scores of their comrades fall under enemy fire.

The American soldiers passed through these towns. The sight of them seemed to buoy the spirits of the devastated men and women around them. Many approached the soldiers with words of hope and gratitude, though very broken English was all they had to offer. It soon became quite apparent to Will that there were few able-bodied men left in these towns. Men were scarce to be seen, aside from the soldiers. The Frenchmen who remained were elderly or in poor physical condition. The strain of the war showed in the lines that creased their faces and in the anguish in their eyes.

My Dearest Bonnie,

It may seem impossible to me yet to imagine taking the life of an enemy soldier, but as I see the pain on the faces of the elderly, the women, and the children—how can I stop short of doing all that is required on my part to bring peace back to their war-torn land? We had heard for months which grew into years of the war and the struggles that many were facing, but now as I am here and I look into their eyes, they become more than a vague idea of human existence overseas. I see them. I see the depth of who they are—and I see the weight of their pain. It is even more difficult to see the hope they have in us. They have struggled for so long and are still standing strong with courage. We must not let them down.

Bonnie, I have at times doubted the foundation of the Allies that has led me to journey across the sea to fight, but I can no longer wonder if our cause is just. If I should never make it home, I will not regret the effort to which I have dedicated my last days.

Yet, if I am able to return—if we all return someday victorious—the scars of the battlefield may remain, but we will have conquered the inhumanity of the wolves, and there is no greater cause.

With all my love,

William Linden

Dearest Bonnie,

I am unable to tell you where we are or much about the war, but there are advances being made on both sides. At times it seems that the progress is scarcely perceivable. I ache seeing young boys holding guns with such fear in their eyes. Many of them joined the war by lying about their age, desperate to be a part of this effort and yearning for adventure. I can only imagine how many mothers sit home alone each night praying for their young sons to come home—and then I think of the children who watch each day for their father's return, only to have a letter delivered containing the most devastating news.

Do not worry for me, whatever may come. I will continue writing you as best I can, though it is not always easy to get mail sent out or to receive it in a timely manner.

I have come to realize that some things in life are unexplainable. Our entire world is torn apart, and yet, there is beauty, even in the broken things. I see it in a comrade who puts his own life on the line before he is willing to watch his friends fall under enemy fire. I see it in the courage of the people we have come to protect. I see it in the European men who have already struggled through four years of this deadly war, and they still find reason to carry on. I see it in the hope for a new tomorrow—the hope in the eyes of even the most downtrodden.

Pray that tomorrow may come.

Ever yours,

William Linden

Sweet Bonnie,

We are now approaching the front lines. I do not say this to trouble you, but I do wish you to know. There are times when we pass through beautiful fields that seem untouched by the battles, but tonight we camp not far away from the conflict and gunshots can be heard through the darkness.

I have been raised to a position of command. It troubles me to know that I am responsible for the lives of many of these men, some older and many with families awaiting their safe return. It is not a position I could have desired, though if I can help in any way to bring a speedier success to the cause of the Allies, I could have no hesitation in doing so.

I often wonder if the solution to all of the senseless chaos that now engulfs our world would be to require the leaders who declare war against each other to sit near the battlefield with the very men they have sentenced to die on their behalf. How many of them would open their eyes and see the error in their lack of sufficient reason? What need have they for these men to suffer for their cause that calculates to be greater than the child longing for her father to come home, or the wife for her husband, or the soldier for his own life which he has been called upon to forfeit to a war which he may not even believe in. Yet, I believe in our cause. It could not be otherwise. Where evil has risen, good men must stand forth or all will be lost.

My men are full of courage—as am I. A new strength of resolution became unwavering in each of us from the first moment we had the chance to meet those who are in such desperate need for us to stand between them and this savage devastation.

May all the world rest peacefully one day.

My love and affection,

William Linden

Chapter 28

WILL JOINED THE FIRST WATCH that night, unable to sleep. The sound of gunshots polluted the clear, starlit sky as Will marched along the lines of his sleeping comrades. He had come to know each of them through the days, weeks, and months of their training in the States and on their journey to Europe. The men and young boys all had their own stories to tell. There were loved ones who prayed for them every night, and each had a hope of life *apres la guerre,* as the Frenchmen would say, which meant "after the war."

Apres la guerre, Will thought as he marched. How many men would live to see such a time? How many would ever be given the chance to make something more of the life they had been given, or would it be stripped from them before even another day arrived?

Will knew he was not afraid to die, but he struggled knowing that many difficult decisions lay ahead. "Apres la guerre," he murmured. The war had to end. He would have to make certain his men had the best chance to make it through until that day came, but never at the expense of taking down the Central Powers. What was one life worth? To the Central Powers, a life of the Allies was merely an obstacle. To the leaders of the Allies, it was a man to count in their favor. But to a child, a mother, a father, a wife—it was a man or a boy who held the power of all their joy, wonder, and hope. It was a man who stood with courage in the face of death. Men who had dreams, thoughts, ideas. Men who could accomplish great things. Men who could change the world.

Will finally retired to his bedroll while a sliver of moon was still high in the sky. He lay watching the sky above, unable to sleep, tossing and turning for hours before he sat up and stared out toward the distant sound of the battle. Tomorrow, and the next day, and the day after—and every day after that, until the bloody battles ended, would decide the future of nations and gen-erations across the world, but it would also determine what would become of each individual man under his command.

Will gave up on sleep. He pulled his rucksack toward him. From it, he withdrew a stub of candle, some matches, and his fa-ther's leather-bound book. Will stared at the crumpled paper that still lay wrapped around it, carefully tied up years ago by that small, lonely eight-year-old boy. Will gently removed the paper. He had never had a greater desire to know what lay inside the book. He had often felt as though not knowing what lay within had kept his father alive in some small way, that there was still a part of him to be discovered when the time was right. Will needed his father now more than ever. The binding cracked softly as Will opened the book and turned to the first page.

For my son,
William Linden

Dearest Will,

I know that for now, it is unlikely that you are able to understand the changes that have been wrought upon our lives. You are still so young. You can't imagine the anguish of a father who is unable to provide for his wife and for his small children whom he has failed to provide for and to protect.

Will, in this life, there are many things that are beyond our control. There were decisions I have made that, had I done differently, would not have led us into these devastating circumstances in which we now find ourselves. The sorrow for what has come to be is a burden no man could rightly bear, but how I could have done otherwise, I know not. I lie awake each night tormenting my mind, wishing there had been another way—wishing I might have found it before the time had grown too late.

How I wish I could give you everything that ought to be a secure and wonderful part of your life—to light up your eyes as I have not seen since we first lost our home and since we later lost your mother. Not a day passes that I don't miss her and long for the past to have been so different. I count it as the greatest blessing that I still have you, little Will. I am so grateful for that singular mercy, but how I ache to see that I am unable to give you better, though I yet hope this soon might change. I know you are too young to understand now, but someday, as you read this, perhaps it will mean something more.

I suppose you will remember the days we used to walk to the city hall together in Bradbury. You loved to sit with me in the office behind the large oak desk in a chair by my side. I worked as an advisor during that time and helped make many pivotal decisions regarding the progress and expansion of Bradbury—particularly working in the construction and development with the occasional opportunity to help effect changes in laws. I had been in that position for nearly four years, my influence becoming rather substantial and of high regard.

It was during this time that I was approached by Mr. Stephens, who owned a large portion of the land and buildings in Bradbury, including our rented home. He had developed a proposal, one which I came to feel was morally and ethically improper and, in time, would prove to be a devastating blow to many in the city. I couldn't agree to use my influence to persuade its acceptance. Mr. Stephens insisted forcefully, but I refused and excused him. The next day, I was arrested on accusations of fraud. Evidence had been falsified against me, yet it was not enough to force a conviction. Unfortunately, I was dismissed, unable to work for the city any longer. I returned home that night after being released from jail only to find an eviction notice taped to our door. We had just celebrated Christmas.

Your mother was a good and strong woman. She continued to believe that things would eventually improve, even as we struggled to find the barest means to survive. We came across a small home on the outskirts of the city that we were able to rent for a minimal price while I searched for work, yet persistent slander had ruined any hope I had of obtaining employment anywhere near Bradbury.

We had no choice but to move and settle elsewhere, hoping the rumors had not spread beyond the town, but your mother was nearly due to give birth. She continued to remain optimistic, but the strain of the situation and the drafty house in which we lived had made her very ill. It was impossible to move her until the baby was born. We soon ran out of money and were no longer able to pay the meager rent. We received another eviction notice with only days to move.

That same night, your mother became feverish and deathly hot to the touch. I ran house to house begging for help—a carriage, even a horse to borrow—any means by which we could travel to the hospital. I offered the last few coins we had with the promise of labor to make up the rest, but it was to no avail. For hours I knocked on doors, only to be turned away. I was desperate. When no other prospect remained, I crept into a stable and borrowed a horse and carriage. We made it to the hospital, but little could be done. We were too late. Sick and feverish, your dear

*mother managed to give birth to a baby girl. The strain of the birth cou-
pled with the fever was too much for her weakened body. She fell asleep
and never awoke.*

*Officers arrived only moments after her passing to arrest me for trespass
and theft of the horse and carriage. I was taken away as your sweet
mother lay quiet and still upon her bed. I never even got the chance to
hold little Emily. The tiny little girl had barely made it into the world,
sick, her breathing labored. The doctors assured me they would do all
they could as I was led away. I returned the moment I was released, having paid the last of what little remained to us. Emily had been sent away.
I knew I had no means to care for an infant, but how my heart broke!
How had we fallen so far! How had I allowed this to happen—to you, to
your mother, to your beautiful baby sister? I have failed each of you.*

*I returned home to find you anxiously watching through the small, drafty
window, frightened, cold and hungry. We packed the few things we
owned and set off to begin a new life the best we could.*

*I am sorry for it, for everything you have had to endure. I only hope that
someday, things will be far better than the wretched existence we have
come to know. At least for now, we have each other. I feel such shame
that I could not have provided for you, for your mother, and for your
baby sister, Emily.*

*There is true joy to be had somewhere in the world, though at times, it
can be desperately hard to find. Perhaps, little Will, you will have to be
the one to create it. I haven't the heart left in me to do so.*

*Work hard, my dearest Will, and stand strong in this weary world. You
must not ever give in to the darkest side of human nature, for men are
easily overcome. Never be afraid to stand for that which you know to be
right and honorable. You may lose everything of monetary value, but
there is nothing worth having if you are not the sort of man who can
wake each day knowing exactly who he is and that for which he stands. If
you are not a man built upon a strong foundation of integrity and princi-
ple, then life will hold little real value no matter what honors you obtain.*

I am certain a great journey lies ahead—and if it is hard, if it lacks many of the comforts life has to offer, then the person you become will be worth every step of the way.

All my love,

Samuel Linden

Will stared at his father's name for several minutes. There was more written on the pages that followed, but it was already more than he could take in. Will carefully rewrapped the journal and slipped it into his satchel. He blew out the candle and again lay staring up at the stars. Eventually his thoughts tumbled together and he sank into a deep sleep.

The next morning dawned with a promise of rain in the thick clouds that had gathered overhead. A gentle trickle dampened the ground by the time their supplies had been packed and the men trepidatiously began their journey to the front lines.

Chapter 29

THE HORRORS OF WAR proved the characters of the men who marched upon the field. Courage could no longer be feigned. Detestation coursed with its utmost power through heated veins beneath chilled, wet skin and muscles taut with terror. Anger screamed silently inside each anguished mind against the enemy as men fell—good men, young men, old men, brave men—the innocent, the proud, the gentle, the father, the brother, the son—pulsing in bitter sorrow for those lost and in remorse felt for those left behind. Homesick, afraid, courageous, and determined. Those who fought discovered the greatness of mankind—the wonder and the horror.

My Sweet Bonnie,

I've written several letters that I have stowed away unsent. I could not find it in me to post them. I have attempted in my writing to protect you from the devastation of the war-torn world around us, but as it occupies so much of my mind, all else that I have attempted to write came out empty and hardly worth the time it would take you to read it. As it is necessary to constantly be giving encouragement to the men around me, I find it painful to hold the rest of my thoughts and emotions to myself as

I must. Therefore, I hope you will not mind if I lay before you a little of the predicament in which we find ourselves and the thoughts I must continually conceal as we gaze toward enemy lines.

If there is to those men who dream up such wars as we are fighting such a purpose worth devoting the lives of thousands of young men, the beloved youth of their own nations, then why are they not here fighting beside them—watching the light fade from tender eyes that once knew laughter, love, and sorrow as bullets tear through the beating heart and blood pools over the broken ground beneath them? What purpose—what cause—could be worth even one such life if it were not to bring down the very men who would create such destruction from the beginning? Will there ever be an end to men raging as wolves in positions of power, lacking even the most menial sense of humanity within their souls?

How can this be—that we raise our weapons against men so much like ourselves, and in a single moment, we end a life—a series of generations that would have followed after? We break a mother's heart; we shatter a tender wife's dreams. The man whose face is so near that we can see both the fear and courage in his eyes, his only sin being in his wearing a different uniform, under command and in a single moment, we decide that this very man will never return home to the small children that press their faces against the cool glass of a window some hundreds of miles away—never again to see their father or their brother, never to know the joy they had before known and always to wonder how life might have been if war had never come to be known. Should we not be striving— giving everything in our power to protect and preserve the lives that are so quickly betrayed by their mother nation in her own name?

The days drag on and the weeks pass in such turmoil. The stench of blood and death fills these once beautiful fields. The skies grow dense with smoke. It seems that little gain is made on either side. At times, I fear there will never be an end until every man has sacrificed his final breath.

We have seen what good can be found amid such devastation. I have not yet lost any of the men who serve under my command, though two men —James McCannon and John Olden—have been sent to recover at a nearby hospital. James will not be returning to the war, but we are not certain of John's condition. We think it very likely that he will survive, and I have high hopes that he will be sent home for a full recovery.

If there is any good that has come from the great misfortune that war brings, it would be the undeterred camaraderie that has developed among the men as they sit each evening in the dark trenches wondering if they or the fellow beside them might never see the sun rise upon another morning. We do what we can to keep our spirits high, and it is only to you, my sweet Bonnie, that I feel I can express the truest sentiments of my heart as they relate to the ravages of war around me. We sing. We talk of the future. We share stories of home and of those awaiting our safe return. At times I wish I could share much more of about my comrades with you, but I fear for their safety—and if I were to lose any of them, it would be a pain almost unbearable. I do not wish you to have to carry that burden as well if it must one day be carried at all.

There are times when we are assigned to recover and bury the dead. There is no assignment so painful as laying to rest beneath the dark, cold soil those men who had only days before laughed and talked in the trenches beside us, speaking with great hope in the future, when only days or even hours later, their futures would be so brutally torn away from them with such senseless purpose.

As we carry each lifeless body to its ultimate resting place, it is nearly impossible to avoid a final glance at our comrade's face. Occasionally we move the body of an enemy soldier who has fallen where ground has been taken by the Allies. It is impossible to describe what it is like to look into a face, frozen with the expression they bore in their last moments. Easily seen is the agony of pain, the dread of death's final grasp upon them, the sorrow for all that is now lost. We lay them to rest.

Among my men is a man I had known well in Bloomfield. His name is Joseph Bronson. Years ago, I came across him and his brother on a fateful morning. They were being attacked by wolves. Both brothers survived, but the elder brother was injured and still walks with a limp. Joseph volunteered to serve in place of his elder brother. Oh, Bonnie, I could not bear to watch him fall under enemy fire. I know the mother, the brother, the nieces and nephew who are all waiting for him to come home.

All I can wish now is that I will be wherever I am needed to alter the possible course of history to resolve these tragic events. My greatest duty is to bring an end to the war, and next to that, I could wish for nothing more than to bring each of my men safely home.

If it were to happen that I, too, am able to one day return, I would wish to have the chance to create a new dream of my own, one in which I could only hope you will play a greater part.

All my love,

William Linden

————————————————————————————

My Dearest Love,

We have heard of certain horrors of the war, but this last week, we were introduced to the worst brutality imaginable. We had been transferred to a new location along the battlefield. Our location, I am certain, would do

*no good to include as it would be cut from the letter before it reached you,
but it is enough to say that we were relocated to a new front line.*

*We had scarcely arrived the previous morning, and now as I think back
on it, it may have been our arrival that triggered the devastating events,
as the increase in soldiers on the Allied side would not have been unnoticed by the Germans. We found ourselves under heavy artillery fire as
dusk set in. Cannons blazed at short intervals, driving us down into the
trenches. We awaited the approach of the enemy which often followed
strong artillery fire, but instead, we were facing something far more in-
humane and deadly. We prepared a strong defensive position and again
found ourselves under attack, but this time, a thick, toxic gas sank deep
into the trenches.*

*I cannot bear to describe to you the scene that unfolded. My men had not
yet encountered mustard gas, but we knew of it. They worked in quick
camaraderie as we retreated, climbing out of the trenches while gunfire
raged around us. The enemy presented a formidable attack.*

*Choking and weeping, the men struggled to higher ground only to find
themselves easy targets for the enemy. We came out of the trenches, gasping—unable to breathe and unable to see. The burning in our lungs was
suffocating as we tried to escape the hail of bullets.*

*Five of my men fell. None were left behind. Gunfire had injured four of
them and one, unable to see, stumbled and fell into a shallow trench,
causing a bad break to his leg.*

*Blinded and suffocating, the men refused to succumb. Some men carried
their comrades until they too collapsed and had to be carried. The excruciating pain they endured and the courage they displayed were greater
than I had ever before seen. We endured an unthinkable hell before we
made it to safety. The men set to work, binding the wounds of the injured*

while I gathered any who were able to return and search for survivors from other units.

The mustard gas had devastated our Allied lines. There were few left alive for us to bring in. Those in the deeper trenches had been unable to get out as quickly. Some were crawling, unable to see and choking on the poisonous gas as they struggled away from the sound of the gunfire. For most, it was already too late, but there were a few who still had a hope of survival. Those men we lifted, struggling ourselves for breath. The men were brave, though terrified, many falling to gunfire even as they struggled to carry comrades they had never even met. We brought in as many as we could, which resulted in several more injuries to my men, and among the badly injured was Joseph Bronson. The sight of that good man being ripped by shrapnel is an image which I will never be able to erase from my mind.

Joseph and I were carrying a young Irish boy we found gasping near an exploded bombshell. The boy writhed in pain both from the gas and from a large wound on his right thigh. As we carried the boy to safety, another shell exploded near us. Shrapnel embedded deep into Joseph's leg, tearing a bloody hole through his sodden uniform. I received only a small part of the blast in my right arm. Joseph was gasping in agony, but he was relentless and determined as we were forced to our knees, pulling the boy beside us, resting only when either Joseph or I would collapse for a time. At long last, we made it to safety.

The young Irish boy died at our side before help arrived.

The medical station was in chaos. Agonizing screams rang through the air, a painful relief from the anguished gasps of those struggling to breath. Supplies ran short. Reinforcements were slow to arrive. As the trucks rolled in at last, I made a final count of all my men. Many had *torn limbs and deep wounds, but not a single one had been lost. All had returned, though some are yet in critical condition.*

We worked through the night. Several men keept watch for enemy movement while the rest of us did all we could to bandage injuries and wash the burning gas from our eyes and skin. It was a long, horrific night, yet the full horror of that night was not fully realized until the following morning. As the sun rose, a few of us carefully made our way back to search for survivors. There were none. Death was everywhere as the Central Powers pushed their lines forward.

I have known great sorrow in the darkest moments of my life, but I can tell you of none greater than the moment I looked out upon the battlefield strewn with scores of men who had died in the most horrific way. Those good men would never return home. I felt as though the anguish of all whose hearts would be broken upon receiving the news was raging so deep inside of me that it could never be rooted out—not with tears, nor words, nor anything ever to come in this life. It is a burden that could never be lifted away in all the time I have to walk free in the light of day while their empty bodies rot, heaped upon by dark, cold earth in silent, unmarked graves in which their journey came to its final end.

We are now receiving treatment in a makeshift hospital. My men suffer more than should ever have been asked of any man. Joseph will be sent home. It is likely he will survive if he is able to get an amputation in time. Pray for him, my dearest Bonnie. I pray with each burning breath I take. I weep thinking of the pain and sorrow these men wake to, if they wake at all. Yet, to hear how they count themselves fortunate knowing that many men were lost that night while our entire group made it out. God willing, they will all live beyond their injuries. Some will never walk. Some will never see the sun rise, but they can feel the warmth on their faces. They can breathe the air, though with burning lungs. They can return home to those who love them.

They have all offered their lives, and now, most have given a part of themselves. The most bitter to watch are those who have lost their sanity, as some have. They stand about, confused and afraid of everything around them, with no comfort to be given.

The men suffer deeply, but they try to find reason enough to be grateful. Those who can have set about to cheer those who have lost so much more —those whose friend or brother never made it back.

I had hoped that all my men might return safely home, but I did not expect it so soon. Only a few of us will even have the option to stay and continue the fight.

I escaped major injury, but I currently have only minimal use of my right arm. I have asked to be temporarily reassigned to other duties until I can be of more use to the effort. I cannot return home knowing what our men are facing while being too far away to give aid.

This war must end. We are not beasts, nor are we mere animals, yet this war is making such beasts of men.

I'm grateful for your letters. The goodness you send seems at times to be the only tenderness that remains in this world. I look forward to each word, to some light and some reminder that there is more to the world than the barbaric cruelties heaped upon this foreign land. I hope that before long, I, too, will have more pleasant things to write and that the war will soon come to an end, never to be known again.

All my love,

William Linden

Dearest Bonnie,

I am recovering well and have recently been given a special assignment. I will soon be back at the front lines, once again in a command position.

Though many of my men have returned home due to crippling injuries, many of them were awarded medals for courage and bravery. Those who stayed behind to continue fighting in the war have all been promoted to positions of leadership. A new unit of men has been assigned to me, many of them from the United States. Dearest Bonnie, pray them all safely home.

The nights have long been cold. With the frozen ground beneath us, it is hard to stay warm, but I suppose that is one of the great advantages of trench warfare. We easily stay out of the bitter winds that sweep across these open fields.

We are well for now and feel blessed to be so.

With fondest affection,

William Linden

Sweet Bonnie,

The whole face of the war is changing — new weaponry, new recruits, new strategies. The wonderful flying machines are a part of the war. They are incredible to see, and to think that men were able to create something so wonderful, and yet, it pains me. Everything good in the world has been turned to be used for evil or to fight evil. Our fliers rise high overhead spying on enemy lines. If the fighting here below is calm enough, we can hear the gunfire far above us as the battle continues in the skies.

We arrived on a new front just two days ago. A terrible battle had already taken place. Several lay dead beyond our reach, and among them were several horses, injured and dying. One particular mare had fallen only a few hundred meters from our trench down at the bottom of a small hill. She lay whinnying, an almost human sound—agonizing and terrible. One soldier from another unit slipped out of the trenches to try to reach the poor creature. He was nearly close enough when he took a bullet to his shoulder. He somehow made it back to safety, but the wound was deep. Had the bullet been even a couple of inches to the left, he would have breathed his last.

We endured the sound as best we could, but after another hour, it was driving the men to insanity. It was foolish on my part, but the poor creature's agony was too much to endure. When I felt there was a chance of getting to her unseen, I crept out of the trench. Though it wasn't far, there was little to use for cover as I crawled to the edge of the hill. I knelt just behind the broken stump of a tree, knowing that the shot used to put the horse from its misery would also alert the German army. I fired and ran.

I count it only by grace that I made it back to safety with a storm of bullets raining around me. It was a night of relief as the poor creature no longer cried out in agony.

Men dream up such horrible wars and the innocent always die, both animals and men. The more of the horror we see, the more I am determined that we will fight until there is an end.

All my love,

William Linden

Sweet Bonnie,

How I long to see you! I feel strongly drawn to the duty that requires me to be remain on European soil, but if it were to end—how swiftly I would return home!

Aside from several cases of shell-shock among the men and some minor injuries from shrapnel, we are all well. Some of the strategies used at the beginning of the war depleted numbers quickly, but I think much was learned. Men are still lost along the front in high numbers, but the war is vastly different.

We hear rumors on occasion that progress is being made in the effort against the enemy, but with the constant bursts of gunfire, cannons, shrapnel, and smoke, it hardly seems possible.

It has been so very cold, a blessing, as it seems to have slowed the fighting. Each day we live to the next, we rejoice—and each day that our comrades live, we rejoice all the more. Our lives mean so little if we can not be among those for whom we fight.

Stay safe and well, my dearest Bonnie. You give me much to live for.

My love,

William Linden

My Dear Bonnie,

Oh, what wonderful news we have heard! I'm sure that by the time this letter reaches you, it will already be known in the States, but Russia has *withdrawn from the war! Is this not a most jubilant moment! The men are dizzy with excitement, and a warm hope fills the trenches. We will win! We will end this nightmare forever! We have been warned that attacks from the Germans may strengthen against us with the news of the armistice with Russia, but never have the men been more prepared. They have hope at last when for so long, the battle seemed endless before us.*

Perhaps within a month, or maybe two, it will all be over. If nothing else, I hope to celebrate Christmas in a world at peace.

With fondest affection,

William Linden

Sweet Bonnie,

The days, weeks, and months drag by in such agonizing monotony of death and fear. We have had little good to report for a time. The summer burns hot upon us and still there has been no more sign of the war coming to an end. The men struggle not to fall prey to the gloom that surrounds us all, yet for every man who succumbs to the anguish, there is another there to lift him up. Throughout my life, I have seen men face the unbearable and I, as well, have had to endure much on my own, but it is amazing to observe what men can forge through if only they do not have to suffer alone.

I often wonder what the world will say of our time. I wonder what the history books will have written upon their pages of this troubling era and the vicious, brutal hostilities mankind rages upon itself. Time may prove heroes of some, but how could it ever vanquish the devils that continue to rise? There's a darkness so thick that it seems as though it is hardly penetrable, forged deep within the hearts of men.

As I ponder the record of our time that is yet to be written, I find myself troubled that it may never be written at all. I worry that these battles and ultimately this war will never end until the last of all human blood flows from our veins to seep into our weary mother earth, having been spilled for no greater cause than that of the pride and foolishness of man — destroying all that once was good. There will be no more creative thought, no more joy, no more love. Perhaps with sorrow so deep, it would be best if all were to pass away. There could never be joy enough to equal the grief of the loss of a single child — and thousands, perhaps millions, have already been claimed to the vain frailties and pride which seem a vast part of human existence, for what man has any right to decide the fate of another man's son?

I can only hope that all will be well again in time, and until then, we stand ready to continue the cause until it is finished. Your letters continue to sustain me and offer me a reminder that there is still good somewhere in this darkened world.

All my love,

William Linden

My Dearest Bonnie,

A change seems to have lit this forbidden ground at last!

I'm uncertain if things are changing all along the front, but today we were aided by great metal machines which, we were informed, are a new development called "tanks." We had seen some earlier in the war, but many improvements have been made since that time. They are still prone to malfunction and many don't make it across the front lines, but those that do bring such a change to the battle! It is now possible to get right up to the enemy, and once the tanks have made it near enough, firing behind enemy lines ceases and the enemy retreats with such haste! The tanks seem hardly able to be defeated.

Tonight the men are celebrating, and yet, it is difficult. We gained ground, but there were still many lives lost on both sides. Their dead and ours lay in graves not far from each other. How many generations have already been lost? How many innovators, engineers, scientists, mathematicians, artists, musicians? How many of these same men, whichever side they are on, would have made an extraordinary difference in the world for the better?

We will never know.

We are nearing the end. I can feel it. We once dreamed of a great victory, but there is no victory in war. Too much is lost regardless of which side ends the conflict. Yet it is better to fight and to die than to be forced to serve those who would destroy our priceless freedom. Such a thing must never be.

Dearest Love, keep the home fire burning and maybe soon, I will be there beside you.

With tender love,

William Linden

_____

My Dear Bonnie,

I can hardly write for the joy I feel bursting within me! I now at last may hope to reach home not long after this letter reaches your hand—what a grand, wonderful morning this day has brought to us!

Earlier, we had heard that an armistice might be reached within the coming week. How we wept and laughed—often both weeping and laughing in the same moment for the sheer, unspeakable joy that pervaded every bit of our souls within us. Last night, as my men and I marched out, the temperature dropped severely. We had only minimal preparations for the cold as resources are waning. Yet, not far from where we were stationed, we saw an old barn. Though it was deathly cold even inside the structure, a large pile of manure produced such wonderful warmth as it decomposed. The smell was terrible, but the men were all in agreement that after surviving so long in the war, we were not going to die from cold so near to the end.

We piled our thin wool blankets around the pile and settled inside. We staved off frostbite and even caught a little sleep between shifts of guard duty. No morning has ever dawned with greater beauty. When we reached a nearby village later that day, what news! What wonderful news! The war is over! We have won! What a blessed day!

When we first heard the news, the men cheered and stamped about with such enthusiasm before the entire unit melted into tears of joy, sobbing, then laughing with such uncontrollable merriment and joy. What a sight it was to see an entire unit of grown men, bathed in manure, weeping, laughing, and dancing around in the frosty morning air.

Truly, the harder our circumstances, the greater our joy when at last success is known.

From your letters, I gather—and I very much hope I am not mistaken— that you still desire to see me, as I long so very much to see you, but I do

not wish to assume it may be so if I have misread your intentions. The
first morning I am back in Bloomfield, I intend to rent a carriage and
journey to Pravda. If you are not opposed to my visit, I would be grateful
if you might tie a yellow ribbon around a branch of the gnarled oak tree
that sits at the edge of town. If I see the ribbon, I will finish my journey
to your door. If not, I will return to Bloomfield, still grateful for the
friendship we have shared and for your support throughout the years in
this, the darkest hour which has at last come to an end.

My dearest Bonnie, I am coming home.

With all my love and affection,

William Linden

Will stayed behind only a few days to ensure that all travel arrangements had been secured for his men before he, too, departed from France.

The journey across war-torn France and over the rolling ocean seemed impossibly long to Will. He found himself anxiously sitting forward, wishing the hours to fly by as they had no intention of doing. Time after time, he found himself getting to his feet and pacing, before reminding himself to try to enjoy the journey. These were the last moments with his comrades before they made the harbor and boarded their separate trains. He would just have managed to relax a moment or two before he would again find himself on his feet, anxiously watching first the billowing waves, then finally, the curving of the train along the tracks ahead.

At last, he stepped onto the platform of the Bloomfield station. His uniform was clean, though a little rumpled from the journey, and glittering with medals from his service. Nearly all of

Bloomfield had arrived to welcome their soldiers home. Many of the men had served, and most had come home.

Joseph Bronson stood beside his brother Jacob, their red hair making them easily spotted among the crowd. Joseph leaned heavily on a crutch, but he smiled jovially. His leg had been amputated, but he looked as though he had recovered well otherwise. He balanced himself on his good leg and passed the crutch to his brother then wrapped Will in a tight hug. He swallowed hard as he grimaced at his former commanding officer.

"What a war, eh? It's good to have you home, Will."

Mayor Ringwald and Amelia swept him into their arms. All through the evening, Amelia could hardly look at him without breaking down weeping and slipping quietly from the room, returning a short while later, her eyes red but joyful.

"We heard such stories. I almost thought you might never make it home," she told him, trying to laugh away her tears. "I don't know how I could have gotten through it if we had lost you." She turned away again and hurried into another room, returning with a smile only to soon find herself melting into tears yet again.

The whole town celebrated through the evening and late into the night. A great feast lay spread across several tables in the town hall. When all had eaten their fill, they pushed the tables back against the walls and the dancing began. Will excused himself and slipped away. He took a walk down by the river trying to clear his mind in the cool, fresh air. He walked along the path through the trees near the town square and came to rest on a cold iron bench.

He was deep in thought, watching the icy water churn against the rocky bank. The sound of wood tapping on stone made Will turn his head. A man with dark red hair and a missing leg came hobbling down the path. He settled himself on the bench beside Will and together they sat for most of an hour, sharing the memories that played before them while not a word was spoken. It was still so vivid. It was still so haunting.

Near midnight, they both stood, shook hands, and each turned his way toward home.

Chapter 30

BRIGHT SUNLIGHT AND THICK LAYERS of frost greeted Will the next morning when he and Mayor Ringwald went out to hitch the team of horses to the carriage. It was scarcely done when Amelia called them both to come in for breakfast.

Will struggled to sit still long enough to a make it through a single sweet apple muffin and a cold glass of milk. Amelia finally took his plate and packed him a satchel full of food.

He settled onto the box seat of the carriage and took hold of the reins. For over a year he had fought on the battlefields of France, yet he now felt greater apprehension in this moment than at almost any time during the war. He clicked his tongue to the horses and set off toward Pravda.

The horses grew tired of the inconsistency in Will's driving. He urged them forward only to once again slow them down. He was anxious to arrive, yet worried at what he might find when he did. Suppose she had found someone else in his long absence? Suppose she had simply lost interest? Perhaps there was nothing tied to the gnarled oak tree. He dreaded coming over the final rise of hills, and yet, he would again find himself growing anxious at the slow pace and would urge the horses back to a trot.

Will barely felt the cool air rushing over him, turning his

cheeks and nose bright red. His heart pounded heavily the entire journey.

He fretted nervously. When he was nearly there, he got so anxious that he had to stop the team altogether and walk around for a while before continuing on his way. He worried that perhaps the letter had not even reached her in time, or perhaps yellow ribbons had been too scarce since the war. Maybe she was sick and unable to get to the tree. How foolish he had been!

Will slowed the horses just before he came over the crest of the last hill. He said a silent prayer, gazing heavenward, then he clicked his tongue and urged the team forward.

They clattered over the rough road and the tree rose into view.

There stood the same gnarled oak tree beneath which his father lay, and on nearly every branch was tied a delicate yellow ribbon.

Chapter 31

WILL SPED THE HORSES to a full trot. They cantered onto the main road of Pravda before he reined them in. He stopped in front of Madame Belle Lucille's Dress Shop before he realized that it was Sunday and the shop would likely be closed for the day. He didn't expect to find Bonnie at home so he tied the horses to a post and set off on foot through the town.

The sun had warmed away much of the frost. Though the air was cool, many people strolled through the streets in the crisp morning, still celebrating the end of the war. Children played, the church bell rang, and all were in a rather jovial mood. Will greeted several men and women as they passed him by, some returning to pass him yet again to get a second look at the stranger who had just arrived.

He recognized the mayor easily enough as the man approached.

"Good day to you, sir," he greeted Will. "It has been some time since we have had many strangers in Pravda. Are you just back from the war?"

"Yes, sir, I am," Will said as they shook hands.

"Well, you are more than welcome. Do you intend to stay a while?"

"Yes, certainly I would like to. I am in need of employment and housing, if there is anything available."

Will pulled a few documents from the pocket of his coat and presented his credentials to the mayor who looked over the papers with a satisfied, "I see," and "Yes, I do think you will do quite nicely."

"Quite nicely for what, sir?" Will asked.

"Well, you see, our clerk was injured in the war—now he is alright," the mayor added quickly, surprised at the anxious concern on Will's face, "but he and his wife have moved closer to the city where he will be able to get better care while the poor fellow recovers."

"He married?" Will asked, pleasantly surprised. "May I ask who it was he married?"

"Yes…" the mayor said slowly and curiously, "he married our own Miss Eleanora. They have been so happy—I must ask, do you know them?"

Will smiled. "I suppose in a way. Now you say the position is open? What might I have to do to apply?"

"A returned soldier with medals of honor and a degree in economics and business? We could only hope you would accept the position." the mayor smiled warmly.

"Yes, sir!" Will said, slightly taken aback. "Gladly! And thank you. When do I start?"

"I will expect you in two days' time promptly at eight o'clock in the city building which is…" the mayor turned toward the center of town and indicated the large stone structure, "right over there beside our new town hall. We have fallen quite a bit behind on the paperwork during our clerk's absence, but I trust we will be running smoothly again in no time. Now we only have the matter of finding you a place of residence. You are alone, are you not? No wife?"

Will shook his head. "No, sir. I am unmarried."

"All the better! We may be able to do something about that as well," the mayor chortled. "But as far as lodging, we do have a home available. It is an older home, but quite lovely. It has been empty for some time now. It belonged to an elderly widow. We could arrange to take a portion of your earnings for your rent, if that might suit you. I happen to know the man who owns the place. It is mostly furnished, though I'm certain it is in need of a few improvements. Come with me. I would be glad to show you the place and you can decide whether or not you would be willing to consider it."

The mayor took Will's arm and guided him up the street. He didn't stop until they had reached the fence in front of a beautiful stone home with a weathered porch and a crooked gate. Will's heart sank a little. Somehow, being away, he felt that things would never change, but Miss Margery had passed away, and how sorry he was to know it.

Will turned to the mayor. "Yes, I think it will do nicely."

"Wonderful! I will work up a deal for you on rent. Would you like me to introduce you around town?"

Will was feeling more than anxious. "That is kind of you, but I thought I might explore a little on my own, if you are not opposed."

"Not at all! Not many of the buildings are open—as you know, it is Sunday, but there will be a celebratory dinner this evening, and you will be my personal guest. Oh, and one more thing..." He again grabbed Will's arm and turned him about. "There is someone I would love for you to meet."

Will was feeling entirely impatient by this time as he searched the crowds around him, yet he allowed the mayor to direct him back up the street.

"Ah, there," the mayor said confidingly, indicating a lovely young woman. He cleared his throat and called out to her, "Miss Leanna, come join us for a moment, if you will."

Leanna, the town beauty, met the two men on the sidewalk. She smiled pleasantly up at Will.

"Leanna, we have here a new stranger who has just come into town. I thought it might be well to introduce you. Leanna, this is…" The mayor looked down at the credentials Will had given him, "William Linden. William, this is Leanna."

"It's a pleasure to meet you, Miss Leanna." Will gave a slight bow.

"Well, yes. This is good indeed." The mayor nodded to them both. "I must leave you now. I have a bit of a matter to settle regarding your accommodations. Leanna would be happy to show you around, I am sure."

The mayor left. Leanna smiled. Will now felt more distressed than ever.

He gave another small bow. "Truly, I am glad to meet you, but I have another matter to which I must attend. Would you forgive me if I were to excuse myself?"

"Yes, of course. It is a pleasure to meet you, William," Leanna said charmingly. She pressed her hand lightly against his arm before she turned away.

Will struggled not to run as he turned toward the city square. He had been searching the crowds of people since he had first pulled into town, but had seen no sign of Bonnie. He searched the base of the tree where he knew she usually took her lunch during workdays, but he could not see her.

He was just trying to decide where he might look next when he heard a familiar voice behind him.

"Hello, Will."

Will turned, his heart bursting with joy. There was Bonnie, so sweet and lovely in a soft blue dress, her hair pinned at the back of her head with a thin yellow ribbon running through it.

"My dear Bonnie!" Will exclaimed. He bowed nervously. Bonnie stepped forward, pulling him into her embrace.

A lovely banquet lay prepared in the town hall when Will arrived that evening with Bonnie gently holding his arm. A few men in the crowd wore military uniforms, but Will felt more comfortable being back in civilian clothing.

Their arrival drew a great deal of attention. The mayor hurried over.

"William, how good it is to see you again. I see you have met another young lady from our small town, but, Bonnie dear, I hope you will not mind if he is introduced to all the available women in Pravda." the mayor spoke swiftly as he tugged at Will's arm.

"Well, actually, I..." Will started.

Bonnie smiled, "I think that is a fine idea." Her eyes twinkled. Will groaned inwardly. For years he had not been able to spend a single moment with Bonnie, and now, he was to be forced away once more. It was unbearable.

"Well, then," the mayor said, proudly leading Will around the room and introducing him to everyone as they went, taking particular care to extol the virtues of all the available young women in attendance that evening.

As the feast began, Will found himself unhappily seated between the mayor and Leanna, who laughed twice as much as she talked and simpered the rest of the time.

Occasionally he managed to catch Bonnie's eye at a table two rows away, seated between ornery Mr. Gordon, who looked older and more bad-tempered than ever, and the shameless Deputy Cornelius. Between a helping of turkey and potatoes she glanced up. Will glared playfully at her as Leanna stroked his arm and laughed her silly girlish laugh. Bonnie grinned and calmly went back to eating, ignoring the attempted advances by the deputy who tried repeatedly to engage her in frivolous conversation.

The feast lasted an unbearable hour before the tables were cleared away and music for the first dance began. Will turned toward Bonnie, but a gentle hand on his arm stopped him. He glanced down into Leanna's pretty face.

"You will save the first dance for me, won't you, William?" she said sweetly.

Will sighed inwardly again as he smiled. "Of course. I would be delighted." He bowed stiffly, but Leanna seemed unaware of his discomfort. She wrapped herself in his arms, beaming all the while.

As the first dance ended, the mayor hurriedly approached with another sweet-faced young lady.

"I hope you don't plan to keep him to yourself all evening, Leanna," he said jovially. "Miss Martha has been begging to be introduced."

Leanna smiled graciously after only a slight hesitation before she slipped off to the side and was quickly claimed by another gentleman.

Will remembered Martha quite well, though it was apparent she had no recollection of him. He was amazed at how she had grown, but her eyes were much the same. Her father was the milkman, though the dairy had been taken over by her brothers years ago after her father had been injured in an accident on the farm. She curtsied and he bowed as the dance began.

At the end of the dance, Will found it difficult not to let out an audible groan as he turned, once again, to see the mayor escorting another young woman toward him. This continued through most of the evening until Will realized he might have to be content with only glimpses of Bonnie, who was claimed at nearly every other dance by Deputy Cornelius.

Will felt enormous relief as the band took a short break before the last dance of the evening. The mayor now approached him alone.

"Well, William," the mayor said, rather pleased with himself, "you have met all of the available young women here in Pravda. Which girl do you wish to claim for the final dance of the evening?"

Will smiled the most sincere smile that had crossed his lips since first being pulled from Bonnie's side. "I wish to dance with Bonnie."

"Miss Bonnie?" the mayor paused, "really?" He seemed rather bewildered. "You're quite certain? You know you could have any young lady you choose."

"I hardly think I could find a more wonderful young woman, wouldn't you agree?" Will asked.

"Well, why, uh…yes. Yes, of course," the mayor said, his confusion evident.

"Oh, and do you think I might make a request of the band for the final number?" Will asked. "I know it's a lot to ask, being a stranger and requesting the final song."

The mayor's face lit up. "No, no. I think it's a marvelous idea. What would you like them to play? I will go submit your request personally."

"Could you ask them to play "Let Me Call You Sweetheart?" It's a favorite of mine." Will confided.

"A lovely selection. I will go request it right away."

Will stood a moment in the middle of the dance floor. The music started gracefully as he searched the room for Bonnie. His heart sank a little as he saw Deputy Cornelius approaching her, but Bonnie recognized the song. She looked up and saw Will's face, earnestly beckoning her to him. Bonnie stood and walked straight past the deputy and into Will's outstretched arms. Will pulled her into his warm embrace. Then, taking her hand in his, they danced.

Chapter 32

NEVER HAD WILL KNOWN HAPPIER DAYS in all his life. He returned to Bloomfield late that night and told Mayor Ringwald and Amelia of all the wonderful events that had transpired that day. They celebrated with him and expressed their desire that, in time, they might meet Miss Bonnie. Will hoped such an occasion would soon be opportune.

The next morning, Mayor Ringwald, Amelia, and Will set off with his belongings loaded into the wagon. It was a pleasant trip on a bright, sunlit morning. At last he was able to show them some of the parts of Pravda that had meant so much to him. Will told stories and pointed out many of his favorite spots as they passed by. He showed them the gnarled oak tree still shrouded in yellow ribbons and told them the story of his last night with his father. They passed by the barn where he had spent his first winter in Pravda. It had been kept up well, though Jimmy was certainly no longer in the main stall. He indicated the old schoolhouse and described the many books that lined the shelves. He told them of the broken bottle with bits of chalk that had been hidden beneath the largest bush beneath the window. He showed them the sturdy blue spruce from which he had observed the town below. Will also named each of the residents and told many stories of the people he knew so well.

It was pleasant to remember, and it was nostalgic to return. How much need he had found while he had observed the town in his youth, and how much more he felt he might do now.

He directed the Ringwalds to the stone house, which the mayor had arranged to be his living quarters. It was strange to Will to now have the chance to see inside Miss Margery's old home. He knew every bit of land in and around Pravda, but he knew almost none of the buildings from within. It felt peculiar to finally be invited to live and work among the people to whom he had so long been invisible.

The Ringwalds spent the day helping Will with cleaning and chopping wood and doing what little unpacking there was to be done. It was a three-bedroom home, which seemed quite extravagant for a single bachelor. As there were no other options, it suited Will quite well.

Several visitors dropped by throughout the day. Most of them turned out to be young women with whom he had danced the previous night. Each graciously welcomed him with a bit of food—a jar of preserves, some baked goods, or some garden produce. Will felt embarrassed with all of the attention while Mayor Ringwald and Amelia exchanged knowing smiles with each introduction.

By early evening, the house had been made livable. Mayor and Amelia Ringwald hitched the horses to the carriage to return to Bloomfield.

"Visit often," Amelia said. She hugged Will tightly before allowing him to help her into the wagon. "We'll always have a place ready for you when you come."

Will sat before a warm fire that night feeling a bit apprehensive about his new job which would begin the following morning and anxious to see Bonnie again, but there was one other matter that had troubled him for many months.

Will located his stationery, which Amelia had prudently set on an old desk in the spare bedroom. He sat down and, in the dim light began, a letter that he had been anxious to write for some time.

Dear Madam or Sir,

I am writing to your orphanage make an inquiry regarding a baby girl whom I was informed entered your care in the springtime nearly fifteen years ago. Her name is Emily Linden. She is my younger sister, born to my parents, Samuel and Eliza Linden, in a troubled time. It is my hope that I might find her and that, if she is willing, I may bring her home.

Sincerely,

Colonel William Linden

The next morning began with the first snowfall of the year. Will woke earlier than necessary and leisurely took his time walking to work, mailing the letter on his way. He still arrived nearly fifteen minutes before he was due. The building was open, so he showed himself inside and found his way to the mayor's office.

The mayor greeted him with the same enthusiasm he had shown on their previous encounter. "Welcome, welcome, William! It is a pleasure to see you. Have you gotten settled in comfortably? I would expect so. It is good to have a clerk in the office again! I expect you don't have experience in such work at this time, but I don't doubt that you will catch on rather well. Follow me. Let me show you around."

It was one of the larger buildings in Pravda, but there still wasn't a great deal to see. Within the hour, Will was settled at his new desk, sorting through the backed-up paperwork.

Clouds of dust flew from the papers as Will shuffled the neglected documents. Though excited to get things in order, Will soon rose from his desk and took half an hour to shift the furniture and reorganize the room. When he returned to his chair, his desk faced the window and a wintery landscape greeted him each time he looked up.

Will dived deep into his work but still did not lose a moment in leaving it all behind as the bell tolled noon. He waited just outside Madame Belle Lucille's Dress Shop until Bonnie appeared.

"Miss Bonnie, may I accompany you to lunch this afternoon?" he asked.

"Of course, Will," she said, taking his arm.

They ate outside on a bench in the falling snow. The air, though crisp, was not unbearably cold. They finished their meal then took a short walk before returning to work. Will could not imagine a more stark contrast than being transferred from the distress of brutal war to the utter joy which he now held in each waking moment.

Having no doubt of what he wanted, he decided to patiently take his time to win Bonnie completely. They ate lunch together each afternoon and attended social events in the evenings. Often, if there was nothing to attend, they sat by the fire in the schoolhouse reading together for hours, sharing their favorite books while Miss Faux sat busy at her desk, preparing the next day's lessons and enjoying the sounds of the stories that filled the room.

Still, the best part of the day came just before dawn each morning. Bonnie met Will at the edge of Pravda and together they walked the streets addressing every need, great or small, that they saw along their way. Will then escorted her to Madame Belle Lucille's Dress Shop before happily tending to his duties at the city building.

Winter turned to spring and the snow melted away from the fields. Warmth returned to Pravda and the grain began to grow.

In late spring, a letter finally arrived for Will while he was working in his office at the city building.

Colonel Linden,

We apologize for the delay in responding to your query. It has taken us a good deal of time to track down the young woman you mentioned.

We have found your sister, it seems. She has not yet been apprised of your desire to find her, though we do not doubt that it will likely come to her as a rather pleasant surprise. We were able to locate her at a boarding house in Manhattan near the factory where she is currently employed.

We know little of her previous years, but she has kept her original name, Emily Linden, and lives at the enclosed address.

Respectfully yours,

Roger Gordon
Assistant Director
Lifehouse Orphanage

Will leapt from his chair and raced down the hall to the mayor's office. He tapped lightly on the door then, with forced calm, strode into the room. Everything inside of him was bursting with excitement until he wished he might run about and shout his emotions to the world.

Instead, he said simply, "Sir, would it be possible for me to take a few days away from work as soon as it might be convenient?"

The mayor leaned back in his chair. He nodded and crossed his hands over his plump middle. "Why, of course, William. I think you might feel free to leave as early as suits you. Might I ask the reason? Not an elopement, surely." The mayor winked with a chuckle.

Will couldn't hold back his smile. "No, sir, but I have found my sister whom I have never met, and I wish to bring her home."

The mayor sat up a little straighter and gazed at Will in sheer amazement before leaping to his feet. "By all that's wonderful, what news! Go, my boy. Bring her here. Nothing could please me more. Take the rest of the day off and don't return until she has been brought in. Go, dear boy. Go on your way!" He clapped Will on the shoulder and waved him on towards the door.

Will rushed from the city building. He stopped the mail wagon, which had not yet departed and begged them to wait only twenty minutes before heading back, promising to pay them well for the delay if he might have a ride into Bloomfield. Will then stopped in for a moment at Madame Belle Lucille's Dress Shop. He hugged Bonnie tightly as he told her the news.

"Bonnie, I mean to bring her here if she is willing. How I could dance for joy! I used to believe myself entirely alone in the world. I can only imagine that she has felt much the same. How wonderful it will be to have a family once more! I will be gone but a few days if all goes well. Be safe until I return."

Within the promised twenty minutes, Will was on the mail wagon heading back to Bloomfield. He arrived and hurried straight to the train station. The earliest train wasn't scheduled to leave until late the next morning. Will booked a ticket then turned toward the Ringwald's home. Amelia greeted him with pleasant surprise at the door.

"Will! Oh, how glad I am to see you! What brings you to Bloomfield? I hope all is well." She brought Will inside as he related to her the news and showed her the letter. They prepared a special feast that night to celebrate the occasion. Mayor Ringwald and Amelia laughed with almost the same extraordinary joy that Will felt within his own heart. Will knew that if Emily was to return with him, the Ringwalds would have a daughter at last.

The next morning, Will set off for Manhattan. The journey seemed painfully slow and the miles stretched out long before him. The tracks twisted through valleys, hills, and ravines. He had to change trains twice. By late afternoon the next day, he finally arrived.

Manhattan was something far different from anything he had seen before. He struggled to find his way in the maze of streets. It was almost more luck than good navigation that brought him to a run-down, three-story brick building that matched the address he had been given. He knocked at the door.

A portly woman with thinning gray hair opened it and stood in the doorway. She had a sweet round face and a tired smile. "How might I help you, sir?" she asked pleasantly.

"Pardon the intrusion, ma'am. I am looking for my sister. We have never before met, but I was given this address, and I hope to find her well. Do you happen to know Miss Emily Linden?"

"Emily?" she said thoughtfully. "Emily has no family—a' least that is wha' we believed." She peered at him closely. Presently, she stood back and nodded, "Yes, well, I see now, she does.

You look jes' another version of herself. Does she know?"

"Not yet, ma'am. I just found out myself not long ago, and I hoped to surprise her."

The woman's wrinkled face lit up. She beamed at him. "Wha' a blessed day this has turned out t' be! Come in, come in!" she beckoned. "The girls gi' off work much later, bu' yer welcome to wai' inside. I'm jes' in the middle of bakin' some bread to go with the soup for our evenin' meal. You would be welcome t' join us."

"I appreciate that, and I am not a stranger to making bread, if you might allow me to help," Will offered.

"I would be grateful for a bi' of help. Kitchen is this way."

They worked the next two hours together. Mrs. Simmons, not easily satisfied that he would provide sufficient support and stability for Emily, asked Will many questions. It was a great relief to Will when she finally smiled and nodded and her interrogation subsided.

Will made use of the quiet moment to get to know the older woman. Mrs. Simmons, as she was called, had worked in the factories when she was younger but had married well. Her husband, unfortunately, had been killed in an industrial accident. Lonely and unwilling to live a useless life in their large, beautiful home, she had sold it and purchased an old office building, which she made into a ladies' dormitory. She felt it to be very important that the young girls who worked at the factory should have a safe place to stay at minimal expense.

"You do all this for them?" Will asked.

"And fer m'self, don' you see?" Mrs. Simmons was just pulling the bread from the oven. "I need them a' leas' as much as they needed me. We gi' each other through. It's the way life's s'posed t' be, I'm certain."

"Well, on behalf of my sister, I offer my greatest appreciation. I am beyond grateful to know such a woman as yourself has been looking after her. For your kindness to her alone, I owe more than I could ever repay."

"You owe me nothin'. She's a swee' girl and one of my favorites—always looking out fer the other girls, and fer me, as of'en as a weary workin' girl can think of i'. They'll be home soon. You wai' 'ere. I'll bring 'er in."

Will waited with trepidation, pacing the floor anxiously. The walls soon echoed with the voices of young girls, tired but cheerful.

Mrs. Simmons' voice was clearly heard through the thin walls. "All of you, gi' on upstairs t' wash b'fore supper, all excep' you, Emily, dear. I need you t' join me for a momen' in the kitchen."

Will turned as the door beside him opened. There stood a lovely petite young woman—a nearly perfect feminine model of himself.

"This young man has somethin' t' tell you," Mrs. Simmons said, her voice tender. Her eyes danced with excitement as she watched the two of them.

Emily looked into Will's face and for a moment he was speechless.

He took in a deep breath. "Emily," he said gently, "my name is William Linden. I am your brother. I haven't long known that you were alive or where I could find you, but I feel as though I could burst with joy from the wonder of finding you—my own sister. If you wish it, as it is the greatest hope of my own heart, I have come to take you home."

Emily stood frozen. Will tenderly reached out and took her hand in his. "I promise I will always take care of you as long as you will allow me to. You will never again have to be alone."

Emily covered her face then melted to the floor, sobbing into her hands. Will knelt beside her and pulled her into his arms, weeping into her thick, dark hair, his heart broken with joy.

Hot bread and soup had never tasted so good. Emily cuddled against her brother throughout the entire meal, tears streaming down her face. She frequently looked up into her brother's face, seeming so afraid that she might at any moment wake to find that it had all been only a dream.

Emily did not even wish to leave her newfound brother long enough to pack her few possessions. The other girls kindly teased her as they brought down her bag. Will and Emily both wrapped Mrs. Simmons in a warm embrace as they departed. Will placed his arm protectively around his younger sister, and together they made their way back to the train station.

Will had been in the city less than a day, and oh, how he already longed for the clean fresh air of the country! He could hardly wait to show Emily everything that he had grown to love. She was so courageously allowing herself to be swept away to an unknown place with such hope in what the future might bring. Will never had to ask. He could see the hope in her eyes, and he was determined that she would never again lack anything she truly desired.

Emily received a warm welcome into the home of Mayor and Amelia Ringwald as though she had been there all her life. They held a wonderful feast in her honor and shared stories late into the night. Emily seemed more content just listening rather than talking.

The following day, Mayor Ringwald and Amelia escorted them both back to Pravda. Will saw Emily settled into one of the bedrooms of his rented house. He then excused himself while she slept off the wearying journey.

Will ran down to Madame Belle Lucille's Dress Shop and found Bonnie working. She looked up when he came in and quickly rose to greet him.

"You made it back! Is she here?" She jumped from her stool and hurried to him.

"Yes. She is sleeping. Oh, she is wonderful! I could hardly be more happy." He pulled Bonnie into his arms. "I can't wait for you to meet her. May I speak with Madame Belle Lucille for a moment?"

"Of course. Follow me." Bonnie led him to the back of the shop where Madam Belle Lucille sat weaving ribbons into the lace of a rigid ladies hat. "Madame, Mr. Linden has asked to have a word with you," Bonnie said as they approached.

Madame Belle Lucille rose and greeted him with an elegant curtsy. "Mr. Linden, what might I do for you?"

"Madame Belle Lucille, some wonderful events have recently transpired in my life and my sister has come to join me here in Pravda. I wish to surprise her with a beautiful dress—blue, I think. Something to make a young girl feel lovely."

"I see, and what an excellent idea. Do you happen to know her measurements?" Madame Belle Lucille asked.

"I'm afraid not, but she is very similar in size I would think to young Miss Sarah Ellison who works here."

"That will be perfect then. Is this to be for formal occasions or everyday wear?" she asked.

Will paused a moment, thinking. "I would like to do one for both sorts of occasions, if that would be alright. Perhaps as you see her, you might determine the best color for the second dress. How soon until they might be done?" he asked.

"Give us a few weeks. I'm sure Miss Bonnie can apprise

you of the progress." Bonnie squeezed his hand and nodded.

Will returned home and prepared a late evening meal. He found himself suddenly worried that it might be difficult to come to know this young woman who shared nothing of his history except for his bloodline. Emily woke and joined him in the kitchen. His fears were proven entirely unnecessary. They talked all through dinner and late into the night as they sat before the warm fire roasting chestnuts and popping corn. They finally fell asleep in their chairs next to the fire, not stirring until the sun rose the next morning.

Emily saw Will to the door as he was leaving for work. He hugged her and left a soft kiss on her forehead as he set off. He had invited her to join him and Bonnie for lunch at the park, and Emily promised to join them. She arrived at the city building just a few minutes before noon. Will brought her into the mayor's office.

"William, she is wonderful!" The mayor turned to Emily, taking her hand. "Young lady, we are honored to have you join our small but thriving community. I don't suppose you are wanting to find employment as well? You know, it was I who found your brother the job he has now when he first entered our town hardly a few months ago." He jovially winked at Will.

"I do would hope to work, if there was anything available," Emily said with a confidence that surprised the mayor.

"Oh, but Emily, there's no need..." Will began, but the mayor was deep in thought and cut him off unintentionally.

"Well, I say, there is likely to be something we can find that needs doing. What kind of work would most interest you?" he asked.

"I've worked a great deal as a seamstress, but I wish to be done with that for a time. I would most like to work with flowers—growing and arranging them. I don't suppose there is such a job available?"

"Well, I suppose we could accommodate you, if you're certain you don't mind the dirty work? The groundskeeper for the city has long been asking for a bit of help as he's grown older. He is a stubborn man, but I think you will get along with him quite well. The pay isn't much."

"That's alright, I would just be glad for the work," Emily said resolutely.

"Emily, you know there is no need for you to work." Will said when they headed outside the city building.

"But what would I do with myself? I'm not sure how I could manage to fill my time otherwise. I do prefer it, especially now that I will no longer have to be stuck inside a dark, miserable factory for long hours. I'm looking forward to having a reason to spend a good deal of time outside, if it would not trouble you."

"No, not at all. The world can always use more flowers." Will wrapped his arm around her shoulders. "And now, I have someone I wish you to meet."

Bonnie was just getting off work for lunch when they arrived at Madame Belle Lucille's shop. Madame Belle Lucille peered through the window. She gave Will a quick nod then turned back to her work.

Emily and Bonnie were delighted with each other. They developed a close friendship from the moment they met. The duo became a trio and their routine continued, meeting at the edge of the woods early each morning, walking the town, attending to duties at work, meeting for lunch and gathering together in the evening to read and attend social events.

Their friendships grew and soon the relationship between brother and sister seemed as though they had never been apart.

Will often found himself amazed at the stunning similarities between themselves, and other times he was startled to discover another side of her that he had never expected—particularly when she livened up the household or the town with a little of her prankster enthusiasm that he had never quite developed.

Thanksgiving approached with great anticipation. It was an especially happy event in the Ringwald home that year. Not only would Emily finally enjoy her first Thanksgiving with a family of her own, but two other guests had accepted the invitation to make the long trip and join in on the festivities.

"Miss Bonnie, Mr. Wilson—you are most welcome! Thank you for coming." Amelia greeted them both warmly. "Will, Emily," she said pulling them both to her, "it's good to have you home."

Two nights before Thanksgiving, Will had nervously paced the path in front of the Wilson's cabin, trying to find the courage to invite Bonnie and her father to join them for the Thanksgiving festivities. Will had tramped the snow so thin, gathering his courage, that Clyde Wilson finally stepped from the misshapen cabin.

"I suppose you have come to speak with me," he said, not unkindly as he observed Will.

Will had only seen Clyde Wilson a few times, most often from a distance. Now he cleared his throat as the man approached.

"Yes, sir. I have come with an invitation," he said, extending his hand. Clyde's appearance was ruddy, but behind the face of the broken man that he was, Will saw a gentle kindness—often hidden, as he knew, by his uncontrolled need for alcohol.

"Come, sit with me for a moment." Clyde Wilson indicated the steps of the porch. Will sat down beside him.

"You've been forming an attachment to my daughter, I am well aware." He watched Will's face intently.

"Yes, sir. Very much so," Will replied in earnest.

"Yet, you have not asked for her hand—is that to come any time soon?" Mr. Wilson gently probed.

Will cleared his throat twice before he managed to speak. "Yes… I, well…Yes. Absolutely, and I hope it will not be too far off. I don't wish to ask her until I know she is ready—until I know she will feel completely comfortable with her decision, whichever way she should choose."

They sat silently together a few moments listening to the clatter of the larks in the trees.

Will again turned to him. "Sir, I do hope to obtain your permission. Is there anything you would like to know—or anything that I might do that would help you to feel comfortable giving us your blessing?"

Mr. Wilson sat back for a time looking up at the clear blue sky. "I would simply need to know one thing, and then I wish you to make me a promise before you make any promises to her."

"What is it you would like to know?" Will asked.

"I want to know how you honestly feel about my daughter. I believe I have no reason to worry, yet I still want to ask—do you truly like my daughter?"

Will was startled. "Yes, sir—I adore her. I love Bonnie deeply."

Mr. Wilson chuckled a little. "I can see that, but that is not what I asked. I asked if you like her, not if you love her. Love is an emotion that sometimes can be a little less than dependable, but I wish to know, do you like her enough to wake up by her side each morning, to be able to look at her across the breakfast table—no matter the effects of time and age—to hold her hand through the most bitter circumstances and to give her the entire man that you are—the best of the man that you are. Do you truly like my daughter enough to never wish for more?"

Will took a moment as he, too, looked up into the clear blue sky. He had never thought of his relationship with Bonnie in such a way, and yet the answer to him was so obvious. He turned to Mr. Wilson with complete confidence.

"I absolutely could never wish for more than the wonderful girl whom I have grown to like, to love, and to adore. If I ever had the incredible joy of having her as my own, I would spend the rest of my life doing all I could to earn the woman I could never deserve. I love her, and I will never stop liking her. That is my sincere answer."

"Good. Well, I expected no less." Mr. Wilson patted Will on the back as he stood. He stared at Will a moment. "Then all I ask is that you promise me one thing. I wish the man that becomes a part of her life to be much better than the only man that has been in her life. The addiction that holds me in bondage is unbreakable. Promise me that you will never turn to alcohol, no matter what may come. She deserves better than what I have been." Mr. Wilson's demeanor had changed. This strong man, so accustomed to drink, now looked down at the dirt beneath his feet, sorrow in every line of his face.

Will stood and clasped Mr. Wilson's hand in both of his. "Whatever regrets you may have, you have raised a wonderful girl, for which you should be very proud. I owe you so much for that. I will honor your request."

Mr. Wilson looked up and smiled. "Then you have no need to ask my permission. I offer it to you freely."

Will felt as though the weight of his fears had lifted from his shoulders. He breathed a sigh of relief. "Well, that makes my next question all the easier. If you happen to be available, I would like to invite you and Miss Bonnie to join my family and me for Thanksgiving dinner. They live over in Bloomfield. I would be happy to bring a carriage around Thanksgiving morning, if you both would care to accompany my sister and me on the journey."

Such overwhelming joy still swept through Will's heart each time he spoke of his sister. It still seemed unreal, yet so beautiful to him that he should have any relation he could claim—and one who had so quickly become dear to him. He felt nearly complete with the Ringwalds, his newfound sister, and Bonnie so often at his side. It almost seemed to him that the past he once knew must have belonged to a very different little boy.

Mr. Wilson hesitated only a moment, then he replied simply. "We would be delighted."

Will had arrived as promised Thanksgiving morning. Despite Mr. Wilson's acceptance, Will found himself surprised when father and daughter emerged from the run-down cabin. Bonnie's father had done a great deal of cleaning up since he had spoken with Will two days before. Clyde Wilson strode up to the carriage, dressed in a handsome suit with his hair freshly cut and Bonnie at his side.

It was a merry trip in the crisp fall air. Upon their arrival, Will took great pleasure in introducing Bonnie and her father to the Ringwalds.

They all worked together to prepare the meal. Once ready, they sat close around the Ringwald's table and feasted on steaming mashed potatoes, a large turkey, thick brown gravy, cranberry sauce, fresh bread spread thick with strawberry preserves, and a variety of delicious home-baked pies. Afterwards, they all retired to the main room to roast nuts and share stories in front of the fireplace.

Will had brought along a special surprise, and he now found it difficult to wait much longer. He hurried out to the carriage and returned with two large boxes. He set them both in front of Emily.

"I have a bit of a surprise for you," he said. "I'm not sure if it is what you would have picked for yourself, but I had some help, so I hope you are pleased."

Emily teased him a little first, but she was far too curious to wait long. She untied the string that bound the first box and lifted the lid. She gasped then laughed in delight. She ran to Will and wrapped him in a great hug.

"Will! Oh, Will! It is lovely!"

"Pull it out!" he said, grinning.

Emily nearly danced as she ran back to the box and pulled out the elegant blue dress. She held it up against her, spinning in a circle. "Oh, Will! Oh, my sweet brother. I have never had anything so beautiful!"

Will could barely sit still. He felt almost more excited than Emily. "There's still another box. You must open that one too."

Emily would hardly let go of the dress. Hesitantly she slipped it back into the delicate paper lining. She then pulled the string from the second box and lifted the lid. She gasped. Her hands covered her mouth a moment, then slowly, she reached down into the box and stroked the soft fabric.

"Emily, show us!" Amelia said laughing.

Emily reached both hands into the box, and as gently as lifting a child, she lifted a beautiful, soft pink dress from inside the box. The light fabric of the top layer swirled as it draped down the side of her arms.

She looked at Will as though unsure if it could really be for her.

"I hope it fits—please Emily, go try it on. I think we all wish to see how lovely you will look," Will said.

Emily looked back at the dress and simply stared in wonder at the beautiful gown.

Bonnie laughed. "Come, Emily. I have been anxious to see you in that dress for the past several weeks. Let me help you put it on." She took Emily's arm and led her away.

Emily nearly pranced down the hall as they made their way into a nearby room.

While the rest of the group waited with anticipation, the sound of a bell rang somewhere inside the home.

"That's the front door. I'll tend to it," Amelia said rising quickly.

She was back a moment later. "Will, you have a guest!"

In walked a jovial red-haired man with one leg and a hand-hewn crutch. "I heard you were in town, Colonel! I hope you don't mind my dropping in unannounced."

Will leapt to his feet and embraced his comrade. "Why, Joseph Bronson! It is wonderful to see you! I'm especially glad you have come. I have brought some people I would like you to meet. This is Mr. Clyde Wilson. I don't suppose you remember when I spoke years ago of Miss Bonnie? This is her father."

Mr. Wilson stood. "A pleasure to meet you."

Just then, Emily appeared with Bonnie just behind her.

"And this," Will motioned to Emily, "is my dear younger sister, Miss Emily."

Joseph looked entirely confused as he turned to meet Emily. He stopped at the sight of her, bewildered and amazed. "Your sister?"

Emily flowed into the room, the soft pink skirts swirling around her feet, her whole face beaming.

Joseph swallowed hard.

"Emily, this is Joseph."

Emily smiled brightly, obviously feeling beautiful and happy.

Will noticed Joseph's hand tighten on his crutch. "Miss Emily, I am most pleased to meet you." Joseph said with a nod of his head.

"Joseph, I do know of you! Will has told me many stories from the war. I am very happy to meet you at last." She curtsied, a little clumsily, but with great confidence.

"Joseph, would you consider joining us for the evening?" Will asked.

Joseph could hardly turn his attention away from Emily. "Well, they were expecting me back...but, I suppose they won't be too alarmed if I am a bit late returning."

"I trust to that," Will said, clapping him on the back. "Emily, that dress is specifically for special occasions, and this Thanksgiving, we have more to give thanks for than almost any other time we have known in our lives. Why don't you consider wearing it through the remainder of the evening?"

Emily twirled a time or two. "I suppose," she said, grinning. "If I must."

It was remarkable what a difference a lovely dress made for Emily. She perched herself lightly on the edge of a chair, her eyes still twinkling, but a lady-like air radiated from her.

Joseph and Bonnie were introduced at long last. Joseph winked and nudged Will, who grinned, but Will soon had the better of Joseph. He teasingly kept attempting to engage his former comrade in conversation, but not long into each conversation, Joseph's attention was diverted and he was again hanging onto every word Emily spoke. Will found that he did not mind at all. He knew no better man, and Emily seemed genuinely impressed with his fellow soldier. She was still young, but a beautiful friendship had begun.

It was late before the tired group arrived back in Pravda. Will held Bonnie tight in his arms a moment before escorting her and her father to their door.

"Thank you for coming. It was a wonderful day," he said, bidding them farewell.

Will and Emily stayed up by the fire talking and drinking hot apple cider until nearly morning. They fell asleep with their chairs facing each other just as dawn broke over the horizon.

The whole town enjoyed an extended holiday over the long weekend. Will, Emily and Bonnie spent a lot of time making gifts and traveling to find the perfect Christmas tree somewhere deep in the woods. They arrived back at Will's place and positioned the tree in the front room just as night settled in. They stayed up late into the evening, decorating the vibrant green branches with what few ornaments they had and making more from anything they could find. When they had finished, it was a beautiful vision to behold.

Will and Emily walked Bonnie home, enjoying the swirls of snow at their feet as they trod along. Emily waited patiently at the gate while Will bid Bonnie goodnight. Then, Will and Emily walked home in the crisp evening together.

Chapter 33

THE HOLIDAYS WERE ESPECIALLY highly anticipated by most of Pravda that year following the end of the war. , yet a dreadful sorrow hung over a few homes where men had not returned. These families received special attention with many visits from kind-hearted guests who hoped to help fill a little of the void. The festivities around town seemed to lift even the saddest of hearts, beckoning all to find joy in the season.

Will felt as though the anticipation was more than he could bear.

Christmas morning came at last. Crystalline swirls of snow danced in the breeze. Will woke early and ran fretfully from room to room, rearranging decorations and trying to divert his mind. Emily teased him mercilessly while she attempted to help him get ready.

Dawn broke at last across the eastern horizon. Will leapt down the stairs and out into the cold morning. He ran until he was within view of Bonnie's gate. He slowed himself to a walk and calmed his breathing.

"Miss Bonnie." He bowed with a smile when she opened the door.

Bonnie reached her arms around him in a loving embrace.

"Merry Christmas, Will!" she said happily.

Will escorted Bonnie into Pravda and they took their usual morning walk, though Emily did not join them. They left a bundle of twigs scattered beneath Mr. Gordon's tree—a larger bundle than usual as it was Christmas. They swept a few front walks and left a platter of bread and several packages of home-baked sweets. They came to the edge of Pravda then turned back.

When they reached the town square, Will suddenly diverted their course. He gently guided Bonnie up the sidewalk toward the large blue spruce. "I have something I want to show you," he told her, smiling nervously.

Bonnie glanced up at him, curious as she allowed him to escort her down the path.

Will slipped his hand into hers and led her around to the back of the tree. There, beautiful and nearly as tall as herself stood a perfect white snow bunny. Bonnie stared in awe.

Wrapping his arms around her, Will pulled her close. "For so long, you have brought joy to those who have had such little reason to smile. You silently taught all around you to see the beautiful things even in difficult and troubling times." Bonnie cuddled her head against his chest.

Will took a shaky breath. "Bonnie, I could wish for nothing more than to be allowed the opportunity to continue your mission forever by your side. I would do everything I could to add a little more happiness to your life and to help you to find joy no matter what comes our way."

Will stepped back and knelt down on one knee. Delicate flakes of snow swirled around them in the early morning breeze.

"My dearest Bonnie, I love you. I will always cherish you. It would mean more to me than any other gift in this world if you would allow me to take you as my wife." He looked hopefully up into her tear-filled eyes. "Sweet Bonnie, will you marry me?" Will reached into his pocket and in his gloved hand, he held a thin golden band with a pure diamond glittering in the morning light.

Bonnie knelt before him in the snow and wrapped him tightly in her arms. "Oh, Will! Yes! Oh, yes, of course I will!" She reached her hands up to his face. "How much I love you." Bonnie kissed him gently on the cheek. "I could wish for nothing more."

Will leapt to his feet, pulling her up with him, and swung her around in his arms, laughing and weeping.

Witnessed only by a great snow bunny on that perfect Christmas morning, Will and Bonnie shared their first kiss as the snow fell around them. They stood beneath the same blue spruce from which a young boy had first seen a lovely young girl—a girl who had never needed to say a word to change his world forever.

Chapter 34

THE WEDDING WAS SET to take place on a Saturday in late spring. Both Pravda and Bloomfield prepared for the event in excited anticipation.

Bonnie and Emily seemed to frequently go missing with the excuse that there were many preparations needed for the wedding. Will wasn't quite sure what preparations were still needed. Bonnie had chosen to wear her mother's wedding dress and much of the town had volunteered to help with anything else that needed to be done. Even through the busy preparations, the trio still took their morning walk together through the town, but the girls rarely appeared before late in the evening, particularly as the date of the wedding drew near.

Many of the citizens of Pravda had thought it a bit strange when the young couple had announced their chosen location for the ceremony—on the edge of town beside the gnarled oak tree, but as the day drew near, the area was made ready.

May blossomed beautifully that year. The anticipated day came at last, warm and fragrant.

Will barely slept through the night and woke long before the sun had risen. Not quite himself, he burned half a dozen eggs before Emily came down and, laughing, excused him to get dressed while she set about cleaning up the mess. Will arrived back down in the kitchen ten minutes later quite misshapen in his appearance.

Emily teased him for a time while attempting to force him to sit still and eat a bit of toast. She straightened his coat, retied his tie and made him change a brown shoe for a black o that both shoes would match. Will paced around the front room and sat for a moment or two then paced again while Emily went to get herself ready. Unable to wait any longer, Will went out and strode through the town.

When Will returned, Emily sent him on an errand to pick up more eggs. She would be leaving soon to meet Bonnie at the city building so that she could give Bonnie some help getting ready without being seen by the groom.

Everything sounded like a dance to Will's ears as he walked to the mercantile. His shoes tapped lightly on the pavement, the carriages and wagons creaked along behind the clopping hooves of horses, and somewhere in the distance, the faint tinkling of hundreds of strands of glass strung high up in the boughs of a tree could be heard over the rustling of the leaves.

At half past ten, nearly the entire town emerged dressed in their finest. It would be one of Pravda's grandest events in several years. Mr. Wilson greeted Will on the street in front of the city building. His suit was clean and pressed and his hair freshly trimmed.

"My boy, don't you think it's time you get on up to your place?" he said. His face seemed serious but his eyes twinkled.

"Yes, sir. And again, thank you," Will said as he heartily took Mr. Wilson's hand in both of his.

"On your way then, lad," Mr. Wilson said, waving him off.

Will turned and forced himself to walk as calmly as he

could toward the gnarled oak tree at the edge of town. Many from Pravda and Bloomfield were already waiting, seated in the lines of mismatched chairs brought from several different buildings.

Reverend Amos stood only a few feet from the tree. Emily and Amelia stood to his right and Mayor Ringwald had taken his place on the left. Reverend Amos beckoned Will to join them. Mayor Ringwald embraced Will as he strode to the front. Amelia smiled and waved, biting her lip as tears streamed down her face. Emily winked and raised her eyebrows mischievously.

The wedding guests chatted eagerly. A few more people filled the seats until the bell above the schoolhouse tolled eleven o'clock. Silence fell with nothing but gentle whispers to be heard. The entire group turned toward the city building. Mr. Wilson strode down the steps, and beside him, dressed in lace with her thick dark hair curled and pinned up with delicate white flowers, was Bonnie. A thin, shimmering veil covered her face, her lovely smile and bright eyes barely visible beneath it.

Will watched in awe as she approached, escorted by her father. Never had he known a woman full of so much beauty. How it amazed him to know that in a moment, she would offer herself to him, entirely and completely.

Mr. Wilson kissed Bonnie affectionately on her forehead before placing her hand in Will's. He gave a gentle nod, then turned away, taking his place in line.

Neither Will nor Bonnie could stop smiling as the ceremony began.

Reverend Amos spoke for a time on the sanctity of marriage, of love, of good times, of hard times, and of the union that could bring them through it all. At last he turned to Bonnie and asked, "Miss Bonnie Wilson, do you take Mr. William Linden to be your lawfully wedded husband through sickness and health, through joy and through sorrow, as long as you both shall live?"

Bonnie looked directly into Will's eyes. She smiled. "Yes, I do."

A tear streamed down Will's face and he choked a little as Reverend Amos turned to him.

"And do you, Mr. William Linden, take Miss Bonnie Wilson to be your lawfully wedded wife through sickness and health, through joy and through sorrow, as long as you both shall live?"

"Yes, yes I do!" Will said. He raised a hand to his face, overwhelmed with joy.

The reverend gave a light-hearted chuckle. "I now pronounce you husband and wife." He patted Will on the shoulder. "Well, William. It is done. You may now kiss the bride."

Another tear coursed down Will's face as he lifted her veil.

"I love you," Bonnie whispered.

"And I will always love you" Will said before gently pressing his lips to hers.

No celebration had ever been so wonderful in all the history of Pravda. A delicious buffet of food had been set up as a picnic in the town square. Every family had brought something to add until there was far too much food to be eaten.

Bonnie stayed near Will's side, his arm tenderly holding her to him as they greeted and thanked everyone who had come.

Emily was quite preoccupied. She sat rather close to Joseph and rarely managed to divert her attention, though there was much happening around her. Something new and rather unexpected had suddenly been set in motion the moment she and Joseph found themselves inclined to introduce the father of the bride to Joseph's mother, Mrs. Bronson. Will watched curiously as his new father-in-law and Joseph's widowed mother took several turns around the square together before settling themselves beneath a blossoming tree, talking well into the afternoon. Even Joseph, so absorbed by the lovely girl at his side, had noticed and glanced at them occasionally with obvious merriment.

Bonnie had observed the developing friendship as well. She smiled and motioned for Will to look at the older couple beneath the tree.

"He has changed a good deal lately, you know," she told him, watching the couple across the green. "You helped him to see how much he has been missing. He wants more than anything to see joy in life again." Bonnie cuddled against Will as he held her close.

For hours, the citizens of Bloomfield and Pravda lay in the sun, laughing and talking and eating enough to burst. A pile of gifts continued to grow beneath the large blue spruce.

At dusk, Emily approached Bonnie. "It is all ready. The carriage is parked near the west end of town. You may even be able to slip away unnoticed." Emily gave Will and Bonnie a wink and gathered her skirts importantly before striding off.

Will looked at Bonnie. "A carriage? Where are we going?"

"Well, I suppose you better just come with me and find out," Bonnie said, pulling him to his feet.

She guided Will around to the back of the city building and out into the street. A few people smiled and waved, but most were quite engaged in dancing and conversation.

At the edge of town, just as Emily had promised, stood a sturdy-looking carriage—and in the seat holding the reins was a one-legged driver in a tall cap that couldn't entirely hide his dark red hair. The driver jumped down and bowed low to the ground, nearly losing his hat in the process. "Would sir and madame be interested in taking a ride in my fine carriage this lovely evening?" Joseph said eloquently. He opened the carriage door and Bonnie pulled Will inside. Will attempted to ask where they were going, but Bonnie shook her head as they settled into the cushioned seat.

"All set then?" Joseph nodded to himself. He climbed back up and took the reigns. "Right then, off we go." He clicked his tongue at the horses. They set off on a nice though rather bumpy ride into the woods.

"We're not really following any kind of path, are we?" Will laughed as again they were jostled by a wheel hitting a raised root. Bonnie didn't reply. She just cuddled herself against Will's side with a contented smile.

Will watched the faint appearances of the stars overhead, filled with more joy and peace than he could have ever imagined.

They were deep in the woods when Joseph reined in the horses.

"End of the line, end of the line. Everybody off!"

Will sat up, confused. "Joseph, we are a little far from town…"

Bonnie grinned. "End of the line, Will. Everybody off." She stood and pulled Will to his feet before stepping down from the carriage. Will followed.

"Madame, I trust you are in need of no further assistance?" Joseph asked. He handed them each a lamp.

"None, thank you Joseph," Bonnie said.

Joseph tipped his hat elegantly and turned the carriage back toward town, leaving the two of them alone deep in the woods. Will stared, confused and rather amused.

Bonnie held her hand out to Will. He took it in his own. She lead him further into the forest, saying nothing. They walked together, enjoying the peaceful spring evening that surrounded them. Bullfrogs croaked in a pond nearby. Cicadas chirped and leaves rustled all around them.

Then, Will saw it. They had come to the thicket. He looked at Bonnie. She reached a hand to his face then rose on tiptoe and kissed him. "Welcome home, Will. This time, I will be here beside you to make sure you never have to feel abandoned or alone."

She guided him to the same small path he had cut through the brambles years before. Then, once more, he found himself back in the clearing he had once known so well, only this time, it was very much changed. Flowers bloomed all around him and the trees were loaded with fruit—and there, across the creek, stood the old cabin, yet it seemed hardly the same. It had been cleaned and fixed up as though it were nearly new with flowers growing all around. Bonnie slipped a folded document into his hand. In the dim light of the moon, Will made out only the bold letters across the top.

"It is the deed to the land, a bit of the past and the future that will be yours as long as you wish. It is our secret hideaway." Bonnie smiled tenderly. "I love you, Mr. William Linden," she said softly, squeezing his hand. Will hugged her tight and kissed her gently on the top of her head.

"Dearest Bonnie, there is nothing I could wish for more." He swept her into his arms and carried her across the threshold.

Chapter 35

LIFE WITH ITS WONDERFUL PASSAGE OF TIME changed many things in the small town of Pravda.

The first child to come to the Linden home was a strong baby boy followed two years later by a beautiful baby girl. Within another two years, a set of twins appeared—one boy and one girl.

Will continued to work as town clerk until the mayor decided it was past time to settle in for retirement, at which time he encouraged Will to run for the position. There was little competition in the race as most of Pravda seemed quite content to cast their vote for the good-natured William Linden.

Days turned quickly to weeks and months turned into seasons passing swiftly by. Will continued his interest in the financial affairs of the nation, often expressing strong objections to the lack of stability that seemed to be growing on Wall Street. Few in the small town of Pravda were into financial investments, but for those few, including Mr. Willet, Will became increasingly concerned and offered his counsel for caution.

Will's first year as mayor proved to be an extraordinary yet challenging time. He felt poorly suited to the task, but he slowly came to better know the needs of the town and was continually seeking the means to meet them. Often he traveled with his family to Bloomfield, staying a day or two to ask guidance from Mayor Ringwald.

"Will, I was approached the other day with a proposal," Mayor Ringwald told him on a warm summer during one of these visits. "The railroad company is looking to expand and put in more rails toward the north, south and west. We were looking over a few of the possibilities and there is a chance they may be willing to build a route near Pravda, passing perhaps only a half mile from your precinct. There is nothing definite in the proposition, but I thought I would ask to see if it is something you think might benefit the town."

"It's possible," Will said thoughtfully. "Travel to and from the town is quite slow and bringing in or selling supplies is rather challenging at times. I think there is a good chance that, so long as it does not to pass directly through, it might be well-accepted— especially if it were to include a station at that point. I'll take comments and see what the leaning of the town would be. I would need to know a little more about it, but from the outset, it seems as though it might offer some significant benefits to Pravda. Let them know we are interested."

Mayor Ringwald nodded. "I can certainly do that."

The railroad was well-accepted by nearly everyone—except Mr. Gordon who didn't like the idea of "a noisy beast passing anywhere near the town." He complained to all who would listen that the world was getting too modern as it was and he quite preferred the natural way of life, twig-fed fires and all. Mr. Gordon was nearly a hundred years old, but he still had a voice loud enough to express his discontent.

The rest of the town offered their strong support, as long as the train did not pass directly through. A station at that location, which became a bargaining point with the railroad, turned out to be an easy agreement.

It became quite the event each Saturday for many to crowd into carriages and automobiles to ride out to see the progress of the railroad. The night it finally crested the hill a mile and a half from town, several hay-filled wagons were loaded up with as many people as they could carry, heading out to go see the track. Within the month, the work had passed well beyond the town and a platform with a station was in the process of being constructed.

By late spring, the station was fully functioning and several people purchased a ticket to ride from Pravda to Bloomfield, just to see what it was like aboard a train. Even Mr. Gordon got in on the fun, though for a man older than anyone even knew, it was understandable that he complained during the entire trip back to Pravda in Mr. Willet's new Tin Lizzie, a neat Ford Model T that had become the pride of the town. Still, having survived, he proudly boasted to all who would hear that he had ridden on the great rail system. "Probably the oldest rider they've ever seen on board," he bragged, his chest thrown out as he limped down the street with his fellow excursionists.

Life mostly went back to normal, though there was a lot more traveling to and from the town now that it wasn't such an arduous journey.

Christmas came and went with its dazzling trees and deco-rations. The new year began with a blizzard greater than Pravda had ever seen before. The children played in the mounds of snow until their cheeks were bright red and their toes half frozen. They would then hurry inside for steaming mugs of hot cocoa and fresh-baked bread to warm them from the inside out.

Will and Bonnie continued their walks through the town each morning, often returning as Emily had just begun waking the children for school. Will mixed up a delicious breakfast while

Emily and Bonnie got the children ready for the day.

Joseph was a frequent visitor, as was his mother and Bonnie's father. The front room of the Linden home often boasted a handful of guests. It was a wonderful surprise to the rest of the town when a double wedding was scheduled for April the following year.

Bonnie eagerly gave her father her consent to remarry with a strong approval of Mrs. Bronson as her new step-mother. Joseph Bronson also had plans for a wedding. He nervously approached Will in late August for his consent in asking Emily for her hand. Delighted, Will gave Joseph his blessing for their marriage and soon the engagement was made.

April was still a bit cool that year, but there were blossoms on the trees and thick grass in the town square on the morning of the double wedding.

Bonnie stood by her father to the left of Reverend Amos. Joseph stood to the right with a place open beside him for Jacob, who would be acting as his best man. The wedding began at eleven o'clock that morning beneath the large blue spruce. Jacob Bronson escorted his mother, Eliza Bronson. They were followed by Will, who escorted his sister, Emily. Joseph reached out to take Emily's hand as she approached. Both couples seemed entirely delighted as the ceremony began, though the exuberant joy seen in the younger couple was matched just as beautifully in the peaceful joy of the older bride and groom.

Reverend Amos gave his same lecture before joining the two couples, and the feast began.

Joseph and Jacob had worked through the year to build a small homestead in Bloomfield where Joseph and Emily had chosen to live. Mr. Wilson worked hard to fix up his old cabin, and by the time of the wedding, he lived in a respectable and rather beautiful home. He fixed up Bonnie's old room for the youngest two Bronson children and often expressed his keen hope of being able now to prove that he could do better as a father. Through the past few years, he had often expressed his sorrow for his earlier failures, begging Bonnie's forgiveness each time he brought the matter up.

After perhaps more than a dozen of these painful reminiscences, she finally became quite impatient with him and told him that she had no regrets from her past and was quite happy with the way things were turning out, so if he was going to try to commiserate, he should go do it where she couldn't hear.

She then took his hand tenderly in her own as they sat beside each other on the front porch swing, watching the children play in the yard. "There is no need to regret the past," she told him tenderly. "You have changed so much, Papa. The man you were doesn't matter any longer—he is gone now. You have worked so hard to become the man you are now, so don't let the past destroy the beautiful future that awaits you. We all do things we regret. I never needed to forgive you. I understood some of what you were feeling, and I never stopped loving you as you struggled through the pain of your trials. Please, let it go."

He wept like a child in her arms that day. Will watched helplessly nearby. There were moments when he felt he could not love Bonnie more than he already did—that she could not become more precious to him than she already was, but she always proved him wrong.

It was a season of joy and peace in the lives of the newlywed Wilsons and Bronsons. It was also an especially happy time for Bonnie and Will as the three families often gathered at the Linden home to celebrate any joyful occasion, large or small, that came their way.

Yet, life hardly seemed content to offer joy alone and before long, something new hit the little town of Pravda just as it had hit the entire nation. As Will had predicted, the instability of the stock market became more perceptible and the financial increase that had swelled the market began to decline alarmingly. Will heard the news. It had been years in coming, but it had come as he had been sure it would.

Most of Pravda had been spared the worst of the effects of the destabilizing market. Will used his connections from his days as an intern to help those who were willing to sell their stocks to be able to do so at the onset of the fiscal change. Mr. Willet, who had highly invested in stocks, initially accepted the minimal loss when Will convinced him to sell—at least until the market turned upward once more. When he saw the prices starting to rise again, he approached Will, frustrated that he had sold.

"It's not such an unstable market," he chided. "The prices are nearly back to where they had been before I foolishly took your advice to sell at a loss. What made you so sure the market wouldn't recover? Now you see how wrong you were, predicting a continual decline."

"Just give it a few days—maybe a couple of weeks before reinvesting," Will cautioned him. "Please, Mr. Willet. I would advise you to sit back and watch for a time. If it rises and stabilizes, then perhaps it is all right to invest again. If not, you will be safe from the risk inherent with this sort of system," Will cautioned him.

Mr. Willet grumbled angrily as he left the city hall.

Several days later, he returned, running into Will's office. "Mayor Linden, something has happened." The older, gray-haired man wiped the dripping sweat from his brow, gasping for breath.

Will looked up from a stack of paperwork, rather confused.

Mr. Willet hurried over to a radio near Will's desk and turned the dial. The words being spoken across the radio waves were clearly an attempt to bolster what was already a lost cause. The market had not only crashed, it had completely collapsed.

A heavy weight seemed to settle over the shoulders of the young mayor. He sat back in his chair and sighed heavily. The American economy had destabilized. There was little to stop its descent.

The newscaster's voice blared loudly into the room, the devastation apparent even in his hope-strewn words. "I owe you an apology," Mr. Willet said humbly.

Will waved it off. "Fred, it's alright. It's hard to see such a thing coming, but what will happen to the nation?" He shook his head. "How will we ever recover?"

Mayor Linden closed the office early. As he made his way home, he saw the town in a way he had never seen it before. He had always seen need, but now, there would be so much more. Some of the people were already aware, and some had yet to hear the calamitous news. A group stood congregated inside Mr. Willet's store, listening to the financial report.

Will slowly walked home. It would be hard, he knew, but Pravda would be alright. There was little excess in the town, but what they had, they mostly owned. There would be devastation across the nation, but he had high hopes that somehow, they would make it through.

Bonnie greeted him at the door, unsurprised to see him returning early. She had heard the news. They stood for several minutes in the doorway, holding each other. The children ran about, playing and laughing, innocent to turmoil in the world that would soon be theirs to overcome.

Will looked around the small front room at his family and

soon found himself on the floor playing with the children. When night fell and the children were tucked into bed, he and Bonnie sat down to list the needs of the town under the impact of the surrounding ruin of the financial market.

Words of hope and encouragement drifted from the radios. For the first few weeks, it seemed as though everyone was determined to believe the smooth voice that floated through the air, but as Christmas approached, the nation and even Pravda had seen the results of the stock market crash. Resources became far less attainable and beautiful gifts wrapped beneath the trees were few to be seen.

Employment became a difficult situation, but businesses issued a trade option instead of dealing solely in cash and were able to pay their workers with food and other items, though minimally at best as work hours decreased.

The men of Pravda gathered on the first Friday and Saturday in December to cut firewood for all who were in need. Joseph Linden, Will's oldest son, was nearly eight and was anxious to join the excursion. Will bundled him up and together they worked to bring in the firewood. The men all helped keep an eye on little Joseph as he walked about, collecting sticks and pinecones which he added to the wagons being loaded with thick logs.

Bonnie organized a collection for any items that families felt they could donate. She, along with several other women, arranged the donations on long tables inside the city building for the community members to look through and select whatever their families might need.

When all of the families had gone through the items, Bonnie and Will were surprised to see several scraps of cloth left behind. Some were just bits and pieces, but a few were larger—discarded curtains and frayed clothing.

That evening at the community Christmas dinner, Bonnie asked for volunteers who would be willing to help provide Christmas to other families outside their community. The stacks of cloth had been set on a table at the front of the room. Nearly every woman in the room volunteered to make several dolls and a few volunteered to make quilts. Some of the men offered to carve wooden toys for the children, having already created several similar gifts for their own families.

Time was growing short. Christmas was less than two weeks away. With fewer work hours to put in for their employers, many of the men and women were free to gather in the town hall to work on their different projects.

Christmas Eve was a joyful day throughout Pravda. The items were collected and a count was made. There were four quilts, seven aprons, forty-two little dolls, twelve wooden Model-T's, five wooden swords, seven carved flutes, and a variety of tiny carved animals. A few coats had also been patched and repaired to be handed out.

A few people helped load the items into a sleigh on top of the large stacks of firewood and sacks of home-grown food. Will, Bonnie, little Joseph, six-year-old Emily, and the twins—Jacob and Lilly—were all bundled up at the front of the sleigh. A second sleigh carrying Mr. and Mrs. Wilson followed behind, bearing a few extra sacks of potatoes.

The journey to Bloomfield was long in the cold winter air, but the children were excited and laughed and sang nearly the entire way with Will and Bonnie joining in the merriment. They arrived in Bloomfield near dusk. Bonnie took the children inside to warm up.

Will, Mayor Ringwald and Mr. Wilson carried all the items inside and sorted through them. Mayor Ringwald, with Amelia's help, directed which items to put into which sacks. Soon they were reloading the sleighs. By late evening, all the gifts had been delivered and the happy trio of men returned to a simple yet delightful feast at the Ringwald home.

There was little extravagance that year as resources had been shifted to help those who needed warmth and food more than gifts, but the children each still had a gift or two to open. They spent the rest of the day taking a sleigh ride, building snow bunnies, sledding down Meadow's Hill and retiring back into the warmth at dark to tell stories and drink hot chocolate by the fire. Joseph and Emily and Jacob Bronson and his family spent most of the day enjoying the festivities at the Ringwald home.

Joseph and Emily stayed that night in an upstairs bedroom. All the children fell asleep wrapped in little quilts before the fireplace. Small heads with tousled red and brown hair poked out from the folds of the blankets. Will and Bonnie slept near them beside a beautiful pine Christmas tree decorated with many twinkling lights.

Chapter 36

IN THE EARLIER WEEKS weeks leading up to Christmas, a new standard had been set for the citizens of Pravda. Unsure of how long the hard times would last, they determined to work together to get through them. There wasn't much that could be counted as surplus, but those who had a little extra reached out to those who were in need. The unity of the town became evident as baskets of food, warm coats, blankets, and other necessities found their way onto doorsteps. As spring came, everyone worked, helping in the fields, planting gardens, and sharing what they no longer needed with those who would have had to go without.

Each Saturday was fishing day, and most of the town set off to the rivers to build a supply of meat for their storage. Will showed the children how to fish without a string and a hook. It took several of the children most of the day to get their first fish, but once they had made the initial catch, they began pulling fish from the river so fast that they often brought in more than their parents. The fish were then filleted and the larger pieces were set out to dry. The smaller pieces were gathered into pots along with whatever vegetables were available. Every citizen in Pravda came together in the evenings for a warm dinner of chowder, which sometimes included fresh-baked bread on the side.

It was a delightful time despite the chaos and the panic in the world around them. Yet things were far from perfect, even in Pravda. The tension of the nation could not have been entirely avoided. Still, most of the citizens living in that little town had determined to make the best of it, and by working together, they realized that there had hardly been a happier time.

The nights grew warmer. There were dances and musical performances each Saturday night in the town square following the community chowder feast. Occasionally, a man would journey in on the railroad looking for work. They were broken men, some very young and some quite old. Though there was little employment to be offered, each stranger left with a stomach full of soup and some biscuits for their travels.

Will watched as the stream of railroad travelers became increasingly more downcast and discouraged throughout the spring. At times, he found it easy to forget the dismal circumstances in the world around Pravda. And yet, with every face that passed through the town, so little hope left in their eyes, he again saw his father. He knew their pain. It broke his heart each time another was turned away.

May settled in with heavy, pouring rain drenching the countryside. The wind had been blowing especially hard one evening when a young father, holding hands with a small boy, walked into Pravda, both wet clear through their ragged clothing. They were invited into the town hall and given a warm bowl of soup and a slice of fresh bread.

Will approached the man and boy as they ate.

The man stood. "I don't suppose you would have any employment to which I could offer myself?" the father asked, hardly daring to look Will in the eye. The small boy looked up, a mouthful of bread and a pleading look in his eyes. Will's heart ached.

"What is your name?" Will asked the man.

"Henry. Henry Ivie. This is my son, Carter."

"What skills do you have to offer?" Will asked.

The man looked up, a faint glimmer of hope appearing in his face. "I can build. I can fix almost anything, and any skill I don't have, I would be more than willing to learn. I promise I would do my best, and I wouldn't need much—just a place to stay and enough to eat."

"He works hard, sir. Papa's a good man," said the little boy. He turned back to his soup quickly, embarrassed for speaking up, his head bowed.

"Well, I suppose we may be able to find something for you, if you don't mind being paid in food and other basic necessities. That is all we can offer," Will said.

The man clasped Will's hand in both his own. "I cannot thank you enough! I will not disappoint you." He drew in a deep breath. "What would you like me to do? When would you want me to start? I'll start tonight, if you like," he said eagerly. He stood, grabbing his satchel.

"Not just yet," Will smiled and put a hand on the man's shoulder. "Enjoy your meal while it's warm. We'll need to build you a home first, if you are to stay a while. Do you have any other family, or is it just the two of you?" Will asked.

"It's just us, sir," Henry Ivie replied.

"Well, I will see about securing some land within the town on which you will be able to build a small home in exchange for your labor. Would that suit you?" Will asked.

"Yes, sir! I could ask for nothing more, and thank you." The man looked down at his son. Both had tears in their eyes as they embraced.

Will left them to eat. He found Farmer Merril with Mrs.

Merril just finishing their soup.

"Mr. Merril, I have a proposition for you that I wonder if you might be willing to consider. May I join you?" Will asked.

"Of course, Mayor. What can I do for you?" asked the old farmer.

"Your dry grain field on the west end of town has not been used to grow crops since we've experienced a couple of dry summers. Would it be possible for the city to purchase that land? We can't offer much financially at this time, but we may be able to work out an exchange. Perhaps we could provide the labor to create a canal to divert water to your other fields, if it is something you are interested in considering. What we can't pay now, we would owe to you when resources are available. I can give you time to think over it, if you like," Will said, standing to leave.

Farmer Merrill stood as well. "No, no. I think it is a fine idea, and with all you've done to pull the town through the present situation, I'm certain whatever you have in mind would be quite satisfactory. When would you care to secure the land?"

"As soon as possible. We are going to put it to use immediately," Will said. He glanced at the far table where the newcomers were just finishing their meal. "Would you be willing to meet even now? I'll gather everyone who would be involved and we'll work up the sale."

"That would suit me. It's difficult to sell land, but if we could work the building of a canal into the deal, it would be a great benefit to the farm."

Will called a meeting that evening. Before they had adjourned, the land had been purchased by the city with a unanimous vote from the trustees.

Early Monday morning, those who were not otherwise employed headed out to the forest. Mr. Wilson directed the men on tree selection and Henry Ivie helped to prepare the wood. They spent nearly a week gathering and stripping the logs. Will made a deal with Mr. Johnson, who owned the sawmill. It was a simple barter. The mill had fallen into disrepair and Henry was more than happy to offer to fix it up once he had built himself a place to live.

The house, which was built on the corner of those few barren acres, was tiny, but it offered protection from the weather and was sufficient for the Ivies. Henry Ivie began working to repair the lumber mill. The young father and son soon became an integrated part of the community, grateful to be welcomed and happy to have work and a place to stay.

With the changes brought on by welcoming Henry Ivie and his son, Carter, the amount of work to be done grew. The city employed men to put in a canal system to water the fields. Will also directed that another split in the channel be directed toward the barren grain field that had been purchased by the city.

The town seemed glad for a new project and many pitched in. The canal was nearly complete before mid-June. The water from the river northwest of Pravda was channeled into the canal down to the farms and to the vacant field now purchased by the city. Will portioned the land into two sections, one slightly larger than the other.

Several more men were invited to remain in Pravda as they arrived off the trains looking for work. Will organized a group to dig trenches in a grid across the smaller section of the town's newly-purchased land. Seeds were gathered—some bought with minimal funds—and an extensive garden was planted.

Henry Ivie finished his work on the mill by late June. Will gave him the assignment of overseeing the building of several more small houses on the larger section of land beside the town garden. For their work, the men were promised shelter and enough wood and food to get through the coming winter.

Work at this time proved to be more than just a means for obtaining basic necessities. It gave the men a sense of purpose and value and the chance to bring their families together again. Many sent for their wives and children once they had steady work and a place to live. As Pravda grew, more projects were designed and carried out to match the need and to keep the town moving forward.

The growing number of children had quickly overcrowded the small schoolhouse. Lessons for the older students were relocated into the town hall and a second teacher was hired to work with the younger children. Two more rooms were soon added onto the schoolhouse and a larger town hall was in the process of being erected.

The lumber mill was once again in full operation. Several more small homes were built as more families came to settle in Pravda. So far, Will had brought in two other builders. He had also hired men to dig, plant, and help at the lumber and grain mills. A few necessities such as cloth, nails, window panes, and glass bottles were still a little hard to come by. The excess that was produced from the land or in the mills was sold in other towns whenever possible to pay for things that could not be traded for in Pravda.

Everyone worked hard, even the children, and yet there was still time to celebrate—to dance and to enjoy life.

Thanksgiving that year was especially enjoyable. It wasn't as fancy as in years past, but because the entire town had worked throughout the year to make it possible, they enjoyed the feast together.

Preparations for Christmas began once again. The men

went out to the forest to collect wood for the winter while the women gathered and cleaned all the donated items.

Making use of everything as they did, there was little left to be collected, but there was still plenty of room for creative gifts to be given. When the needs of Pravda had been met, the town set about making items for those passing through on the railroad.

Furs from the previous hunting season were turned into coats and the extra leather was used to mend worn-out shoes. Hats, scarves, socks and gloves were knitted. Work and lodging were given to as many as was possible, and those who were sent on their way left with a good meal and warmer clothing.

On Christmas Eve, nearly everyone had gathered in the new town hall where a warm fire blazed in the large stone fire-place. The building was not yet entirely complete, but the outer shell was finished and the flooring nailed into place. There were soups, biscuits, potatoes and an occasional mincemeat pie arranged on mismatched tables which had been set back against the wall. Everyone talked and laughed and sang carols as they ate their fill.

The events of the evening had nearly drawn to a close when Mr. Willet burst through the door. He and several other men shuffled in under the weight of heavy sacks. Will welcomed the men as they brought their load to the front of the room.

Will stood in front of the fire with the bulging sacks at his feet. "Tonight we have a special gift for every citizen of Pravda. It has been a long year, but through these last twelve months, I have seen the remarkable courage, love, compassion and camaraderie you have extended to neighbors and friends—and even to strangers who have become friends." Will saw Henry Ivie lift his glass and nod in humble gratitude at these words.

Will continued, "We could ask for nothing more this

Christmas than for the wonderful friendships we have formed and the strength and unity of our small town." The children were edging closer, curious as they stared at the large sacks. "But since we already have that friendship," Will continued, "it seemed as though there might be room for just one other gift."

Will bent down and opened one of the sacks, still speaking. "We were able to trade some of the goods produced by the town for something we could not grow ourselves. To bring a little light into the cold, dark winter," Will stood up holding a beautiful round orange in front of him, "we have ordered a single orange for every person in Pravda. Before you leave, please, feel free to select one with my appreciation for the work you have all done to get each other through this trying year. Have a merry Christmas."

The hall erupted with cheers. As several adults joined together in singing Christmas carols, every person came forward one by one, starting with the children, to receive an orange. The scent of sweet citrus filled the entire hall as a few oranges were peeled and shared around, the others set aside to be shared and enjoyed later.

A chill breeze drifting through the room caught Will's attention. He looked up to see a small boy slip in through the doors at the back of the town hall. The boy looked to be about his son Joseph's age—perhaps eight years old. The boy was dressed in many layers, all filthy and ragged. His arms were wrapped tightly around himself as he silently made his way toward the fire.

The boy stopped abruptly. He seemed fixed in place. Will followed his gaze. The young boy watched intently as a family passed around an orange, each taking one slice. The boy was still for several minutes, just watching, his eyes longing and sad. At last, he turned away and drew near the fire where he sat, nearly hidden in the shadows.

Will picked up an orange and slipped it into his pocket. He left Mr. Willet the task of distributing the remaining oranges. Will passed through the crowd to the buffet table and prepared a large bowl full of steaming soup by which he set a biscuit. He carried the food as he made his way over to the fire. The boy looked up when Will sat beside him.

"I'm sorry, sir," said the boy nervously. "Is it alright if I stay a little longer? It's been awful cold. My feet were nearly frozen and my hands too. Please let me warm up a bit. I promise, I won't be no trouble." The boy shook his head to emphasize the point then wiped his cold red nose on his sleeve.

Will smiled. "You are more than welcome to enjoy the fire. I just thought you might enjoy some food as well." He set the soup and the biscuit in front of him.

The boy reached out slowly. "For me, really?"

"Yes, you are hungry, aren't you?" Will asked.

"Yes, sir!" The boy pulled the bowl toward himself and began eating as quickly as he could bring the spoon to his mouth. "It's wonderful, sir. Truly wonderful," he said, his mouth still full of food.

Will sat back and watched the boy eat until the boy slowed a little. "What's your name?" he asked.

"I'm Lawrence." said the boy. Will watched as Lawrence slipped the biscuit into his pocket.

"Lawrence, where is your family?" Will asked.

"They's all gone, except my brother," Lawrence said. "There was an accident when I was four. We was living with our Aunt, but she couldn't take care of us no more. We been looking for work. We can work real hard."

"I see, but where's your brother?" Will asked.

Lawrence went quiet. He hesitated a moment before he

spoke. "I don't know if he would want me to say."

Will leaned forward confidentially. "I promise, I only want to help. Whatever you need, I'll try to help you get it."

Lawrence chewed the last few bites of potato from his soup slowly. "Well," he said after he swallowed, "we don't got no place to stay, so he's out looking around, trying to see if there is an empty barn or maybe an old house we could sleep in for the night. We don't mean no harm," he added, seeing the concerned expression on Will's face.

Will smiled. "I know you don't. Come to think of it, I have something for you and your brother." He reached into his pocket and pulled out the orange. "And I believe we can find you a place to stay—somewhere warmer than a barn, if you like."

Lawrence stared with wonder. He looked up at Will questioningly. Will nodded. The boy carefully took the orange into his cold, red hands then raised it to his nose and smelled its sweet fragrance. He closed his eyes for a moment and sighed. He tucked the orange against his chest, cradling it tightly to him.

"Why don't you go find your brother and bring him here. There's more soup and plenty of biscuits." Will said. "Then we'll look for a warm place for you to stay."

Lawrence nodded excitedly, still cradling his orange. He ran back through the crowd and disappeared outside. Ten minutes later, he was back with a boy who looked to be about twelve years old. Lawrence pulled his brother to the table and pointed to the soup and biscuits. The older boy hesitated, looking around nervously. Lawrence spotted Will and pointed him out to his brother. Will came over to the table where the boys stood looking over the food.

"Get yourself some food and come warm up by the fire. I'm sure you've had a bit of a journey getting here. What is your name?" Will asked.

Lawrence nudged his brother who at last spoke. "I'm Andrew," he said. The boy held out filthy hand, feigning the confidence of a young boy forced too early to try and become a man.

Will shook the boy's hand. "Welcome, Andrew. Lawrence, maybe help him get some food then go enjoy the fire. I'll make arrangements for you to have a place to stay."

Will caught Bonnie's eye. She had been watching Will as he talked with the boys. She came to join him where he stood.

"You don't even need to ask. They are more than welcome to stay with us," she told him. She slipped her arm around his waist as they stood watching the boys.

Lawrence had a second helping of soup, grinning the whole time. Andrew nervously watched everyone around him. Both boys finished their soup and returned their dishes to the table. Lawrence began prancing up and down. Will was close enough to hear their conversation.

"You'll never guess what he gave me! And it's just for us, all our own! I'm sure of it," Lawrence said. "Look!" From somewhere in the folds of his ragged clothing, Lawrence pulled out the beautiful round orange which he slipped into Andrew's hands.

Andrew stared at it. "It's so beautiful," he said at last. The two boys sat together, side by side, staring at the orange. Neither showed any desire to peel it. They took turns lifting it to their small noses, enjoying in the sweet scent.

Chairs and tables were put away and the remaining food was packaged up to go home with the families that were most in need.

Lawrence and Andrew looked uncertainly at Will who made his way toward them as the fire was put out for the night.

"If it is alright with the two of you," Will said as he approached, "my wife and I would like to invite you to come stay with us."

Lawrence looked at Andrew and nodded fervently. Andrew stood. "We would like that very much, sir."

"Come along then. Let's head home," Will said. He ushered the boys over to where Bonnie and the children stood waiting near the main doors of the town hall.

"Bonnie, dear, the boys have agreed to stay with us," Will said.

"Wonderful," she said and nodded with a smile. "Come, along now. It's time to get some rest."

Upon their arrival back at the Linden home, Will immediately set about getting a tub of water heated for the boys. Bonnie went to work finding more suitable clothing for the two brothers. It was nearly midnight before the work was done, but at last the children were all tucked into bed, including the two young boys who lay wrapped in wool blankets near the fire.

Chapter 37

CHRISTMAS CELEBRATIONS came and went. By the new year, Lawrence and Andrew began to realize that the Lindens had no plans for them to leave any time soon. Will purchased each of them a pair of shoes with the little bit of money he had managed to scrape up. Bonnie acquired some thick brown cloth and set about to sew them each a new set of clothing for school. On his way to work, Will took them to the schoolhouse and introduced them to Miss Faux, who still taught as schoolmistress.

Spring came followed by a warm summer. The boys were now a regular part of the town. They took turns helping with the fishing and hunting as well as working in the gardens and fields. They labored hard alongside Will and little Joseph Linden, but they also found plenty of time to enjoy a good game of baseball as often as Will could get one organized in the town square. Joseph and Lawrence were only four months apart and spent nearly all their time together, quickly becoming quite infamous as the town pranksters, egged on by their Aunt Emily each time she came for a visit.

It was a hot, dry year. The water diversion through the canal helped the crops survive through the burning late summer heat, for which Farmer Merril never lost an occasion to thank Will for having initiated the waterway. Again came the harvest followed by another long winter.

Resources grew harder to obtain with each passing year. Some members of the town occasionally indulged in self-pity for the things they lacked, but as it only brought on selfishness that helped no one around them, Will continually drew their attention back to the many things they did have and the need to find joy and contentment even when the challenges around them at times seemed insurmountable.

It was difficult for anyone to truly complain to their good mayor, knowing how much he had given to the town and to the two boys who might easily have been left to fend for themselves. Will had unwittingly set a new standard. When trouble arose, his encouragement for civility and understanding was quick to reunite the town.

When, on occasion, there came demands for loans to be repaid—from both within and beyond the town—Will refused to give up until terms had been negotiated. There were a couple of times when an outside bank refused negotiation. The first time, Will stepped in. He used the bit of savings he had gathered during the last few years to pay off the required debt, as there was nowhere else for the family to live. The second time, Mr. Willet, who had heard of the situation, came unexpectedly with the cash in hand to cover the debt.

Each day was filled with hard labor, but the busy life helped the weeks and months to pass quickly by. Overall, everyone found themselves quite content. The stream of men passing through their town looking for work served as a sorrowful reminder of how much the residents of Pravda really had in comparison to the poor souls for whom they were unable to do more.

Two more children were born into the Linden home over

the next three years—a boy, Zachary, followed by little Eliza. The house that had once seemed too large now seemed quite small. Will spent many hours after work adding on two more bedrooms for their growing family. How it surprised him when he often returned home from his office to find that a good portion had been completed while he was away, each board fitted perfectly with the skill of a master builder.

Another year passed and several more. The nation still suffered the distress of the financial collapse—a depression so pervasive that it rocked nearly the entire world. It seemed as though it might never end and that there could never be a darker time, but if only that might have been true.

News began to trickle in: unrest in Europe, a new war, the Axis powers rising and death and destruction in the many countries that had been invaded. At first there were only rumors, but it could not be doubted that something was terribly wrong overseas. Still, the United States was once again determined to stay neutral.

Yet, for all its devastation in the countries that had fallen prey to the new war, the worldwide economy seemed to be slowly improving as requisitions were made from both sides of the conflict for machinery, bullets, and cargo.

Will watched with trepidation as the snowball effect began, rolling across the entire world, sucking one country then another into the gloom and terror that accompanied the war. Feelings of anti-interventionism in the States had, for now, kept their soldiers home. The deaths from The Great War were comparatively few across the United States in relation to the rest of Europe, but the painful memories from those casualties were neither foreign nor desirable in the least.

Yet, for all its neutrality, America could not have avoided the conflict.

On December 7th, 1941, the world was rocked by an unprecedented attack against a neutral party. Japan, afraid that the United States would eventually find it necessary to slow the Asian offense in the Pacific Theater, sought to destroy much of the American naval and air power.

The death toll rose quickly on Pearl Harbor beach. Within barely a few hours, over 2,400 American lives had been claimed by Japanese bombers. In the scope of the attack, nearly two hundred aircraft were destroyed and the Navy fleet stationed at Pearl Harbor sustained formidable damage. The United States had little choice. Opposition to joining the war disappeared in that unforgivable attack. America entered the second World War.

The day the announcement was made, many of the young men of Pravda enlisted—Joseph Linden, Lawrence and Andrew the first among them. The boys had not even hesitated. All three enlisted in the Air Force. Their patriotism called them to their duty. They, like their father, could not refuse the call.

Memories flooded over Will. It was too much to bear as he imagined his sons being subjected to the horrors that he well knew lurked upon those battlefields.

The first few days after Joseph, Lawrence and Andrew had departed, Will disappeared for hours at a time into the woods. He found himself on his knees pleading for the world, for the nation and for his sons. He returned late, cold and exhausted each evening, broken and afraid for what he stood to lose. He often visited the gnarled oak tree, kneeling before his father's grave, begging his father to somehow strengthen him now. So much had already been required of him from early in his life, but this was far more than he could bear. How could he ever endure the anguish that would come if he were required to give up his sons as well?

The months passed slowly. Pravda listened insatiably to the

news as often as they found time away from work. Thirty-two men and boys had left Pravda to fight in the war. It was impossible to pretend that they would all come home.

The first devastating letter, edged in black, came to the Willet home just before Christmas the following year. Charles Willet, the shopkeeper's son, the bookworm who had helped so many people with their groceries, the man who had married and had fathered two sweet little girls, the same man who had enlisted in an earnest desire to do his duty, had been killed in combat. For Pravda, the tragedy had just begun.

Eli Merrill was the second whose life was lost. Eli was Jason's eldest son—Farmer Merrill's grandson. Each death broke the heart of everyone throughout the town. The bond of unity had become their greatest strength, and yet it brought unimaginable sorrow. In Pravda, there wasn't one son, grandson, nephew or father lost that the town did not mourn together while reaching out to support each other in their grief.

Jason Merrill died in combat not long after. His wife, now widowed, and having lost one son already was left with only three sons, two of whom had already enlisted and the youngest alone remained home.

The war was dark and left none unscathed. Through the next year, three more letters were delivered and all of Pravda wept.

The first was delivered to Miss Faux—her only brother had been lost in the Pacific aboard a ship that had been sunk by a kamikaze pilot. The second arrived at a small home on the edge of town. Deputy Cornelius was now gone. Newly married that spring, he had no children, but his tender wife was devastated.

The third letter was delivered to the Linden home. It bore three names. The gratitude expressed for their service by the United States military brought no consolation. Will fell to his knees and wept with Bonnie beside him.

MIA—as had been written on the letter to Deputy Cornelius's wife. Not even a body to be returned. Lost over enemy territory. The plane fallen in flames.

The letter outlined the importance of the mission in which the aircraft had been destroyed, carrying seven men including Lawrence, Jacob and Joseph. They had served honorably and had given their all, lost in the European Theater.

Will could bear no more. He held Bonnie close that night as they both wept until morning. They had not yet had the courage to break the news to the rest of the children. The next morning, Bonnie helped Will to pack.

"Just please come home if you can," she pleaded. "I know you have to go, but please, try to come home." She held him tight. Will kissed her tenderly and held her to him. The whistle blew. The train was preparing to depart from the station. Mayor Ringwald and Amelia had come to bid farewell. They would be staying with Bonnie and the children for a time until Bonnie would be able to manage again on her own.

Bonnie tried to smile as she waved, but instead she turned away, refusing to look back as Will boarded the train. The wheels creaked and the train lurched. It began to pull away from the station platform. Bonnie suddenly turned back, wiping the tears from her face. From his open window, Will heard her strong yet gentle voice calling out, "I love you, William Linden. Please, make it home safe."

The train gained speed and Pravda disappeared from sight.

Chapter 38

CASUALTIES MOUNTED HIGH on both sides, and yet there were far more gruesome stories reaching the Allies. Many doubted the rumors, but Will found himself deeply troubled at the consistency of the reports. Will was soon aboard ship, heading back across the sea to Europe.

My Dearest Bonnie,

Even as I departed, I questioned whether I was wrong to consider leaving you, especially in such a time as this when our hearts are in so much need of comfort, yet, the anguish and the pain we feel is compounded with each battle in which the sons of many tender parents are left broken on the battlefield, never to return.

If I could, I would give everything I possess, even my life, to save our sons safely home, but it is too late and it can never be, so I must do everything in my power to save the sons of mothers and fathers who would do just as I, if only they were here.

It seems as though there is no limit to the cruelties men are willing to heap upon others if it were to seem in the least way profitable. How can mankind be so savage? We hear such reports that are beyond comprehen-

sion. At moments I despair that, even should we conquer this over-whelming evil, another will rise up in its place, more terrible than before. It seems to be the trend throughout the whole of history — never learning the value of humanity beyond exploitation for an infinitely smaller gain. I do not understand how this can be, yet I am ready to give my life to find a way to bring it to an end.

Please forgive me. I must aid the Allies in bringing an end to this war. As reports of the devastation and inhumanity reach us, I feel an anger so incomprehensible that I fear it will change me, that the darkness of the world will find its way into my soul. Help me to remember all that is good in the world. Help me to see a time beyond war, murder, tyranny and death.

How I wish that I had words of comfort to write to you, as never before have you needed them more than now. All I can do is pray for you as I do always. Though I am not there to hold you, I hope that somehow you will feel the comfort and love I would give to you if I were there.

Your devoted husband,

William Linden

My Dear Bonnie,

We have landed, though I am unable to tell you of our location, but we will be moving toward the battle within the week. I have no fear of losing my life but for the pain I know it would cause you and the children.

I am confident in the justification of our cause, and my courage never falters. War throughout the whole of history has shaped the world. If those pursuing that which is unjust were to win, then a world full of sor-

row and suffering is all that would be left to our children. It must not be so. The joy I have known in the freedom of the United States is owed to those who have fought before me, as I must fight now.

Bonnie, I cannot endeavor to tell you the sorrow I feel when I think of the possibility that I may never return to hold you once more. No sweeter joy could fill me than that which sweeps over me with each memory of you. I may walk into darkness, but still I carry your light by which to see the hope and the good in the world around me.

I know these things are hard to endure, but I would rather die for a cause that is noble than to allow this evil that now engulfs the world to gain an even greater advantage.

I hope for nothing more than for an end to the conflict and to soon find myself home in your arms. Yet, if it so be that I am never to return, know that I love you with all my soul. If ever there is a way for heaven to touch the earth and for fallen men to walk among those they love, then I will be there, tenderly kissing your cheek with each sunrise and guarding you through the darkness as you sleep. If that ultimate sacrifice is to be required of me, then I will wait on the other side of this mortal veil, and when at last it is time, my dearest Bonnie, I will guide you home.

My love forever yours,

William Linden

Will's letter arrived at the Linden home on a cold winter morning.

The next day, another letter was delivered, its edges marked black.

Chapter 39

THE MAIL CARRIER HAD COME around to gather the outgoing mail as Will received the order to prepare his men to march out. Will sealed the letter and handed it over. He surveyed his men, huddled in small groups for warmth. A dark foreboding wrenched at his soul. Will retired to his tent and bowed his head in fervent and silent prayer. Then, rising, he gave the order.

It was a long march. The storms were bitter with a penetrating, icy wind that froze the damp clothing to the men's skin and chilled their weary feet inside their boots. They marched with pride, with determination and courage, yet on every face was the expectation of death, the dread of life soon to depart. They knew. They were their motherland's sacrifice.

The men's boots grew heavier with each step, fear begging their courage to forfeit into retreat. Each breath drew them nearer to an ultimate destination, the end of every dream they had once imagined for the future, severed unforgivably and unchangeably.

Far in the distance came a rigid humming. It was the anthem of death. The nearer their approach, the more the sound evolved into blasts of artillery and rapid gunfire broken momentarily by explosions and the anguished cries of men. It was the symphony of death, orchestrated by the least humane, the most animal among all the creatures of the earth. It was the sound of the greatest and most unfair of all barters made—human life in exchange for power.

The men they joined at the front lines were weary, wind-beaten, discouraged and emotionally defeated. The dead lay in long lines, hair and skin crystalized with ice, their filthy uniforms soaked with blood.

Will looked at his own troop of good men. Their faces were ashen, wide eyes staring straight ahead, muscles tense as they continued their march. Johnny Alton, a farmer's son from Kansas and a brand new father, lifted his head a little with each step. He was near enough that Will could hear his continued encouragement to those around him.

Then, unexpectedly, Johnny took a deep breath and began to sing, *"On Jordan's stormy banks I stand…"* The other men at first just listened, grateful for the small distraction. *"…and cast a wishful eye…"*

Slowly his voice grew in strength. Others joined in and their courage swelled with the power of the song which they knew would likely be their final anthem.

"…to Canaan's fair and happy land where my possessions lie."

The sound of their footfalls faded as the din around them grew, and still they sung.

"…I am bound for the promised land…"

The lines of the fallen grew around them. Will felt his voice giving the commands and he saw the men respond. It seemed as though they were buried beneath a body of water, trudging in slow motion, already half dead.

"…I am bound for the promised land."

Hopeless, lost, buried and drifting. The men raised their rifles, ducking for shelter as shells exploded around them. It was a bloodbath, worse than Will had never before seen.

"…Oh, who will come and go with me?…"

The final scores of the lives once lived began to be counted. The first explosion near the ranks claimed two, immediately followed by artillery fire and another explosion. Foxholes became a confusion of those who breathed and those who had just breathed their last. Blood dripped as red as poppies, turning black as it mixed into the icy mud of its weeping mother earth.

"…I am bound for the promised land."

Each moment pulsed in slow motion—fire, explosions, screams, death. Always death. The brother fell, the father, the son. They had come to renew the ranks in the devastation, but their task was futile as they were condemned to execution. Johnny Alton never ceased to sing courage into the men around him until a bullet ripped straight through his heart. He fell lifeless upon the cold, hard ground. Death tightened its grip, the steel vise purging the last dream as blood poured from the gaping wound.

Will pressed on with his men, nearing the tree line that might help protect the soldiers who remained, returning fire as they ran. Tanks blasted holes in the ground from both sides.

The battalion had just made it into a bit of forested land when an explosion jolted the entire unit. Will's body jerked sideways. He slammed into a tree and crumpled to the ground. His breath grew shallow. His head throbbed and hot blood trickled down his frozen face. Blood pooled around his right leg. He felt the strength his fading and his vision growing dim. Somewhere near him, Will could hear one of his men screaming in agony.

"Paul!" Will attempted to call out, but his voice was faint. His breath came in strained gasps. "Paul!"

Will struggled to push himself to his feet. He was shaky but able to walk. He listened for the sound of his men. Will's legs buckled and he toppled over. Blood stained thick through his uniform. He managed to stand again, disoriented, sick and weak.

"Paul!" his voice rasped in a desperate cry. Will pressed on, stumbling as blackness blotted out his vision. He fell over bodies, roots, and holes—each time rising again and walking further, forgetting after a time what it was that he was searching for. The sound of artillery fire grew distant, and all he could remember was the name "Paul" still on his lips. Will crumpled to the earth.

Chapter 40

WILL SAW ONLY DARKNESS surrounding a small dancing flame near his face. He was cold. His body screamed in agony. The flame faded from his vision and he sank into darkness once more.

A cold breeze fretted across his skin and a tiny strip of sunlight tumbled through dark, drab curtains. Will woke, his vision still blurred. The pain in his right leg and the pounding in his head continued to pulse with each heartbeat. Small footsteps pattered somewhere near him. He heard voices and footsteps growing closer. Will tried to move, but the smallest change sent his body into convulsions.

A gentle, wrinkled hand pressed softly on his chest. Will found himself looking into the face of a small gray-haired woman. Beside her stood a young boy. The woman spoke, but Will was uncertain if his brain had been too damaged to make word comprehension difficult or if she was speaking in a language that was foreign to him, but her intent was easily understood. "Rest." she seemed to say. "You are injured. You must rest."

The woman turned to the boy and spoke a few words. The boy ran off. He reappeared a moment later with a bowl that curled with steam. He handed it to the woman and sat down, watching anxiously.

The woman lifted Will's head, carefully touching only the left side. She then raised a thick wooden spoon to his lips. The liquid was warm and felt pleasant in Will's mouth, but each time he tried to swallow, the broth burst from his lips and dripped down the side of his face. Patiently the woman tried again and again, and a small trickle began to seep down his throat.

Exhausted, Will fell asleep and didn't awaken until the room had grown dark. He heard again the patter of footsteps. Soon after, the elderly woman approached with a bowl of broth. Little made it down to his stomach, but it was more than he had managed before and Will found great relief in the small portion that settled inside of him.

Sunrises and sunsets were lost as Will slept and woke only long enough to swallow small sips of broth. He tried to speak—tried to move, but each time he soon found his mind sinking back into the darkness from which he had awakened not long before. It had been perhaps many days, or even weeks—Will could not tell. Strength slowly began to flow back into his muscles. He woke for longer periods, and after swallowing what broth he could, he lay back, weak and tired but unwilling to sleep. The young boy sat in a chair beside him, talking with hardly a breath to halt his words, sometimes reading to Will from tattered books.

Will was certain now that the language was quite different from English, but he tried to listen and tried to understand. Desperate thoughts overwhelmed him and plagued his mind. He had to ask questions, to know of his men, to know of the war, to somehow express his gratitude to these strangers who watched over him were nursing him back to health.

Will struggled to sit up and push the covers away. He was anxious to test his strength. His right arm would not respond. The boy ran to Will, urging for him to lie down. Will tried to motion that he would like to sit up, but the boy again shook his head and pressed his hand against Will's chest, speaking rapidly in his foreign tongue. Will took a breath then tried again, almost falling over.

The boy shook his head sadly. He placed both hands on Will's chest until Will stopped resisting and lay still. The boy then raised the blanket covering Will's right side.

Will felt himself grow faint. He saw for the first time the price he had paid that fateful day. A bandaged stump wrapped with bandages hung uselessly at his side. The pain on the right side of his body pounded through his veins from head to foot—even, it seemed, in the arm that was no longer there. Will motioned for the boy to lift the blanket from his right leg. The boy did. Will sighed in relief. Though bandaged, the entire leg remained attached. Will attempted to raise his leg a little. The pain was unbearable, but the leg responded. Will pulled his left arm from beneath the blanket and fingered the bandages wrapped around his head. He paused over his ear and pointed. The boy shook his head. Will nodded that he understood.

Again, the boy beckoned for Will to rest, but Will had one more question. He pulled the blanket back from his chest enough to show a part of his uniform. He pointed at the uniform and then out through the window. The boy shook his head slowly. He pointed at Will's uniform and held up a single finger, which he again pointed at Will.

His men had fallen. Will lay back. The boy indicated that he should sleep then quietly left the room.

Will wept.

Chapter 41

SEVERAL WEEKS PASSED. Will struggled to remain in bed as his body healed. The boy, Peter, had stayed by his side and diligently worked to teach Will to read and speak the language of that region with the help of his older brother, David, who came in occasionally when he was not needed elsewhere. Will discovered that the distraction of learning helped him to put aside both the physical and emotional struggles that burdened him. With a great deal of patience and effort, he found he was growing accustomed to the new language and was grateful to be able to more easily communicate with the boys and the elderly woman who were caring for him.

Will asked the boys many questions. They, in turn, told him their story. The war zone had erupted unexpectedly near their hometown. Their mother had hoped it might soon subside or shift towards the west, but as it continued to approach, she packed the boys to move them to their grandmother's while she remained behind to help. The boys left while the battle raged not far off. They could hear the cannons and gunfire. Fearful but curious, they skirted around the war-zone. David had stopped the rough-hewn sleigh at the top of a hill, watching the bursts of light a short distance away. In an enormous explosion that lit up the sky, they saw a soldier struggling through the snow a great distance away before the man collapsed.

They hurried down to the soldier and were surprised to find him still breathing, though nearly dead. The cold and the snow had helped stop the flow of blood from his badly damaged arm and leg. The boys struggled to drag him onto the sleigh, packing snow around his wounds.

When they arrived at their grandmother's, another man was called on to help to bring the bloodied soldier inside—a man like Will, the boys told him. A man in an American uniform who had been there a few weeks longer. The boys then explained how their grandmother had done her best to heal the deep wounds. Will's leg had been healing well, they said, but an infection was spreading rapidly through his torn arm. It had to be cut away.

"It is good you were already asleep," Peter told him. The thought made Will sick yet grateful beyond his ability to express in his poor grasp of the language.

Will could not imagine the two young boys working in the cold with bombs exploding so near them as they struggled to pull the lifeless form of an unknown soldier to safety, nor could he imagine their weary grandmother working tirelessly to preserve what little life was left in his torn body.

In his broken grasp of the language, he told them his story—of his comrades, of life before the war, of his children and of Bonnie. The grandmother, Tiana, often came in to listen and to ask questions, her hands constantly busy with two long needles and a ball of wool yarn.

Will tried many times to get up from his bed, but Tiana or Peter would rush in and force him to lie back down. Several weeks passed before he was permitted to stand. Peter brought him a thick branch that had been scraped down to the smooth wood. Will gratefully took it in his left hand and used it to balance. His legs were stiff from the time he had spent unable to walk, but his right leg had managed to survive the shrapnel only to ache excruciatingly with each step.

To celebrate his first steps, Tiana presented him with a handmade set of clothing. Although far from new, it was a welcome relief from the filthy and bloodied uniform that had been cut to expose his wounds.

Will practiced walking for as long as he could endure each day, rising as often as he could manage, and falling when his strength failed him. The pain at times left his muscles contracting with tormenting spasms.

The first week showed little progress. By late in the second week, Will found that he had enough strength to stand for nearly an hour and to walk around the small cottage for a short time. Peter encouraged him with every step and tried to pull Will back to his feet each time he fell. Another week passed, and then another.

The boys walked alongside Will as the trio took a walk in the fresh air at sunrise and at dusk. The weather, though still rather cold, had lost the bitter chill. Will was surprised to realize how long of a ride he had survived that night in the sleigh. It was obvious to him now that they were a great distance from where that devastating battle front, but how far, he was uncertain.

They walked an extra length one evening as the weather warmed a little. Will was excited to see his progress as his limbs strengthened and his endurance grew. When he and the boys returned, Tiana stood in the doorway with a tall, dark-haired man at her side. Will didn't know the man, but from the first words the man spoke, Will recognized the language.

"Hello, Yankee," the man said with an American accent.

The two soldiers sat on the porch in the fading light that

evening. Captain Hammond had been the pilot in a bombing mission, but the plane was struck and went down over enemy territory. He and his crew had hidden in a barn when the Germans came to find the missing airmen. The farmer pacified the Nazis until they left. The old farmer then housed and cared for the small unit of American soldiers as they recovered from their injuries. The men soon discovered that dozens of soldiers had been hiding in that town and in several towns nearby. Captain Hammond had stayed for nearly three weeks before joining two other soldiers who were determined to make their way back across enemy lines. They made it as far as the shipyard before they were discovered by a German patrol. His companions never made it out. Captain Hammond took a bullet to his shoulder but somehow managed to stow away aboard a ship before it left the harbor. When the ship docked, he waited until dark then crept out of hiding and stole into the back of a wagon. He had arrived half-starved, sick and feverish in the small town just a few weeks before Will was pulled in on a sleigh, blood-soaked and barely alive.

"Have you written home?" Captain Hammond asked.

Will shook his head. "It would do more harm than good. I'm certain that news of my death must have reached them. Suppose I were to write to say that I was coming home but never made it back? I will do all I can to return, but until I am safely back in the States, it may be best if I do not raise their hopes."

"But there *is* reason to hope," Captain Hammond insisted. "You are alive! Give them something to believe in."

"I can't do that to them. We've already lost our three sons. I couldn't make them lose me twice."

"Is that why you joined? Your sons were lost to the war?" Captain Hammond asked.

"I joined to end the conflict. I couldn't bear to watch more of our young men die. So many boys and men from our town will never return. Those who do return will likely never again have a normal life," Will said.

"I'm afraid no one will ever know what normal is after a war this bloody. I only hope that an eventual change will take us far from what we know now."

Captain Hammond stood to leave. "Heal quickly. I'm anxious to see Alabama soil and the little family I left behind." The captain hesitated a moment before continuing. "There is a group of soldiers that have gathered here—some are deserters and some were separated from their platoons. We intended to journey home together in a day or so, but I am willing to stay behind and wait until you are ready. You are in no condition to travel alone."

He glanced at the bandaged stump of an arm that hung at Will's side. "We can head back to the States within another month or two, though it would be an uncomfortable journey until you are fully recovered."

Captain Hammond left. Will sat on the porch for several hours, trying to piece together the world that had fallen apart around him. It was no use. He felt powerless and dark with despair. The cold night air made him shiver. He pushed himself to his feet and hobbled inside.

Late that night, a sudden pounding on the door woke everyone in the small cottage. A voice echoed through the room. "Tiana, it's me. I need to speak to Colonel Linden!"

Tiana opened the door and Captain Hammond rushed inside.

"Is it over? Has the war ended?" she asked in her own tongue.

"No, not yet," Captain Hammond shook his head. "But I hope the end will come soon. No, this is something else, but it is very important."

Tiana berated him for scaring them all. Will sat up on his straw bed in the corner and attempted to get to his feet. Tiana shook her head and pulled up a chair beside him and sat down. She stared hard at Captain Hammond, quite unable to forgive the scare he had given her.

"If you have something to say to the colonel, then you can tell me, too."

Captain Hammond sat on the floor in front of Will's makeshift bed. "Colonel, I'm sorry to do this to you, but I want you to tell me about your sons. What are their names?"

Will rubbed the dryness from his eyes. "Captain, please. It is not the time." He placed his left hand against his head. "I can't let myself indulge in remembering just yet. It leads me only to despair and I can't let it overcome me. In time, perhaps I will have the courage to face it, but please, not now."

Captain Hammond drew nearer to Will and Tiana. "As a captain, I cannot order you to tell me, Colonel, but I need you to do this. What are their names?"

"Captain, please. I can't speak of it. We will discuss this another time. Please go." Will leaned wearily against the cold wood of the wall behind him.

"Then tell me this, Colonel, did two of your sons have a different surname—Major and Lieutenant Hale?"

Will jerked upright, almost losing his balance. Tiana caught him, but Will hardly noticed. He stared at the captain. "What are you saying? Tell me! How do you know them?"

"Major Lawrence and Lieutenant Andrew Hale, right? I'm sorry I hadn't realized it earlier. I hadn't known a set of three men called Linden, but they were as close as brothers with a Captain Linden—Captain Joseph Linden, all of the air force."

Will's mouth opened and shut several times, but no sound came out.

Captain Hammond placed a hand gently on Will's left shoulder. "Colonel, I know the last thing you wish for is false hope, but I have to tell you. They bailed out over enemy territory in the same area as my crew. I know your boys. They made it to the ground, though Major Hale was severely injured. I can't tell you where they are now, but there is a chance they may still be alive."

Will collapsed back onto his bed. He turned his face into the straw and wept. The sobs that raged through his body were both tormenting and wonderful. Hope and fear cascaded through him. For several long minutes, he was unable to control the agony and the joy that swept over him. His sons had survived, and perhaps they were still alive if they had not since succumbed to the brutality of the war. The anguish of not knowing burned hot as acid through Will's veins for hours that night until his mind at last fell into a restless sleep.

Will woke before dawn the next morning. Captain Hammond was still asleep, leaning uncomfortably against a wall where he had rested through the remainder of the night. He stirred as Will hobbled toward the door.

"Where do you think you are going?" he asked, suddenly alert. "You can't make that journey now. You are not ready."

"I've little intention of leaving just yet, but I need to build my strength. I need to find my boys. I need to know if they are alive." Will struggled to open the door. "Come, walk with me."

Will asked question after question, hardly waiting long enough for a complete answer. Captain Hammond told him the story the best he knew.

"My crew landed near the mountains in an isolated bit of

country behind enemy lines. Many soldiers found refuge there. My crew was not the first. The same base that took out our plane had hit several others throughout the war. Our mission was to take out that base. We dropped our bombs at night, but the accuracy was a little off and we only achieved minimal damage. Your sons must have been in the second wave of bombers sent to finish the mission.

"After their aircraft had gone down, we saw the patrols before we saw the men from the plane. German patrols often searched the small villages if a plane had gone down somewhere nearby and the bodies had not been found. At that time, we were hidden in a stuffy barn loft where we had a good view of the road below. We watched the Germans, nervous as we always were to see them, until they had gone.

"We knew more soldiers must have been shot down. Under Colonel Simmons' orders, three of us set out to find our fallen Allies. Some of the men felt it was too risky, but Colonel Simmons felt it was our duty. He took the lead. At one point we spread out, close enough to see each other, but far enough to allow us to cover more ground. We wore civilian clothing marked only with our wings pinned to the front. We hoped that, though they were likely in hiding, they might see the pins before the Germans found us.

"Colonel Simmons nearly stumbled over them. Captain Joseph Linden and Lieutenant Andrew Hale had struggled for miles carrying Major Lawrence Hale. It may have been the only reason they had not been found by the Nazis, not having made it nearly as far as the Germans would have expected by the time they had found the wreckage.

"It turned out that Major Hale had piloted the bomber that night. The fuel tank was hit as they dropped bombs over the base, a direct hit to both the base and the plane. The Boeing caught fire.

The major had refused to leave the pilot's seat until all the other men had made the jump. By the time he jumped, the plane wasn't far above the tree-line. His parachute didn't have a chance to open. He suffered a severe head injury and two badly broken legs. It was a miracle his own men found him before the Germans. Lieutenant Hale and Captain Linden had located him within half a mile of the burning wreckage.

"We each took turns carrying Major Hale until we arrived back at our hideaway. He was delirious, but he was still alive. Several days later, Colonel Simmons decided it was time that we rejoin the Allies to help end the war in any way we could.

"I haven't seen your sons since we attempted that fateful trip to rejoin the Allies, and it is a bloody war. I have watched too many men fall to pretend that I don't think there is a good chance your sons may have since lost their lives—but then again, there is a chance that they are still safe.

Will listened with tears pouring silently down his face. He walked as far as he could before he lost his balance and fell. He rested for a time then pushed farther on. It took nearly twice as long to return to the small cottage as it had to make the outward journey. They continued the process several times each day. Will struggled not to give in to his failing strength as he determined to push onward.

Each morning, news came flooding in from the war. More battles, more atrocities and greater inhumanity. Spring came and the weather grew warm. The Allies had at last gained a little success in their approach to Berlin, raising greater hope with each day that passed.

May came and ushered in the anticipated news at last. Some people screamed their uncontrollable joy. Some wept, some laughed, and some stared breathlessly into the sky. The war was over. The Allies had conquered the Axis powers. Hitler had fallen. The broken world could at last begin to heal.

Peter and David danced around the room, cheering with all their hearts. The adults shed tears of joy.

That same day, Will and Captain Hammond packed a little food and bid Tiana and the boys farewell. They turned their feet southward, their dreams of soon reaching American soil displaced in their search for the three lost boys.

Captain Hammond carried the map which was little more than a rough sketch drawn by Tiana. The words written on the rough paper of the map were difficult to read. Still, it offered them a general sense of the journey that lay ahead.

They headed down a dusty path through wide, empty plains that led into the hills. For nearly three hours they trudged on, pausing only once to refill their water supply in a shallow spring.

The landscape was lush and green with charming cottages and villages spread sparsely along the way. The picturesque landscape did Will some good. It gave him a great deal more to focus on than the shooting pain that burned through his right leg with each step.

High noon passed. The day began to cool slightly.

"It's time we stop," Captain Hammond said, turning abruptly from the path. He sat down on a fallen log and unhooked his water pouch, taking a long drink.

"It's still light. We can't stop yet," Will stood determinedly in the middle of the road.

"You've been growing very pale since we passed the last town. It's time for you to rest—and don't try pulling rank on me."

Will continued to stand in the road for several minutes, staring out to the furthest point at the end of the valley.

"It will do you no good to push your strength to the breaking point," Captain Hammond insisted. "It will just slow you down the next day and the next until you are forced to stop."

Will knew his strength had ebbed hours ago, and his vision had grown blurrier the more they pressed on.

Captain Hammond held the water pouch out to him. "Rest awhile. If you are looking better after a time, we'll continue until nightfall."

Will finally agreed. He sat on the ground and took a few deep gulps of water. A few hours later, he woke with a start.

"You shouldn't have allowed me to sleep," Will chided Captain Hammond.

"You obviously needed it. You'll be better off if you take care of yourself." The captain stood and pulled Will to his feet. "There's still a little daylight. We'll walk a while longer and find a place to rest for the night."

They ate a bit of the flatbread Tiana had packed for them. They continued walking on until the last bit of light faded from the sky. That night, they slept beneath a large tree near an open field.

Will woke before daybreak as the hazy sky began to glow. He nudged Captain Hammond and got to his feet. Every bone in his body ached both from the hard ground and from the exertion of the previous day.

They feasted again on a bit of the flatbread as they walked, rationing their supply but maintaining enough strength to cover a good distance. The pain in Will's leg hadn't gone away, but it eased a little as they continued forward.

The two men arrived at a harbor less than a week later. Much of their speed was owed to two travelers who had allowed the pair to hitch a ride on a horse-drawn wagon until their paths turned contrary ways.

Captain Hammond secured passage for the two of them and asked for updates on the fallout from the war. Although the war had ended, there still remained a great deal of political unrest and damage. Will gave a description of the three young men to any who would listen. No one they had met recalled seeing the boys, but the chance of finding them by chance across Europe was almost nonexistent. Yet, as he reminded himself, Captain Hammond had by chance stumbled across both father and sons.

With his comrades, Will had sailed on the large steam vessels that carried soldiers across the ocean, but he had never ridden in a smaller boat. The threat to capsize seemed imminent in the choppy waters. With one injured leg, he managed to stand only for a moment or two before losing his balance and toppling to his side. He spent most of the journey sitting near the ballast, ill and watching anxiously for land to appear.

The ship docked in a small harbor. Will struggled to stay upright on the swaying boat long enough to cross the deck to disembark. Captain Hammond supported Will until they were at last on dry land.

"We are only about sixty miles from the town in which your sons took refuge. If they have already begun to travel, it will likely be a very slow journey, considering Major Hale's condition when last I saw them."

They spent several hours asking around the small fishing village for any news of the three young soldiers. Many recalled seeing Allied soldiers pass through within the previous few days, but none recalled any that matched the descriptions of Joseph, Lawrence and Andrew.

At last they concluded that the boys had never made it to the docks. Captain Hammond indicated that it was likely that they had to move more slowly due to Lawrence's condition. He found the road that he was certain led to the rural hideaway. Daylight was already fading and the air became cool as evening fell. They soon had to stop and make camp for the night.

It had been a long day, but they hadn't walked far. Not yet exhausted, Will found it difficult to rest his mind. Within a day, he would perhaps know whether his sons were alive or if he would have to endure the sorrow of their deaths a second time. The thought was unbearable.

Long before the sun rose, Will woke. He still felt the strain of exhaustion but was far too anxious to rest any longer. He had drifted off to sleep only a few hours earlier. Captain Hammond was still fast asleep on the soft grass.

Will reached for his crutch and pushed himself to his feet. He walked up the road a distance to warm his muscles then returned. The captain was still fast asleep. Will paced the campsite a while longer then took another walk up the road. A glow finally appeared over the horizon.

Will turned back toward camp. He was nearly a quarter mile away when he saw Captain Hammond searching for him. Will picked up his pace and called out. The captain turned and waved, obviously relieved to see him.

Captain Hammond sat himself on a boulder and pulled out another slice of flatbread, which he tore in half. He looked up as Will hobbled toward him. He smiled and held up a piece of the bread. Suddenly, the captain froze.

Will hurried to him. "What's wrong? Are you alright?"

Captain Hammond stood, gazing past Will, his face tense, but he didn't reach for the pistol at his side.

Will caught his breath. He turned.

There, just at the crest of the hill, were two tall figures with a third supported between them.

Captain Hammond put a hand on Will's shoulder. "Colonel, just wait. It might not be them."

"Yes," Will said, hardly breathing, "but it might."

He hobbled slowly forward at first, then faster, unable to bear the torture of wondering. He stumbled and fell. The crutch beneath his left arm snapped as he landed on top of it.

Captain Hammond reached down and pulled him to his feet. He slipped the stub of Will's right arm over his shoulder and supported Will as they continued up the road.

Daylight glowed around them, but the figures in the distance were still too far to see.

"Hello!" Captain Hammond called out.

The trio stopped a moment, watching the two men ambling toward them.

"Hello!" one of them called back.

"I am Captain Richard Hammond," the captain bellowed. "Who are you three?"

"Captain Richard Hammond?" a young familiar voice called out, excitedly. "We know a Captain Hammond!"

Will collapsed, falling to his knees sobbing.

Captain Hammond knelt beside him with tears in his eyes. The three figures were coming nearer again.

"Yes," Captain Hammond called out to them. "Yes, you do." He looked down at Will. "And I think you will know my comrade, too."

Captain Hammond lifted Will to his feet. "Go on ahead," the captain encouraged him. "I'll wait here."

Will slowly hobbled forward without his staff to support him.

The sun broke at last over the horizon, and in the hazy morning air, a young voice split the morning, screaming jubilantly. "Father! Lawrence, Andrew—it's Father!"

Chapter 42

CAPTAIN HAMMOND barely had two coins to rub together after he booked the passage for the five soldiers returning to England. They reported in at the nearest base upon their arrival and had to wait another two days before passage to the United States was secured for them by the military.

For all their joy, there was a somber air on the long voyage across the sea. The war and its toll on the world weighed heavily on each of their minds. Lawrence remained silent, painfully uncertain of all that was happening around him, though now and then he seemed to grow more aware for a time before fading back into confusion.

The eyes of nearly every man aboard the military ships filled with tears as the Statue of Liberty appeared on the horizon. The next morning, they boarded the trains. Captain Hammond headed south while Will, Joseph, Andrew and Lawrence headed west. Captain Hammond departed with a firm handshake and a promise to visit Pravda within the next few months with his small family.

The train rocked and blared its whistle as they traveled over the wide rolling hills.

"I wonder if it will be too much of a shock if we all show

up without sending word ahead," Andrew stated thoughtfully. He stared out through the train window, watching the landscape slide by.

"I don't think so," Joseph said looking up from the weathered notebook in his hands in which he had been writing. "There is no woman I have ever known that would keep a spark of hope alive longer than Mother."

Will looked at him, somewhat taken aback at the assertion.

"I believe it, Father," Joseph stated confidently. "She would never give up hope—not entirely."

The sun neared the horizon as the train swept by Bloomfield, the final leg of the journey home. Will and his three sons watched anxiously through the windows as the tiny forms of buildings grew in front of them.

"Father, look!" Joseph cried.

Andrew gasped.

Will buried his head in his hands.

There on the gnarled oak tree, covering every branch, twig and bough, were thousands of tiny yellow ribbons, and hundreds of strands of bright, tinkling glass.

Acknowledgements

Many years ago, I was introduced to a beautiful letter which had been written during the American Civil War—the Sullivan Ballou Letter. Will's final letter home in Chapter 38 is taken in large portion from that remarkable letter. Love so beautiful as was written in the original could hardly be better expressed, so I hope you will forgive me for borrowing that portion of the story from history's archives and from an exceptional love that was never reunited in this life.

www.ingramcontent.com/pod-product-compliance
Lightning Source LLC
Chambersburg PA
CBHW071452170626
46811CB00007B/2553